The Tiny One

The Tiny One

ELIZA MINOT

ALFRED A. KNOPF NEW YORK 1999

THIS IS A BORZOI BOOK
PUBLISHED BY ALFRED A. KNOPF

Copyright © 1999 by Eliza Minot

All rights reserved under International and Pan-American
Copyright Conventions. Published in the United States
by Alfred A. Knopf, a division of Random House, Inc., New York.
Distributed by Random House, Inc., New York.

www.randomhouse.com

Knopf, Borzoi Books, and the colophon are
registered trademarks of Random House, Inc.

Owing to limitations of space, all permissions to reprint
previously published material will be found on pages 257–258.

Minot, Eliza.
The tiny one / Eliza Minot.
p.   cm.
ISBN 0-375-40645-X (alk. paper)
I. Title.
PS3563.I4745T56   1999
813'.54—dc21
99-18516
CIP

Manufactured in the United States of America
First Edition

*To the memory of my mother and my father
and to my husband Eric.*

If you want to know me,
look inside your heart.

—LAO TZU

Contents

PART I   HOME IS WHERE THIS HOUSE IS

  1   Staying with Puddle   3
  2   Still Winter   6

PART II   MORNING

  3   The Breakfast   17
  4   The Bath   39
  5   The Bus Stop   51
  6   The Fire   66
  7   Reading   71
  8   10:00 Art Class   94
  9   History with Mr. Waring   106
10   Recess   115

PART III   AFTERNOON

11   Lunch   127
12   Homeroom   149
13   Social Studies   159
14   Short Recess   174
15   A Special Assembly   182
16   Sloyd   197
17   Math   209
18   The News   226

PART IV   NIGHT

19   After   237
20   Home   248
21   Via   252

     Acknowledgments   255

PART I

Home Is Where
This House Is

ONE

Staying with Puddle

⟋ VIA REVERE. She's just a kid in the morning except
that she's sitting still on her bed in the thick of far-gone winter
with her mouth parted open like a grown woman's in thought.
Life's got her for the first time pinned up against a wall, open-
mouthed. But other than her mouth, and her stillness, the rest of
her's pure kid, but stunned. She's slouched and static, puffy-eyed,
staring at the rug where it meets the wood floor. She's sitting waiting, lopsided, dumbstruck, not even thinking yet what to think.

Her mother would have put her in the gray flannel or Black
Watch plaid dress. Instead Via's wearing an Easter dress that curdles,
but nicely, with the raw winter surrounding her. Its white cotton is
springlike, clean and pleated, cool over her dark wool tights. Lavender smocking is embroidered across her chest, and her young fresh
head grows up out of the starched scalloped collar that petals at the
neck. Her hair's got so much static that she can feel it clinging silky
to her cheek, buzzing, tickling at the side of her chapped mouth.

The Tiny One

One of the cats jumps up beside her and arches to rub along her arm. She pats it without looking at it and with her electricity gives it a little shock so the kitty twitches its whiskers but keeps purring. Via twitches too, her eye, but keeps staring.

She's just a kid and it's morning but nothing's the same. Everything's different now. She's at the beginning of a new chapter. She's perched at the edge of a new era. Grief has been born boring into her soft ripe life full of cartwheels and digging with sticks, leaves and laughter, sky and light, her mother's face and jumps in the air. Grief's been injected like a strange sedative that has the opposite effect—it wakes you up. It's jarred her like shaking her shoulders. It has her. The grizzle of life has rattled her numb. It's like she's been whacked in the head out of laughter and now she sits alone on her bed, looking out, in awe at anything, in awe at everything, stunned.

Hearing the news is like this: The day was like other days and then it happened. Then the news came like those film clips where huge buildings sway gracefully to the ground like someone's sucking them down with a vacuum. It's a whirl of air. It's a night of movement with billowing as the darkness is go everything go, everything moves, disheveled and alive, rushing with sound. Then suddenly it is silent. It's like the sound has been turned off but you're watching a storm. The trees bend like slingshots and the leaves tornado up into the air. Where is the sound? And then it is over.

Then it is over and it's morning. You've heard the news. You'd almost rather hear it again—fresh—than begin a life with what you know now. It is morning. It is a morning when everything is hit white-yellow and windows of buildings shine in dull flashes. The windshields of slowly moving cars turn weak sun in your eyes. You wince. You feel like a fever that's petrified.

It's her older sister Marly's voice in the door behind her. "You ready?"

Then it's her father. "All set?"

They're in the door together but Via doesn't want to turn around to see.

Marly comes and sits beside her. "All set?" she says, like her father just did.

Via nods. She pats the cat Puddle and listens to the purring. "She's purring," Via says.

"Come on," says Marly, nudging her. Marly heads toward the bureau. "I'll get you a sweater."

"No," says Via.

"No what?"

"No sweater."

"You'll freeze, V."

"I don't think I will."

"Well you think wrong," says Marly. "Look at it out there."

Via looks up from the floor to look out the window. She doesn't remember yesterday. Today looks like it's trying to snow.

"I want to stay here with Puddle," Via says.

Marly goes over to her. Marly squats down and looks at her little sister in the eye. "You want to stay with Puddle?" Marly asks her.

Via nods.

"It's not time to go yet," says Marly. "Want me to come get you when it's time to go?"

Via nods again. "Yeah," she says. She's patting Puddle.

Marly kisses Via's forehead as she's standing up. "We'll all be right downstairs if you want to come down," Marly tells her. "Okay?"

" 'Kay," says Via.

When Marly leaves, Via looks back up out the window while she listens to Puddle purr. It's as white as can be out there. Only the rattly knuckled trees are dark and still against the icy snow that's beneath them and behind them. Above the world is the long white sky, open and bare.

TWO

Still Winter

━◌ MUM'S DEAD FOREVER. It happened the day before
yesterday. Yesterday I don't really remember. Today it's trying to
snow. Mum's dead forever and the world's all different, roomy and
huge. Even my own room in here seems like the walls are moving away and the ceiling's moving up. I look up at the ceiling
and watch it and it seems to be slowly moving away. Things look
farther.

The world's so big. It feels so big now. I'd get glimpses of it
before sometimes but not really. I do stuff and feel different new
things. Like I feel like I'm flying sometimes when I see something
really pretty. I get lonely and, like, sing the sad songs from *Oliver!*
up in my tree house alone and pretend I'm being filmed. I try to
run so fast I think I'll pee in my pants. I feel bad and cry and stuff
like that. I wear capes and masks and jump into snowbanks or piles
of leaves. I get all happy and glad at things or like I love my mum so
much I want to pop open my chest like a flower. I feel sorry for

some people usually at the right times. I do things like dance and jump my arms around without being able to help it. But this is so different than other things. I want to explain but I can't really. It's like I'm in a rowboat and the oars are under the seat and I'm not big enough to get them out. So I drift. It's not so bad. The world's a whole different place that no one ever told me about. Or maybe even if they did I didn't listen right to hear them.

A few things are still the same I guess like it's still winter. It's still cold. It gets wicked cold here in Masconomo, Mass. Sometimes I like it. Sometimes I feel like a blister. The ocean's still down at the bottom of the hill. It gets so wicked cold sometimes that the ocean steams and the twirls of steam rising up look really excellent but spooky also like ghosts coming up from the dead.

It's still February. Sometimes for like a whole week there will be no color in the sky. It'll just be white, or gray, but then when the blue does come out from behind the clouds it's a nice light blue way up in the distance and it looks kind of more like a painting. It's still winter. We always hear the wind here since we're on a hill above the water. It flutes through the cracks around our windowpanes. It goes up and down in notes like a song. There are blue days too, bright ones, when the sea looks thick like a navy-blue Slush Puppie and the sky's like a shiny blue Easter egg, when icicles drip and you can hear them all over the place like leaks in a roof or panting animals, when the sun's so bright and the glare of the snow makes you squint like you're an Eskimo.

On those cold gray days sometimes I'd brush up against some-thing large and important all on my own. I'd feel how big life could be, sort of, and how maybe it could change with all of the changes in it. It would be like a winter afternoon and the house would seem like it had fallen asleep. The house would be full of everyone but it would seem like it was empty, everyone asleep or something except for me—Mum and Dad taking a nap in their room, my sister Marly maybe sacked out on a couch in the living room, my oldest brother Pete probably not even woken up yet from the day before, and my other brother Cy who's the youngest except for me and comes after Marly—the order goes Pete, Marly, Cy, then me—Cy's like asleep on one of the sofas in the TV room or up in his own room maybe. The house would be so quiet that I'd pretend everyone was gone. I'd pretend that everyone had disappeared. I'd pretend that the house was all mine, just me, only me to eat the potato chips, to feed the cats, to turn the lights on and off and stuff like that.

All alone and in my house it's like I'm important and have a secret. I pretend I'm an orphan. I walk from room to room like our dog Sparky does. I sit at the piano and kind of play it. I look in drawers that I've looked in a lot before. I walk from window to window and look out. Winter. I watch Godzilla movies on *Creature Double Feature*. I watch *Happy Days*. I watch *The Wide World of Sports* with the wipeout guy at "the agony of defeat." I leave the TV on when I leave the room and I can hear the audience's laughter come tinkling down the hall. I wander around in the back of the house. It's full of things like skis and cardboard boxes and rotting rugs. The banister back there has paint that's excellent to peel. It's soft and gray and rubbery so it comes off in nice loose strips like moist skin. It's so soft I can push my finger against it and see my fingerprint or roll all the strips into a ball like it's Silly Putty. Underneath the gray paint there's a lime green that's so bright that I didn't think they'd invented that color in the olden days. It's nice because it's sort of against the rules to peel paint, but in the back of the house, nobody cares. But nobody's here anyway.

I walk upstairs to the widow's walk which is too narrow to even walk around. The windows are too high for me to see out of. I come back down to the front hall. The snow on the ground outside gets brighter white, almost purple, when it gets darker. Way over at the horizon through the crisscrossing black tree trunks the sunset gets redder and looks like a treasure chest being creaked open. It's like a peek into a fiery treasure that's about to seal shut.

I look out the window at all of this. I look back around inside. The clock in the kitchen twangs so softly every second that I can barely hear it. It's the same hollow twitching sound that the oven makes when Mum first turns it on. The house is so quiet. I wait a little too long to turn on the lights so that the white walls look like blue clay. It's like everybody is gone. Even the cats. Even Sparky. It feels creepy but I like it too. I feel quiet. I'm little. I feel like an Indian being tested to grow older. I feel older like I know things. Like I'm set on an adventure. Like I'm Huck Finn or an orphan and I'm sad to be alone but I like it too since it makes me feel like I'm a tough boy kid even though I'm a girl and still there's a humming inside of me that can make me feel warm. I listen and stay still. I watch the sun go down.

Then when I get bored I go upstairs to Mum and Dad's room and sit on top of Mum. Their room is getting dark. I straddle Mum's mummied body under her covers.

Her face is mashed into the pillow.

"I'm hungry," I tell her.

Mum creaks an eye open at me without moving her head. "Pumpkin," she says. Her mouth's half crushed by the way her head is. She slurps some sleepy drool in. "Where's your sister?" she says.

"Marly's sleeping," I tell her, "I think."

We hear Dad groan from his side of the bed. He's facing the other way so I can't see his face. He's not under the covers. He still has his boots on.

I'm straddling Mum. She's lying on her side so I'm straddling her hip. It's a good saddle. I bounce a little so she'll get squished to move things along. "I'm hungry," I tell her. It's Sunday. Maybe we'll have dinner in the TV room and watch a Bruins game or *Donny and Marie*. "Mum." I whisper it loudly. "I'm hungry, Mum."

Mum's eyes are closed again. "I feel we're constantly, constantly eating dinner," she murmurs, like talking in sleep.

"What?" I ask. While I bounce on her I can't really understand what she's saying because her voice gets disrupted in jerks. "What?" I ask. I move my face down so it's right close to her face. She smells good like sleep and cotton. My head's so close to hers that her hair is up around my face and I can pretend that her hair's mine. When she opens her eyes we're so close-up that it startles me. Then it doesn't. I like it. I smile. Me and Mum are like animals all nosed in.

"Okay," Mum says. She breathes. "Clear away so I can get up."
I don't want to because I like this. "I don't want to," I tell her.
"Good," she says. She closes her eyes. "Five more minutes."
"No!" I yell.

"Via!" says Dad from his side of the bed. I was too loud.

"Shhhh!" says Mum, pushing me away.

"Sorry," I whisper. I'm sitting back up, straddling her. "But come on," I whisper. I tug at her sleeve. "Come on," I whisper again. I sit and wait for a second. I try braiding the fringe of the bedspread that's by Mum's shoulder. I can't do it because the tassels are too short. I stop. I bounce on Mum with just little bounces. "Come on," I say. I've got lots of energy now. I want to, like, run down a hill. I want to get up and run around. "I want to get up and run around," I say, but I meant to say "Come on" again but it came out wrong, so I laugh. I'm laughing at myself and then laughing at that I'm laughing at myself.

"Uh-oh," groans Mum. She detects a laughing fit.

I laugh a little more and then I stop. I get down off of Mum and get down off of the bed. I do a back bend on the floor and stay in the arch upside down. "Look," I say. I'm upside down. "Look, Mum. Mum, look."

"I see," she says. Her head's still smushed in the pillow. "A very gifted small fry."

Then I stop and get up and stand still. It's quiet and it's getting dark and I'm all energetic. I shiver my shoulders. *"Angie!"* I sing. I move my hips. *"I still—"*

"Quiet quiet," says Mum, whispering, but it's a powerful whisper.

I stand still and wait for a second. I watch Mum. I go stand beside the bed where Mum's head is and I look down at her face and the covers. I look at her eyelashes on her closed eyes and I want to pat them like a kitten. I watch her face to see what it's going to do.

She opens her eyes. We look at each other. My mum. "Come

close," she says. I'm busy looking so I forget to listen. "Come," she says again. I lie down next to her and she arms me in. She tries to put part of the covers over me but Dad's weighing them down on the other side of the bed so she can't pull them very far they're stunted like when you pull the cord for a lightbulb to turn it on and it's stuck it won't pull. She stops trying. She pulls me in farther. I feel small and all in her arms. "Mmmm," Mum hums. I can feel her mouth saying it against the top of my head. Her arm around me under my chin smells good like grass and oranges. "Mmmm," she hums, and then I hum it too. "Mmmm," we say. We're like the cats purring. I'm all in, perfect and warm. I feel her chest up against my back. Our hearts click into each other and beat. Mum rocks a little bit and then squeezes me too. "Mmmmm," she says, getting me tighter, "this is the life, my little love. This right here."

SEE SO LIKE I remember something like that and now Mum will never ever be taking a nap in her bed again? And if I didn't remember that time, it would have just, like—*poof*—no one would ever have known? It's just weird. She dies. She goes to heaven. Or wherever. But where do all the things she thinks go? And if I die when I'm eighty and I go to heaven, how old will I be when I see her? Older than her? Where do all of when she thinks of me go?

I hold on to the day before yesterday. I feel like Cy or somebody pushed me in the back along my shoulders and I stumbled forward and stood up so fast that I don't get what happened. It's like the wind being knocked out but I can breathe. Like in movies when someone's lost their senses and they're freaking out and then someone slaps them. Then they shape up. Then they can see straight and stop babying around. It's not like I see straight really now. It's not like I'm only sad either. I feel sad and weird. I'm almost embarrassed that this hasn't happened to me before. It doesn't feel real but it feels really real. Almost like fresh air. That part I kind of like. I don't feel like myself but at the same time I feel me. I'm older now.

The Tiny One

I can feel it. One second it seems like I've known it all along and then the next I can't believe I'm one of those kids who doesn't have a mom.

And I'm just spacey. Yesterday's blurry. It's all so different. Everything looks the same but it's like we've moved. I space out and can't taste anything but I can't stop thinking about the day that it happened. The day before yesterday. I can't stop thinking about how that day began and kept going. I remember so much of it. I remember what I was thinking about. I'll be remembering like searching for a clue or something and then I'll all of a sudden realize that I'm staring at the wall or for a second I forget my name.

Yesterday's blurry. Dad walks into the TV room and I look at him and I think maybe it's a joke. Maybe it's a test. I watch Marly crying down on the sofa downstairs in the front hall and I think this couldn't be true—it's just too much to really be true. There are other people here too like Aunt Nellie and Sasha and Uncle Terry and other older people but I just sit close to the screen and keep my eyes on the hockey game on TV. All the noises of the rink that usually sound so good—the stick clacks and slap shots, the organ echoes, the yells, the blades spraying up ice—all sound like they're making fun of us. What is happening? While we're watching the game my brother Pete brings me chicken noodle soup and some chicken potpie. The white soup bowl doesn't look like we own it. "Where did we get these?" I mean the bowl.

Pete looks at me like I'm dense. "They're the ones we've always had," he tells me.

I look around at everyone. Suddenly I wonder what they're all thinking all of the time. It's only been like a day but yes in our full house someone is missing. I look out the window at the driveway. One of the cars is missing. I ask, "Where's the green car?"

Everyone looks at me heartbroken like I'm a poor kid who doesn't understand anything. "Mum was in it," Marly tells me.

"Oh," I say. I want to tell them that I understand that she crashed in a car but I just thought it was the blue station wagon. I look at the fire burning in the fireplace. What an ugly fire, I think. I look at the rug and think what an ugly rug. It looks like someone spilled it and it makes me feel like I have a stomachache. I want to ask when we got a new ugly rug but I know that we didn't really especially because we've been sitting in here the last couple of days and I'd have seen the workmen bring it in.

There are lots of grown-ups milling around and I don't know who they all are. I know some of them. There's stuff being cooked in the kitchen that I've never seen before. New smells. The cats are hard to find when so many grown-ups are hanging around, hugging, smoking cigarettes in the hall. They speak softly and slowly to me like I'm younger than I am. I don't know what to say to some of them so I don't say anything. They don't get it either. They don't get what's going on. I'm usually always sitting on one of their laps or under one of their arms or on a walk outside with one of them but I don't really notice who it is.

I CAN'T STOP thinking about the day that it happened. The day before yesterday. I want to think about as much as I can that's happened. I think of the day and I go over it in my mind. The day was like other days and then it happened. I want to think about it so much that I also don't want to think about it. But I want to think about it so I don't forget it. I want to hear the story again because there's a thrill in it somewhere that I can't get enough of. I know it's Mum but it's not her. Mum's dead; that was the day. I was in recess. I was at lunch. I listened to Miss Hunt in class. Lulu bugged me but she made me laugh too. Then Dad told me.

How can something so big fit into such a little thing like a day? I can't get it. I don't know what it is. It's how it happened and how everything's different so fast that I can't stop thinking about. I can't really think about her. It's the day that I think about. The day was just another day and then something stopped. Something else began.

I can't stop thinking about it but when I think about it I'll start to think of another thing and it turns into another thing and it keeps going. It's like fireworks with all the different streams that come ribboning off of one exploding thing that I remember. It's like petals to a flower that just keep shooting out of the round thing. Or, no, it's like a path that has lots of little paths going off of it and I can't help it I have to check them all out on my bike. I want to tell what I know so I remember. I trace it in my head, over and over, trace the day before yesterday from the beginning of it and then I do it again to remember, do it again to remember, do it again to remember.

I want to be able to find something in that day to hold on to like a rope swing, to swing with. Trying to hold on to all that I remember makes my stomach jump—there goes something; here comes another. But if I don't do it, I feel even more scared because I worry that I'm forgetting everything, that I won't know anything. I won't have her. I've got to keep her as long as I can. Because I thought I loved everything, but it was all just her. This is what happened. This was the day before yesterday. This was the day.

PART II

Morning

THREE

The Breakfast

⟋ᴖ MY SLEEP WAS all over the place. I woke up in the early early morning sweaty on the floor of the front hall. My drool was on the floor and the sleeve of my nightgown and I didn't know why I was downstairs. I sort of remembered getting up and walking down the stairs to the piano. I sleepwalk sometimes but it's not really sleepwalking; it's just trying to find a more comfortable place to sleep. Sometimes I like the cool feeling of the front hall floor or the bathtub against my cheek. So anyway I woke up and I was down in the hall but the light was on so I wasn't that confused. I had my tights on though which was weird, but it doesn't matter. They felt uncomfortable and hot. The floor was cold on my cheek. Looking sideways I could see a bump in the floor like a flattened speed bump. When we go over a bump in the car Mum says, "Thank you, ma'am." I don't know why. Sideways I watched an ant walk. It was a small creaky little ant so it moved really slow. I watched it go over the cracks in the floor until it went into the dark cave under the brown velvet couch by the window and I couldn't see it.

My head felt so heavy and tired that I scuffed up the stairs to Marly's room and took off my tights and my nightgown in there. She's away at school so sometimes I sleep in her room.

Once or twice I slept in Pete's room but not much. On the wall in Pete's room there's a shield from Africa that looks like a giant turtle shell. There's a spear too that looks like a harpoon. There's a poster that's a blue-and-white photo with a little girl blowing at a dandelion fuzz and underneath it says TODAY IS THE FIRST DAY OF THE REST OF YOUR LIFE. Most of his other posters he brought with him to school. In Cy's room there's a poster of Bobby Orr being tripped by a defenseman after scoring and winning the Stanley Cup. Bobby Orr never wears socks inside his skates. Cy's got some signs too from *Mad* magazine that look like road signs that are a joke but I don't get them. One of them's yellow and it says GO SLOW CURVES and then there are like curvy lines like an hourglass around them. In art class one day Miss Gracie told us to make a sign. Anything we wanted. I didn't know what to do so I did that GO SLOW CURVES. When I gave it to her she laughed. "Where did this come from?" Afterward at home Cy explained to me that it was funny because the curves are meant to look like a woman's body.

When I took off my tights in Marly's room my legs felt cool and free. I didn't get under; I just pulled the quilt up. It's a quilt Mum made. It's all different fabrics and it says Marly's name on it. Mum gave it to her for her birthday once and didn't wrap it or anything. She just put it on Marly's bed so when Marly came home from school she saw it there. Marly was with her friend June. I followed them in to see. June jumped on the bed and put her hands all over it since she liked it so much. "You *luck!*" she said. Me and Mum were standing out in the doorway and Mum thought June said "yuck!"

So in Marly's bed I fell asleep and then woke up again. I thought to go wake up Mum so she'd get up with me but I didn't want to. I'd just go watch TV or something. But first I put my nightgown back on. Then I went into my room to get some socks.

It was Valentine's Day. There was a little heart of chocolates at the bottom of my bed and a package like the ones that hang on a hook at the drugstore with jacks and a ball behind the plastic and one of those paddles that has a red ball on an elastic and you go *boing boing boing* with it for as long as you can. I brought it with me downstairs. In the kitchen I did it a few times—*boing boing boing*—then tried again. Then I hit something with my elbow and it fell off the counter and slid into the sink. It was the tape recorder that Dad gave Mum. I played with it last week when we first got it but it was hard to get at because everyone was wanting to look at it and use it. Now here I was; it was all mine. It was like winning a prize.

I took the tape recorder out of the sink and sat down at the kitchen table. I put it next to me. I spoke into it. I spoke sort of softly because even though I knew everyone was asleep I usually get the feeling that maybe they're all, or one of them, like Mum or Cy, is hiding and watching me. I think maybe they're testing me for something just like I sometimes think God's put us here just to test us to see if we're good enough for something better. Like training. Like maybe when I leave the TV room they all stop talking, then start up again when I come back in. It seems like something tribes might do to their kids.

I pressed the black button with the red dot underneath it. I spoke into it—"Hello. My name is Via Mahoney Revere. I live on Slate Avenue, Masconomo, Massachusetts 01944. I have a mother, a father, a brother, a sister, and a brother. Their names are Mum, Dad, Pete, Marly, and Cy. I have seven cats. They're all black. Their names are Milo, Linus, Jezebel, Incubus, Puddle, Sweet Pea, and Bean. And Incubus. And a black dog named Sparky. I am a fourth-grader at Bayside. I am eight years old. What's your name?"

I played it back. All the words were stuck together and it sounded like I had a stuffed nose. I tried it again. I forgot the address. I tried it again and I forgot to say my name. "Hello. My name is Via Mahoney Revere." I said it again. "Via Mahoney Revere. Via. Revere."

It sounded weird. It sounded dumb. Via. It sounded like I was lying. They were going to name me Olivia but they just made it Via instead because Dad knew someone named Olivia that he didn't like. Dad makes fun of my name. But he's the one who picked it. I thought of my name and I thought of Dad.

WE'RE LYING on the lawn. I'm lying on the lawn with Dad. Everywhere smells like grass. We're about to have corn on the cob for dinner. Dad likes to saw the corn off of his cob with his knife and eat it that way. I like eating it like it's a typewriter, back and forth. Dad's lying on his side and holding his head up with his hand, leaning on his elbow. I sit on his hip like he's a toy horse. He's looking into the woods and chewing on a piece of grass. I can look right into his ear. The low sun through the trees is on his face. It lights up his eye. "Whatever you say, Vivienne," Dad says to me.

"Stop!" I cry. "That's not my name!"

"Don't be silly, Veronica."

I tear up some grass and throw it at Dad. "Stop!" I smile.

"Stop what, Victoria?" He keeps his face straight and serious.

"Dad!"

"Vanessa?"

I swoop down toward Dad's head. "I hate that name!" I cry. I'm close to his face. The black hairs on his cheek look like tiny thorns coming through.

"How could you hate it? Viola's a beautiful name!"

I sit back up. I bounce on him and slap my hands down. "Dad!"

He bucks me up with his hips like a hockey check. "Vera!"

I bounce again. "Dah-ad!"

He bucks me up so that I fall off of him and onto the ground. I'm laughing on the grass. "Valerie, what in the world has gotten into you?"

I'm laughing. "That's not my name!"

He's grabbing my ankle and tickling up my leg but he's still not laughing. "Violet, sweetheart, I think it's time you had your little head examined."

I'm laughing. I can feel grass and dirt streaking across my cheek while I laugh and turn my head on the ground. Dad's voice is behind me and behind my laughing. I look down my leg and I can see his face next to my foot. It's saying "Do you hear me? Vanna? Can you hear what I'm saying?"

WHILE I FIDDLED with the tape player I heard the milkman drive up and drop the milk off on the porch so I put my boots on and went outside to get it without a jacket and while I was out there my nightgown felt like it hardened into a cold thing around me. Mum just gets NuForm. Around Christmas we get eggnog too. Pete loves it. Pete loves the eggnog when we get it. He'll put it on his Cocoa Krispies for breakfast. It looks foamy and gross. Once Mum with puffy eyes came in wearing her bathrobe. She looked down at Pete's bowl and, yawning, opened her mouth to ask to try a bite. Mum'll try anything sweet.

I put the milk in the fridge and took out the one that was already opened that was already in the fridge. I found a whole huge Fun Pak with the different single boxes behind the Sugar Smacks and Froot Loops in the cupboard under the counter. I like the little packs but you don't get the prizes like in the big ones. For a while Cy was sending away for things from the back of the boxes. When they'd finally come months later they were always stupid. Like a sheriff's badge that looked cool and real on the box but then when it came it was way too shiny and plastic and dumb. Cy entered contests too, like Kellogg's contests. They were mostly drawing contests. I'd try to draw things too but I couldn't do it as well since I'm littler. At the Bicentennial Cy did one with a drawing of George Washington crossing the Delaware, all of his soldiers rowing with the oars out like bug legs. George Washington stood up in the front with a bent knee looking out over the water while he ate a bowl of Frosted Flakes. You knew it was Frosted Flakes because there was a big box that said FROSTED FLAKES on the seat behind him.

But the best thing Cy ever got was the weather balloons. They were from the back of a comic book or like *World* magazine. The day he launched them was one of those extra-still days, quiet like everyone's hiding. They were the biggest balloons I've ever seen and they were ours.

ME AND MUM and Dad and Cy are out on the lawn watching Cy's weather balloons. From the terrace and over the garden the water down at the bottom of the hill looks like dried paint that a ball would bounce on. The balloons are white so they almost blend in with the white sky. I'm holding our cat Milo and my neck's getting tired from looking up at the balloons for so long but I can't look away because I'm afraid I might miss something.

Mum points at the three of them with her hand that's inside the pocket of her coat. "Look what they're like," she says. She points at each of them. "The Father, the Son, and the Holy Ghost."

I think of how I could maybe lie on my stomach on the top of one of the big balloons so I could float up with it and bob around.

I pat Milo more and tell him, "Good kitty." Milo's named after our neighbor Mr. Emerson because that's Mr. Emerson's real first name and he doesn't like anyone to call him it. Everyone calls him Mr. Emerson. So we named our cat Milo so we could say Mr. Emerson's name, I guess. Mr. Emerson talks like he's almost from England. Mum says it's because he's from the city and that's how some people his age talk. He has kids that have their own kids. They're not around enough for me to know them but when they are around they know my name. His wife's Tessa. I don't call her Mrs. Emerson. She's my godmother but she's not a Catholic godmother.

WE CAN HEAR Mr. Emerson burp when he's outside working in his garden or something. We can hear it all the way over at our house. He likes chocolates and ice cream. Mum says it's because he doesn't drink anymore. Mr. Emerson gives me jackknives. When I lost one he gave me a new one and told me, "Never lay it down." He teaches me how to sharpen the knives with the sharpening stones and a squirt of oil. I bring them home. "Great," says Dad. Dad flips the flat stone over to look at its other side— "That's a beautiful stone"—and then he takes it forever since he doesn't want me sharpening anything. Dad tells me I can have the stones when I'm older. It's the same with the fireworks and firecrackers that Sasha brought me from Mexico. Sasha is Mum's sister so she's my aunt but she's more like Pete's older sister because she's young and she's my godmother too.

Even though Dad takes the sharpening stones, he doesn't take the knives. Sometimes I can't get enough whittling. I can't stop. I find a good stick in the woods or in the kindling by the fireplace. Pencils are extra soft and it's all over in about four strokes. At first Dad doesn't want me doing it at all. I hear him coming and I go into the bathroom and I don't turn the light on because I don't want him to know I'm in there whittling.

SO I GOT the cereal out, the milk, all that stuff. I had Sugar Pops. They inflated in the milk like miniature buoys. I brought my bowl into the TV room to watch cartoons. I turned the light on and held my hand up against the lamp shade and I could see the outline of the bones in my hand like an X ray. After a bite the Sugar Pops tasted too puffy and too sweet.

I expected to find, like, *Davey and Goliath* because it felt like Sunday even though it wasn't. Usually *Davey and Goliath* is only on Sunday mornings when there's nothing else to watch. It's religious and sort of dopey and slow with their voices and everything but I like watching it. I like watching it because the dog's, Goliath's, brown body looks like a Tootsie Roll the same way Rudolph and all those other clay guys kind of do. They look like fig rolls with coconut on them or like cookie dough.

WHEN I WAS littler I'd walk right up to the TV to look closely at those clay guys like Rudolph. I'd get as close as I could and look at them as close as I could. I'm standing right up at the TV screen looking at the snowman on *Rudolph* move through the snow. I turn around and look at Mum. She's sitting on the couch in her spot. "What are they?" I ask, then look back at them, close-up, and Mum tells me not to stand so close to the screen. I want to eat them or squish them. They look chewy and good. I especially like it when Rudolph or the snowman move across the snow. There's a slight noise they make like whispering, and the fluffy snow swirls around their feet while they slide along. I really want to mush them. Or eat them.

"What are they?" I ask again. I like them whatever they are.

Mum's behind me sitting on the couch in her spot with her legs out with her ankles crossed on the coffee table. She's doing a needlepoint. "They're fun," she tells me.

I don't really know what I should ask. So I say it again. "What *are* they?"

"They're cute," says Mum, needlepointing.

My face is right up at the screen. I'm studying the snowman's body. It's like the Pillsbury Doughboy. It's like chewy food. "I want to eat him," I say.

Mum's doing her needlepoint. "I want to eat you," she says.

DAVEY AND GOLIATH wasn't on anywhere. On *Superfriends* it was the Wonder Twins—"Wonder Twin powers, activate! Form of . . . an eagle! Shape of . . . a waterfall!" I don't like them but I like watching them. They're the same sort of people as Donny and Marie. They have shiny dark hair and white teeth. I sort of mix them up. I always mix up the songs that go *Time keeps on slipping*

slipping slipping into the future and *Slip slidin' away.* Also I used to always confuse tomatoes and cucumbers. I love cucumbers. Mum would give me a block of cucumber and the shape of it and the color looked like the whale's tooth in her room. I'd eat it like a giant carrot while I watched TV. I'd ask the baby-sitter for tomatoes and she'd bring them all cut up in nice red slices on the plate. "Oh," I'd say. I hate tomatoes.

"These are tomatoes," the baby-sitter tells me. Her name is Candy but she looks like her name should be Joan. Her face is always like it was stung by a bee. It looks chewy.

"I know but the other ones that are like them," I tell her. I've been whining all afternoon but Candy doesn't say anything about it so I can really turn it on. I listen to the singsong sound of myself and play with it, higher and lower. "The *other* ones," I whine, "the other ones that are like them, but green."

"What other ones?"

"The other ones that are *like* them," I whine.

"You mean cut differently?"

"No-oh." I hit the wall and rap it with my stick. I brought the stick in from outside to whittle it later with my jackknife. "No," I keep saying, "the other ones that are like them. But *green.*"

"Green tomatoes?"

"No!" I'm rapping the wall. I'm whining.

Candy speaks loudly over my racket. "Green tomatoes?" she says again.

"Oh!"

"I'm sorry, Via, I don't know what it is you want," says Candy.

THINKING OF THAT made me want a cucumber. I got up from the cartoons and went back into the kitchen. I looked in the fridge. There were cucumbers in circles on a plate on the top shelf from dinner the night before. I put one in my mouth. Outside it was winter but in my mouth it tasted like a little bit of spring. It was sweet. It tasted like watermelon. It tasted like summer.

The Tiny One

—

SUMMER'S AT THE CLUB POOL when the sprinkler's stutter sounds like a rattle being shaken really fast. On the other side of the hedges is a wire fence and you can hear the dulled pop of tennis balls bouncing and being hit.

In the pool the boys flip their hair back in slaps when they come up from underwater. In the water you have to time it right to talk to someone because they might be underwater and can't hear you. Cy does a thing for me where he goes underwater and then splashes up for a breath with a happy face, then goes under, then shoots up with an angry face, then goes under, then comes up with a dork face, then goes under, and keeps going like that with different faces.

HANGING ON TO the edge of the pool at the club the air smells like wet sunned cement. I have tea parties with Charlotte underwater or we say things to each other under there and then try to guess what we said. Underwater our voices sound like beasts in cartoons. I have a clear orange squirt gun and I shoot the water into our mouths for a drink and it tastes like warm plastic. In the deep end some boys are going "Polo polo polo polo."

At the snack bar we charge French fries and soft ice cream. At the counter the floor is slimy on my bare feet like in the pool's bathroom. The radio behind the counter loops out music and it's Jimi Hendrix going *If you can just get your mind together, Then come on across to me. . . . We'll hold hands and then we'll watch the sunrise, From the bottom of the sea. . . .* The older boys walk around with their shirts or bandannas on their heads. They wear sweatbands on their wrists for tennis. They take off their shirts to do cannonballs into the pool, and the splash fans out like fireworks. In the water their arms and shoulders are brown and shiny. Their red mouths are wet. When they get out their chests are even and smooth and I want to put my head on them like a pillow. I want to get on them and, like, wriggle around.

On one side of the pool there's a little field with a huge stump toward the middle. We use it as a base for Home Free. The field's full of purple and white clovers. If you pick them and then pull out a line of petal and bite it at its end like it's a blade of grass you can taste the sweetness that the bees are after. There are tons of bees. They really nestle into the clovers.

I step on them to see what it feels like to be stung. Andrew Fiske does it with me. He's a grade ahead of me. Me and Andrew step on the bees and after a while Andrew stops. But I keep doing it. I just do it some days. I go stick my foot in the pool after and then take it out and look to see how much of the stinger's left in there. Sometimes half of their body gets left behind as well. With those ones it's easy to pull the stinger out. The ones that hurt the most are when just a tiny little bit of stinger gets left deep in, like a deep splinter. You can't get it but you can see it fuzzy way under the skin like you're looking through ice.

One sting I get is really bad. It makes me stop for a while. The lifeguard puts baking soda on it. It's right in the middle of the arch on my foot. It swells up so much that I don't have an arch. "And you've such high arches," Mum says. She says if it doesn't go down by morning we'll go see Dr. Hooper.

I'm sitting on my bed putting my little toe to my mouth to bite the sharp nail on it off.

"What are you doing?" It's Marly in my doorway.

"What?" I say. I wonder how long she's been standing there watching me with my foot to my mouth.

"What are you doing?"

"Biting my nail," I tell her. "The one on my little toe."

"Oh," says Marly, then she comes in to inspect the bee sting on the bottom of my foot. Mum told her about it. Marly comes over to my bed to look at it. She holds my foot in her hands. "Oooh," she says, looking. "Poor Via." She winces. She holds my foot gently.

The Tiny One

She runs her finger along the tops of my toes. Then she asks, "Right here?" and she pokes her finger right into the middle of my puffy arch and stabs it. It doesn't hurt as much as I think it should. It makes it itch and ache. It makes it feel hot.

"Get out!" I yell. I'm not crying but I wish I could. I'm sort of smiling because I can't believe she did that.

Marly's smiling. "Sorry," she says, "the devil made me do it."

BUT REAL SUMMER is in Maine on Sky Island with the fog and the sun and padding down the wood dock in bare feet. The motoring boats leave a white trail behind them like they're unzippering the ocean.

There's the ocean at home in Masconomo too but this one with Maine is much more the sea. Our house on Sky Island is right on top of it. The ocean's like a tongue that tongues around under our house. Our house is half on stilts over the water and it's almost part of the yacht club out in front at the end of the wharf. We can jump off the balcony upstairs into the water when the tide's high.

In the living room you can see the water reflecting up onto the ceiling like swimming lights of fish. In my room at night sometimes the moon shines on the water enough that it lights up my ceiling in wavy light. The moon shines into my room and outside it lights up the water so it looks sleek like the back of a fish.

I'M LITTLER and I'm looking out the window of my room in Maine. There's the little rope wreath that dangles from the shade that you pull the shade down with. The wind's making it knock against the window's glass in dull little thuds. I'm looking out the window. There's a white light shining around on the dark water. I tell Mum, "I see a fairy out on the water." I point. "See?"

Mum's changing the pillowcase. "It's the moon on the water, love," she says. "It's the moon. A built-in fairy."

———

AT THE END of the day sometimes Sky Island gets really still so the water looks oily. The dock posts squeak and their squiggly reflections wiggling on the water make the water look like marbleized paper. Sasha would make paper like that. It smelled like vinegar in the dining room when she was making it.

On still nights you can hear everything out there in the thoroughfare between us and South Island. There are lots of boats on moorings. We can hear it all out there. A man coming up on deck in his sailboat, kicking something by mistake in the dark, his gruff voice faint but completely clear like he's inside the drawer of my bureau in my room—"Margaret? Darling? Where's my watch? And where are you?"—in the darkness and then I hear him muffled, can hear him going down below. Or from a porch all the way across on South Island I can hear a woman—"Jonathan? Jonathan! Come look at what Emily's brought us"—then the women's laughter like running feet to my window. Some of the boats have parties or then there are the teenagers, people like Pete and his friends, "Wahoo!" whizzing out in boats into the night, and some girls shrieking, a guy going "Smitty, man, look! Wait! Go back! Scully's ralphing by the ramp!"

IN THE THICK FOG you can't see a thing when we're socked in. You can't even see the ferry landing or the end of the wharf. We can hear all the boats around us, trying to find their way. Everyone honks. If they're not honking you can hear the engines gurgling along like some kind of dragon out there in the white. Dad says fog's just a kind of cloud that's low down on top of us.

I'm on the window seat looking out at the white fog. Mum has an album playing kind of soft. I'm looking out at the white fog. "Is this what heaven's like if we're in a cloud?" I ask.

"No," says Mum. She's fixing the arm of the wicker couch with a pair of pliers.

"No?" I ask.

Mum's snipping a piece of wicker off of the couch's arm like it's a twig. "This is probably a lot like purgatory, though," she says.

"I can't see anything," I tell her.

Cy comes in and stands next to me, looking out. He's holding the bottom of his red T-shirt out so it's like a pouch for a mound of potato chips he's just gotten from the kitchen. I take one. "I can't see anything," I say again.

Cy crunches a chip. "Maybe it's all gone," Cy says, "just us."

THEN COMES the deep end of summer when the ocean's like thick blue suede, and the wind is the finger that smudges darker lines across its fuzzy grain. It gets really windy. You see the gusts come feathering across the blue water.

Real summer is Maine, and Amanda makes me laugh so hard. We can't stop. The clouds move fast above us. We look up at the trees and they look like they're falling because the clouds move so fast behind them. We laugh so hard we fall into each other and I pee in my pants.

I have a black eye from falling on a rock. It started with just one eye and now it's both. It got bigger every day for two days and then it stopped. Now it gets darker. Mum says it'll turn green and yellow even. We were at the cookout and Sam Smith was singing with the guitar and I kept looking at him and his mouth when he sang. Then later I was so happy he was teasing me and I was running away from him in the dark across the rocky beach and I tripped on a rock and fell on another one. It was dark so no one could see. It hurt. My head felt like a sharp mountain. In the van on the way home it was still dark so no one cared. We drove slowly past the old overgrown graveyard in the woods but I wasn't even scared since my head hurt so much. I slept at Beth's in the top bunk. I told Beth's mom it hurt and she put a Band-Aid on a little scratch that was on my forehead because she thought that was the problem. When I woke up I couldn't open my eye. I swung my head over the bunk to look down at Beth, and Beth screamed. I got up and looked in the mirror. It was really puffy and purple. I loved it. When I came home Mum was in the kitchen drying dishes. She looked at me. "Heavens," she said. In the afternoon we went outside and Mum took pictures of it.

Me and Amanda laugh down the road because Mum's coming to pick us up. Amanda's swerving around because she's still laughing. Amanda smells good like straw and pancakes. We stop laughing and we're quiet and then Amanda says a word—"car"—and we collapse laughing on the ground again. It's a dirt road but I don't care if it's all in my hair. My pants are wet because I peed in them from laughing so hard and I can't open my big black eye. My stomach's aching from laughing and I can taste the dirt from the road. We're laughing so hard we're just quiet and shaking. Amanda pulls me up. Her hair's messy from rolling around.

When Mum comes up in the car she looks really serious which makes us laugh again. Cy's in the back and Pete's up in the front. They both look serious too. There are boxes and things in the way back because they're bringing them somewhere.

"You've got to at least go change your pants," Mum says to me. It's not funny to her. Sometimes she's the one trying to get me to pee in my pants. Once she was imitating the girl at sailing who squints one eye all the time even when there's no sun. I fell to the ground laughing at Mum and then there was a puddle of my pee on the gray wood floor. Dad came in and looked at it and said, "That damn dog."

Pete gets out of the car because he's going somewhere else so me and Amanda get in the front. "Dream Weaver" is on the radio. Me and Amanda have our penny candy in bags on our lap. Mum eyes mine.

I ask Mum if she wants any. "Mmmm," says Mum, "how about a piece of that purple licorice."

The purple licorice is rare. The red's always at Cheston's the market but the purple's only there sometimes and it's really good. Like the purple fish. There are always red fish but only sometimes there are purple fish. The red shoestring licorice is good too but it's not at Cheston's all the time. You take the string licorice and then you tie it in a knot then a knot then a knot then another knot then it's like a tangled chewy red golf ball that you put in your mouth.

I look for a purple licorice for Mum. I'm afraid maybe we ate it all. I look into the little bag and shake it around. I want to be able to give her a purple one. "Oh." I reach my hand in because I think I see one but it's just a red one that was shadowed so it looked purple. I look at Mum. "Can you live with a red one?" I ask her.

Mum smiles at the road in front of us. "I can live with a red one. Yes," says Mum.

WE GO to the post office sometimes and the guy in the booth window stamps our hands and arms with FRAGILE or HANDLE WITH CARE or THIS SIDE UP. They're better than those tattoos that you put on with water and then end up peeling off like paint. After the post office we go down to Cheston's to return bottles and cans and buy penny candy with the money we get from the cans. When we're pouring out the half-filled beer cans the old beer's slimy and hunks of gray mold like pussy willows or slugs come out of them. Sometimes there are real slugs. Sometimes there's a soaked cigarette butt and the flat beer's ashy black. The penny candy's in glass dishes behind glass and under a glass counter. You have to ask for what you want. Amanda likes the chocolaty things. Me and Ethan go for the licorice and red fish. The bags for the penny candy are like brown paper grocery bags shrunken to the size of little people like if people only came up to where their knees are. After carrying them around for a while the throat of the bag gets all wrinkled and curled like the top of a Hershey's Kiss. Ethan keeps his bag neat and he saves his candy. Me and Amanda usually eat it all fast. We all buy the little bags of barbecue potato chips and then go eat them down at the ferry landing. You can climb under the pier at the ferry landing and there are different levels to sit on.

WHEN WE GET HOME I change my pants and get my bag and then I'm in the boat with Amanda and Ethan on our way to our sailing class overnight. Our sailing sailboat to the overnight's going fast. The water sprays up at us salty with the sun. The boat dips up and down over the waves like we're riding an animal.

Then we finally get there and we're out on the overnight on Columbine Isle. The salt water makes my hair feel crunchy. Amanda and Ethan and me climb around the stubby hills to look around for the sheep. The sheep graze loose on the island. We're not supposed to chase them because you can give them a heart attack they get so scared.

Me and Amanda and Ethan climb to the top of the biggest green hill. We get up there. At the top the wind's blowing really hard and we all laugh. It flaps our T-shirts and blows our hair and pushes us in gentle shoves. It blows into our mouths. Beneath us the water is blue, out like a rug as far as we can see. To the left the hill goes falling down to the ocean and then right across the way is Minnegan Island. Then to the right farther away are the hills on the mainland. We're way up looking down; we're on a throne.

When we come down from the hill we get our food out to eat. I don't like the bread and I don't like it when it's on the sandwiches. In my paper bag it's all things I like. In one plastic Baggie I've got pieces of steak from dinner. Then I have a bag of Humpty Dumpty potato chips. Barbecue. In another Baggie there's a chunk of a cucumber. The Baggie's fogged over like a bathroom window. The cucumber's warm so I don't eat it all. I have a can of Welch's grape soda. There's strawberry soda too now and I like that but grape's always good. So's orange. If it were me, though, I'd make tons of different flavors—peach, watermelon, banana, blueberry, raspberry. I don't get why they don't. I don't get why they don't make more colorful sneakers either. Like with purple or bright orange or like shiny silver decals that change color in the light.

The Tiny One

I take a sip of the Welch's while I'm still chewing the steak and they all mix around. Grape meat. The soda's warm but I don't care. It makes the bubbles slip around more and feel hot in my throat.

We have a fire already. It smells good in the wind. Since it's pretty light out still some of the flames mix with the air so you can't see them. I've put my pants and sweater on and we've sprayed Off! everywhere and Amanda got some in my face by mistake so my bottom lip's numb. It tastes sort of interesting at first but then it's gross. Philip the instructor is getting a bag of marshmallows out. We get to burn them on the fire and then eat them. Some people deal with the cookies and the chocolate and the layers and everything but I don't care about all of that. I just like the marshmallow, burning it like a comet and then peeling the black crust off so the goop underneath looks like ice cream that someone leaves on a spoon when they don't take the whole bite. I eat the charred crust. It tastes like sweet ashes. Then I do it again. Every time the crust gets a little thinner and tastes wispier.

Philip's the tall instructor with tons of freckles everywhere. He has them on his lips like an old banana. He tells a ghost story that's a little too scary. It's not about a ghost. It's about a sailing instructor who's schizophrenic which means he doesn't know what he's doing. He doesn't know that he's killing the kids he's in charge of. They're all on a sailing overnight just like we are. One by one the kids disappear getting killed in gross ways. The crazy instructor's just as scared as everyone else because he doesn't know he's doing it. It's not fun because what if Philip's that way. Or some of the other instructors. Like Christian, or nice Gwen.

The older boy who lives in another country who's here in Maine for the summer for the first time with his family is really scared. There's a sailing instructor from Spain, Emmiliano, but he's gone now, but when he was here with his accent whenever he'd yell to us "Pull in the sheet" he'd say "Pull in the shit! Pull in that shit! What's so funny? Do you hear me? Pull in that main shit!" The older boy who lives in another country is hugging his knees and not really looking up.

We're scared too but Amanda and I get into the same sleeping bag so it's not that bad. We're laughing because we're so scared. We kick our legs around while we laugh scared inside our sleeping bag.

Gwen the instructor has to calm everyone down and tell us that it's just a story. She's the nicest one. To calm us down Gwen tells a story too and we think it's not a ghost story but, it turns out, it is. Gwen smiles when she gets to the creepy part. The fire's on her face. But she makes it nice. Gwen tells us the story and it's about an old fisherman who crashed into the ledge off of where we are and drowned.

"That's why it's called Fisherman's Ledge," Gwen tells us.

But the story's not over. Gwen tells us about how there's a little light out on the end of the point to warn people of all the rocks on the ledge. The rocks are really jagged and bad. Gwen tells us about how during a big storm once a family was lost out in their boat getting tossed around. They were heading straight for the rocks on Fisherman's Ledge, but they didn't know it. They would have been smashed to bits but they saw the Fisherman's Ledge light just in time and veered away from it.

The next day when they were back in town the dad of the family was down at Cheston's getting groceries and he told everyone about how close he and his family had come to being shipwrecked. He told about how they saw the warning light just in time. Then everyone who was listening to his story looked at him funny. They said that the Fisherman's Ledge light hadn't been working for months. The Coast Guard kept forgetting to fix it. Then, another time, soon afterward, a lobsterman was so lost in the thick fog he couldn't see where he was and his compass was broken. He thought he was pretty far away from the ledge but then he saw a light sort of hovering in the mist. The lobsterman called to the light because he thought maybe it was another boat but it didn't answer. The lobsterman steered away from the light in the fog because he didn't want to hit whatever it was and then, suddenly, the fog began to break up a little bit and he could see an edge of land in the distance that he could recognize. The lobsterman realized he'd practically gone right up onto the top of Fisherman's Ledge except he'd curved away to steer clear of what he thought was another boat that wouldn't answer him. The lobsterman turned around to look behind him and in the shadowy fog he could still see the light again but this time he could make out a figure, the fisherman, holding the light like a lantern, standing on the sea. The lobsterman could see it—a man—and then it just sort of drifted into the misty fog and disappeared.

"See," Gwen tells us, "the ghost of the fisherman protects people. So he'll protect us too."

I SAW a ghost once but I was so little I don't remember it really. Or I do but I remember it from what Marly and Cy say. Our baby-sitter Missy's about to get married and we go with her to go look at a house in Beverly that she might buy.

The woman named Ann selling the house brings us to a room upstairs. The room upstairs is bare with white walls and wood floors and a couch with a white sheet over it that's facing toward the window. Marly and Cy go outside to play catch or something. Missy's holding me, then she puts me down.

The woman Ann selling the house is walking around the room, talking to Missy, ignoring an old lady that's sitting on the couch. I look up at Missy. I remember this. I say, "Who's the lady?"

"What lady?" says Missy. "That's Ann. She's the lady selling the house."

"Not her," I say. "Her." And I point to the couch. "The old lady in black with the crow on her shoulder," I say. The crow isn't really on her shoulder. It's near her shoulder sitting perched on the back of the couch. The old lady isn't scary looking. She looks sad with a wide face like an Indian princess's but wrinkled. Her hair is white and up. She's looking out the window sort of like she's wishing for something. Missy doesn't see her and I think Missy's kidding me because Missy's little dog Bucket is barking at the old lady too just like I'd be doing if I was a dog.

Marly and Cy are outside when me and Missy come back out. The lawn isn't really a lawn, just a triangle of grass with a short hill that's so steep it's almost like a wall. Missy tells them what I said. In the car Marly and Cy keep asking me questions about it.

"Did she say anything?" asks Cy. He means the lady with the crow on her shoulder.

"No," I say.

Marly's in the front and she's turned around resting her head on the seat to look at me. Marly stares at my mouth while I talk. I'm not explaining enough. She looks away from me and turns to Missy who's driving. "And Bucket was barking too?" she asks Missy.

M U M S A I D there was a ghost in our house when we first moved in. I wasn't born yet. It was the guy who the road we live on is named after—Slate. It concerned me. "But was he a kind man?" I ask Mum.

Mum's unloading the dishwasher. I have to listen carefully through the clanking. "I'm not sure what kind of man he was," Mum says.

"I mean, I mean a mean ghost?" I ask.

"He'd just play around," says Mum.

"Like what?" I ask her.

"Mmm. Once we unrolled a bunch of rugs and then in the morning when we came downstairs they were all rolled back up again."

That didn't sound good. It sounded like he didn't want us here. "What else?" I ask her.

"Oh." She's putting the glasses upside down in the cupboard. The cupboards look like windows with their panes of glass. "He'd slam doors. Open and close windows. That kind of thing. Dad had to nail them shut."

"A lot?"

"Oh, every once in a blue moon," says Mum.

"Dad nailed stuff?" I ask.

Mum nods. "Mmmm–hmmm," she says.

I go to Dad. He's out in the garden. He's bending over without bending his knees. He's pulling up grass in clumps and it sounds like Charlotte's pony when it's grazing. I'm behind him. "Sure," says Dad. "I had to nail a few windows and doors to keep them closed."

"Well what happened to him?" I ask.

"To the nails? I took them out, I guess."

"No! To Mr. Slate, Dad!"

"Your mother. I don't know. She went out to the back of the house one day and said something to him."

I go to Mum. "What did you say?" I ask her.

She laughs. "It's a secret."

"Mum!"

"Pip-squeak!"

"Mum!"

"I told him we're a nice family and it was our turn to live here now so it was time for him to hit the road."

"And he left?" I ask.

"Either that or he's being very quiet," says Mum.

FOUR

The Bath

⎯෧ I DON'T KNOW why because I don't think I've ever taken a bath in the morning before school in my life but instead of watching the rest of Wonder Twins I went upstairs and turned the bathtub on. Mum does it sometimes, takes a bath in the morning. I'll go to say good-bye to her on the way to school and she's in the tub. When she leans forward to give me a kiss her face is rosy like it's sweating but it's just wet and warm, her bosom floating full in the water in front of her. When I have my book bag and my coat on and everything it feels sort of weird to be next to the warm water and have all of my clothes on and Mum's naked.

Anyway, I turned the water on and I filled the tub up really high. When I got in it stung at first because it was hot but then it felt good. I sat up and before I put my arm underwater I dipped my finger in the water and then wrote my name with it on my dry forearm.

When Pete would take baths sometimes I'd sit on the toilet

with the lid down to keep him company. I'd tell him his legs looked like a werewolf's and I'd stare at his penis. The whole area would almost float like a lily pad. "Don't stare," he'd tell me, his ears under the water.

In the bath I turned over to lie on my stomach. I kissed my wet arm. I kissed my wet shoulder. I lay on my stomach and pretended like I was swimming. I blew a few bubbles. It feels good to get your shoulders under. I tried to get all of my body under the water. I put my head underwater up to the edge of my nose and lay very still. My ears were under so they were cupped quiet. I let the water get still and flat around my face so I felt like an alligator, waiting, just eyes.

When my ears are under the water I can hear the pipes by the drain by my feet clinking like I'm in a submarine and I can't hear them when I'm above the water. When I flick the side of the tub with my fingernail I can hear it really loud. It's like when you're chewing. When you're inside it, it's loud. When I have a pickle I can't hear a thing—"What?" You have to chew, stop chewing to listen, chew again. I love pickles. But I don't know why they even bother making sweet pickles they're so gross when the dill ones are so good. It's like a dirty trick that no one's pulling on you when you take a bite of a sweet one that's shaped like a dill so it's disguised and there's no way of knowing.

I've put my finger up my bum in the bath. It's all clean. When I first did it I felt the inside all cushiony and it scared me so I quickly stopped. Then I did it again because I could. It was tight and then soft and made my face tingle. Sometimes a long hair gets up my butt hole and it feels like unraveling air when I pull it out.

WHEN I HAVE a cold and my nose is all runny and slick I can stick my finger up almost to the far knuckle. "Look," I say to Cy. "Look," I say again, keeping my finger there.

He turns around to look and Mum does too. "What?" Cy says.

He's looking but he doesn't really see. He doesn't get how far up my finger actually is.

Mum does. She wrinkles her forehead. "Don't do that, love," she says to me. "It's not necessary."

AT SCHOOL my friend Lulu says, "I can make my tongue touch my nose or I can put my tongue up my nose." And she can.

MUM SAYS never to put anything smaller than your elbow in your ear. I've seen Dad cleaning his ear with a toothpick. I've seen him do it with a bobby pin too or with the cap of a pen, with the little pointy part that sticks down from the cap. Dad loves the smell of earwax.

Mum and Pete say you shouldn't cross your eyes because if the wind changes you'll be stuck that way. There's an old lady at church who it happened to. I picture her as a young girl on the top of a green hill, horsing around, crossing her eyes and, up, suddenly the wind shifts into the other direction.

At church there's another lady whose face is scrunched squinty to the side and Mum says it's because when she was leaving her wedding and the guests were all throwing rice at her a grain went right into her ear and froze her face.

The oldest lady of them all, way back in the back pew, always wears navy blue and a hat and her head shakes around. The veil off of her hat quivers. Cy says it's because she has rocks in her head and she keeps moving it to be sure that the rocks won't stay in the same place and sink into her brain. "But don't they bang into her brain when she's shaking?" I ask.

Dad doesn't come to church but sometimes he drops us off and then picks us up after. On the way home we go to the drugstore and pick up the newspaper. There's a row of them like big fallen dominoes turned to papers on the floor by the door. Ours has

REVERE written in blue Magic Marker along the top of it. I usually get a Charms lollipop. I like the blue ones. I like it too because I haven't had breakfast yet and it's like having candy for breakfast. Dad's not with us today.

"Why don't the rocks bang into her brain when she's shaking all the time?" I ask again. I'm talking about the lady with the rocks in her head at church.

Cy's talking to me but he's looking ahead at where we're driving. He's up in the front with Mum. "No," he explains, " 'cause it's like all the rocks are all in their own, like, pouches."

"But then why don't, why don't the pouches hold them still?" I ask.

"Because they're not thick enough," says Cy.

I knew it didn't really make sense but it kind of did.

I ask, "What does she do when she goes to sleep?"

"Um," says Cy. "She probably has a little machine that makes the pillows of her bed shake."

I ask Mum. She's driving. Mum says, "She shakes her head because the rocks are so heavy that she's constantly straining to hold her head up with her poor little neck."

THE WATER in the tub was getting cold so I let some out but not even for long enough to hear the drain begin to gulp. I turned on the hot water and for a few seconds it was cold but then it was warm, then it was hot. When I turned it off the pipes rattled all the way down the wall.

I farted and underwater it came out in a little series so it sounded like when Cy plays Asteroids while we're waiting for subs at Lorraine's sub shop—*badeee doy doy doy doy doy*, underwater. When I try to play a turn I get flustered. I'm shot into crumbles almost right away. I'm good at Space Invaders. Cy gave us all Pong for Christmas one year and it seemed like such a grown-up present I didn't understand how he did it.

ONE YEAR for Christmas I went and took stuff from around the house and wrapped it up to give as presents. I didn't understand where gifts came from then really.

Dad unwraps his red wrapping paper. "Why thank you, Via. I've always wanted my own belt. What a thrill to have it back!"

Mum opens hers. "Well. It's the—what is this? It's the little glass bear from the—" She holds it up to Dad. "Where's it from?"

"Part of the fun," Dad says.

"Really." Mum turns it in her hand. "I can't remember where it's from."

"The sideboard in the dining room," Dad says. Mum's holding it up in the same way, still wondering. "By the china bowl," Dad says.

"Right." She remembers, and puts it down.

WHILE I DRIED OFF, the drain chugged down the water like a big toad. Mum would say hurry up because I always take too long getting out of the bath. Most of the time it's because I just want to get back in the water. Mum would say, "Hurry run get on your nightgown before the Germans get you!"

ONCE I TELL Sasha that the Germans will get me when she's here once in the bathroom while I'm drying off. "For you it's the Germans?" Sasha says.

"It's always the bad Germans who are coming to get you," Mum says.

"For me it's always the Russians," says Sasha. "Quick! Thirty seconds or the Russians will get you!"

I don't think of who it is, just bad people who will get me. Like at church when I'm praying I pray God bless Mum and Dad, Pete,

Marly, Cy, Sparky, Milo, Linus, Jezebel, Incubus, Puddle, Sweet Pea, and Bean, all adopted children, nice people, and then I end up rounding it off to just all the good people in the world who you, God, think deserve to be blessed.

I'M LOOKING at my First Communion book with Sasha. She's eating cream and strawberries out of a white bowl. "Yuck!" I say. I hate cream.

"What?" Sasha says. "You don't like strawberries?"

She knows I love strawberries. "I love strawberries!" I cry.

"You don't like cream?" She knows I don't.

"Gross!"

"One day you will," she says. "Mmmm." She puts a spoonful in her mouth. "One day you'll love it."

BUT I LOVE strawberries and I love any fruit. Once in Maine I got hives everywhere. Mum walks me up the road to the little room that's the summer doctor's office.

The doctor takes my temperature. He's puzzled. "I can only say that it'll pass," he says. "Reactions like this tend to simply run their course."

"Reaction?" says Mum. "Yes. But reaction to what?"

"Who's to say, really," says the doctor.

"But reactions are serious, Doctor, are they not? Her father, for example, could easily die from a bee sting."

"He could?" I cry. I'll have to stop him from going out in the garden. I'll have to keep an eye on that.

Mum and the doctor are looking at me. I'm sitting on the examining table with the white tissue paper crinkling underneath me, itchy.

Then Mum thinks of it. "Well, what have you eaten today?" she asks. "You had Cheerios for breakfast. . . ."

I look at Mum. She's looking back at me like she's saying, *Well?*

"Um." I'm thinking about it. "Um." I think. Then I know. I say, "I had, um, like two plums, no, three plums, those huge strawberries. An apple. Four peaches. Two nectarines. Another, no, an orange—those raspberries from—"

Then Mum and the doctor are both laughing.

THE BOOK FOR my First Communion's called *We Celebrate the Eucharist*. Sasha's looking at it with me while she eats her strawberries and cream. There are blank pages that already say things like "Here I am with my family" printed along the bottom and then up above you're supposed to draw in your family. Or "The world is full of people whom we pray for. Here are some of the people I pray for." I draw adopted children. On a couple of them I draw dots for tears coming out of their eyes and upside-down smiles for frowns. Sasha's laughing because I bring up adopted children so much throughout the book for things like "These are people I would like to make happy" or "I can spread my love with people who need it like . . ." and "Here are some people whom I will pray for who aren't as lucky as I am."

Sasha laughs. "What about the poor kids who don't have a family at all?"

I don't understand. "What?"

"What about orphans?" she asks.

"They *are* orphans!" I say.

"No they're not. They have a family," Sasha says.

"Not their real family," I tell her.

Sasha's still laughing. "What got you hooked on them?"

"They're poor kids!" I say.

"Why don't you pray for kids who don't have any food?"

"What?"

"Or kids that get beat up and run away from home."

"What?"

"Adopted kids are usually given up for adoption for a good reason, you know. They're not just forgotten about."

The Tiny One

"What?"

Sasha laughs again. "Where did it get into your head?"

Mum worked in an adoption place before she married Dad, but that's not why. It's not because Marly used to tell me I was adopted, either. I don't think. Marly used to tell me Mum and Dad had to take me in because Mum found me on the doorstep in a brown basket and when Mum brought me back to her old friends she used to work with at the adoption place they couldn't find anyone who wanted me so Mum had to take me herself.

"But I look like Mum," I'd tell Marly. "And I look like Dad too," I'd say. That proves it.

Marly'd shake her head back and forth. "Via. People just tell you that so you'll feel comfortable with us."

But that's not why either because I never really believed Marly. There's the scar Mum has where I was cut out of her.

Sasha laughs. "Adopted children."

"They're just kids," I say.

I GOT OUT of the bathtub, dripping water on the light blue floor. I twisted my hair in a towel like Mum does but it didn't stay. I sort of wanted to go into Mum and Dad's room and do something like wake Mum up or try on her purple dress.

MUM'S DRESS IS long and purple and has little round mirrors the size of dimes sewn onto it. They're mostly scattered around the neck but then there are some down lower too, all alone. Mum's standing in front of the mirror twisting her head around to look at her back. She's getting ready to go into the city for dinner or something. I just ate a turkey TV dinner downstairs and now I'm watching her get dressed. I don't really know where she's going. I don't care. I just wish she wasn't going. "It's what Indians wear," Mum says. She means her purple dress she's wearing.

"No it isn't!" I cry. I fall back on the chaise. I have lots of energy. I feel like air and trees and running. "It isn't!" I say again. Indians wear buckskin and beads.

"Indians made it," she says.

"They did not!" I kick my legs up in the air and look at my red sneakers.

"India Indians, love," Mum tells me. I don't know about India Indians but I don't ask. One day sometime I'll know. I look at Mum sideways since I'm on my back. "Like Indian print," she says, looking in the mirror. "Like your Indian print T-shirts."

She's going to the symphony tonight. She's happy. Her voice is gentle. "It's like *The Nutcracker* but without the dancing," she tells me.

I see three of her in the mirror. "Then what do you watch?" I ask.

Mum's patting her stomach. "Mmm. You just look around," she says. She lifts her dress up to adjust something underneath. Her underwear is black and lacy. "Like when the chorus sings at school."

"I watch the singers sing when they sing," I say.

"Well," she says, "I don't know then. You just roam around inside your head."

She turns around and looks at me instead of the mirror. "Do I look nice?"

"Uh-huh. Mum. You know something, Mum? You know what?"

"What's that, love?" She's back at the mirror, smoothing her eyebrow with her finger like she's applying a sticker.

"When I grow up, Mum, I'll live in a jungle house with a hammock with walls made of lilacs and all the animals can come live with me."

"Sounds lovely," says Mum.

I kick my leg up and grab on to my shoelace that dangles down at me like a worm. "In a tree."

"Even better."

"In a tree that grows out of the water but you can get to land on a ramp."

"That'd be fun, wouldn't it."

"A glass ramp. No. I'll live in a house all made of glass. No. A boathouse." I'm thinking of things all at once. They're flying across my head like a banner that doesn't have an end. "No. The jungle house. Forget about the animals. Just *some* animals, Mum. Little soft ones. Baby wolves. I don't want big giraffes and stuff in the way. I don't want deer antlers. Baby tigers. But it couldn't be in a tree. And you can come visit me, Mum. But you have to let me wear just a grass skirt because that's what you wear in my jungle house."

"By all means."

"Then we'll go up to the big rock and chop the girl's head off for the gods."

"We'll what?"

"She'll be dressed up really pretty with beads and everything. I'll make arrowheads. We'll throw the girl over the cliff into the water and then the corn will grow."

"Will it?"

"And we'll save the girl's blood and we'll . . . we'll put it in a—no, we'll pour it on the—no, we'll—yeah, we'll put it on the flowers so they'll grow. They'll grow big and really red and really pretty." I try to slow my head down with a red flower up in it, just the flower alone in a garden, red, with tons of petals, no just a few.

"Where did you hear that?" Mum asks.

"What?" I'm investigating petals.

"Where did you get that idea?"

"What?" I'm still on my back with my legs in the air. I'm kicking my feet together.

"Don't 'what' me," Mum says. "Where did that idea come from?" She means the girl that we'd kill. She's looking right at me.

"Nowheres," I tell her.

———

AFTER MY BATH I stood at the sink and brushed my teeth. I brushed them to the tune of "Lucy in the Sky with Diamonds." I can do it really good if I sort of move the shape of my mouth while I'm brushing.

Then I went into my room. I put on my dark red tights because I remembered it was Valentine's Day. I put on a blue-jean skirt. We have to wear skirts or dresses at school. The boys can wear shirts and whatever they want, just not jeans. Next year in fifth grade they'll have to wear a coat and tie. While I looked for a sweater I kind of thought of which sweater Brendan would like, not because it was Valentine's, but just because. I put on my gray one with a zipper at the neck and at the bottom of the zipper's a white metal ring. If I zip it all the way up it's a turtleneck. I got it on the way back from Maine last year at Memorial Day.

WE GO UP to Maine for the weekend at Memorial Day and it's not summer yet so we have to bring our parkas even though at home it's not that cold. All of the colors of the trees, the ocean, everything, are a shade lighter than when we're there for the summer.

I'm picking flowers with Marly for the Memorial Day parade. She lets me pick them but she points to where they are. "Forget-me-nots," she says, pointing. They're so little and blue that they're my favorite.

"Who named them?"

"I don't know," she says. "Here, over here we can pull down some lilacs." She breaks them off for me because they're high up and they're so big. It's not that easy for her to do. She hands them to me. They smell like Mum. I stick my face in them. They're my favorite too.

"Who names flowers?" I ask again.

"Depends," says Marly. She's coming back to me with more lilacs.

In the parade I hold hands with Roy. Roy lives on Sky Island all the time. We walk with the other kids and we're behind people in uniforms walking in rows. I'm wearing yellow tights. First we stop in front of the Legion Hall and Roy's dad reads some things, lots of names. Then we march down to the ferry landing and the guys all in army uniform shoot their guns. It's loud but when they do it we kids with flowers throw our flowers over the edge of the pier into the water. Some kids don't throw them out hard enough over the railing so their bouquets sort of fall against the pier and stay there instead of drifting out onto the water and then out to sea.

It's for the dead soldiers. The flowers and the gunshots are for all the soldiers that are already dead. The flowers floating in the water are what look sad to me. When I look behind us back at the little town there are people standing out on their porches watching. All the people in the store Cheston's are out on the street looking down.

FIVE

The Bus Stop

⌒ CY WAS still asleep. Cy always sleeps as long as he can. Mum says it's because he's growing so fast. When she says it I see Cy in his bed, getting longer. Cy has bad knees because he's growing too fast. We used to be able to play football on the lawn, me on my normal feet, and Cy would run around on his knees so we'd be at the same height. I'd be faster but he'd be stronger. Now he can't kneel; it hurts too much. Even though Marly and Pete go away to boarding school Cy still goes to Bayside with me. It's his last year. He hardly ever takes the bus like me. He says it leaves too early. He rides his bike even in the snow. Our house is really close to school but I like taking the bus. I ride my bike too when it's warmer. Sometimes I walk.

When I left the house Sparky was at the door, wagging his tail, saying good-bye, wanting to come with me. His breath was making fog marks on the glass of the French door. They faded really fast since it was so cold outside. He smeared the glass with his wet nose when he smushed too close.

I have to walk to the end of Slate Avenue to get the bus. I wasn't in a hurry so I walked close by the Emersons' house. One of their lights was still on. It's on a timer because they're away. They went to France. I knew they were away but I walked out onto their lawn and looked into the windows. The snow on the lawn was deep so some snow went down my boot but it wasn't too cold. I looked into the Emersons' kitchen. A small light was on. I wished they were home. The kitchen was so still. The plates were all in their spots. With the light on it looked like one of them could walk right in only it was extra clean looking. I wished they were there. I'd go in and we'd have cookies. Tessa makes cookies. They both like chocolate so usually they're grown-up sorts of cookies that I don't go for. But the smell is nice. I got close to the glass. I wished I could get in. I wished they were home. I thought of Mr. Emerson and me out on the lawn together, standing right where I was standing, the snow gone, earlier in the year.

I'M WITH MR. EMERSON out on his lawn and it's almost summer. We just had coffee ice cream in blue bowls in his kitchen. "Wonderful," he said when he finished. He gave the bowl a little push away from him while he wiped his mouth.

Now we're out on the lawn. It's dark and warm. I can hear the crickets. We're looking up at the stars. Mr. Emerson knows all about them. He's pointing at different things and some of the time I know what he's talking about but some of the time I don't and I sort of pretend I do. But these ones I see. They're a little cluster of stars in an almond.

"Yes, right you are," Mr. Emerson's saying. "There they are." He's looking through the binoculars. Tessa's in the kitchen. He calls to her. "Tessa!"

I look down the side of the house toward the kitchen. I can't see her. The light's yellow and it comes in a thick shaft out the window onto the lawn where it pools. I see her movement make a quick shadow on the lawn. We hear Tessa answer, "Darling?"

"This child's able to see the Pleiades with her bare eyes," he calls to her.

We hear her. "Imagine!" A pot clanks.

Mr. Emerson looks through the binoculars again. He repeats her words softly. "Imagine indeed," he says.

I see their cat coming toward us. He's got something. "Up," I say. "Gray Puss has a mouse."

Mr. Emerson takes the binoculars from his eyes and looks down. "Indeed he does," he says. Gray Puss puts the mouse down on the ground in front of us and swats it around a little. Mr. Emerson talks to him. "Well done, Puss," he says. The dead mouse looks wet and exhausted.

Puss looks up at us. His eyes shine black. He's purring loudly. It's dark. I feel something exciting with his loud purring and the warm dark. I wish Mum was here too—the stars, the dark, Mr. Emerson, the purring, the ocean down below us that we can't really see.

From the sound of his voice I know Mr. Emerson's quoting something. He's looking at the cat and mouse. He says, " 'The earth that's nature's mother is her tomb. What is her burying grave, that is her womb.' " He pauses. He looks over and down at me. "Are you familiar with that quotation, child?"

"Nope."

He's got the binoculars back up in his face again. His other hand's in his pocket. "It's from one of the greatest love stories ever written," he says. "*Romeo and Juliet*. Do you know all about them?"

"Kind of," I tell him. "Not really."

I look out toward the ocean. It's hard to see it at night from the hill we're on because it blends into the sky. We can hear it. I can feel it moving swishing around down there. It's dark and I'm standing next to Mr. Emerson and Gray Puss is purring with the caught mouse. I say, "Ashes to ashes." I say it because of "tomb." I say it because of the warm dark air and the purring. I like the way it sounds into the dark so I say it again. "Ashes to ashes."

Mr. Emerson laughs a little. I don't know what's so funny. "Yes. That sort of thing," he says, then chuckles some more.

THE PRIEST SAYS "Remember you are ashes and to ashes you'll return" before he puts the ashes on your forehead. I love going to school with the Ash Wednesday ashes like war paint. Before First Communion I'd beg Mum to let me have part of her host when she came back, just for a taste. "No," she says, pushing me aside. She's down on her knees trying to pray. The knee rest in the pew is like a low balance beam but padded with a reddish cushion the color of the eraser at the end of a pencil.

"Just half," I'm begging. I want to try so bad. She's leaning forward with her head in her arms so I can't see her face. I try to edge under her arm a little to get in there. "Please," I'm whispering. I really wonder. "Please please," I whisper.

Mum shoots her head up and fakes a very angry face at me and whispers, "No no no, pint size!" which makes me laugh so I stop.

Cy makes them for me out of Wonder bread. He smushes the piece of bread so it's really thin. Then he pushes quarters down on it to make circle indents that he pushes out.

He's the priest. "In the name of the Father, the Son, and the Holy Spirit."

"Amen," I say, and cross myself like the grown-ups.

I LEFT THE EMERSONS' and walked down the hill. The marsh was covered in snow. The marsh rivers looked like dark curlicue roads that get thick and thin. I saw a heron flying up in the air and it looked like a needle pulling thread across the sky. I love the marsh when it's warmer. It's like half land, half sea. The ground is spongy and the prickly grass is hard to get used to like you're afraid of what might be in there. Cy and his friend Mal build rafts out of Styrofoam and wood and life jackets and then use a hockey stick to pole around with through the twirly streams.

As I got closer to the end of Slate Avenue I could see Jeremy was there already at the bus stop. Jeremy Niven's the only other person who waits at the bus stop with me. He comes from across the street. Both of us live up roads off of the main road. I'm on this side; he's on that side. It's like living on different sides of a river. Jeremy's in the sixth grade. Most of the time he wears brown or mustard-colored clothes. In his house there are mustard-colored glass ashtrays on the brown tables. At dinner his mother poured our milk into olive-green glasses so it made the milk look sour and I didn't want to drink it.

Jeremy was playing with his pocket-size electronic football thing. He was biting his bottom lip while he pressed the buttons. Every time he got a touchdown it made the trumpet sound they do at the Red Sox games before everyone yells "Charge!"

He kind of looked up from the game when I approached. "Hi," he said.

The day before Jeremy missed school. I asked him about it. "Were you sick yesterday?"

"My grandma died." His glove was off so he could play. His thumb was going crazy in thumb-wrestling dodges and ducks, pushing the button.

"Oh."

"She was sick," he said. He made a touchdown and we heard the tinselly tune.

"Oh," I said.

"Yeah. She was sick."

I didn't know what to ask. "Did you like her?"

He looked at me. "I guess." He said it off to the side like he was talking to a tiny person on his shoulder.

While we waited for the bus I watched Jeremy play on his electronic football thing and chewed on the thumb of my leather mitten. It has the perfect bouncy feel on my teeth like when you sit on a branch on a tree and it gives a sway just enough but not too much. Not too hard, not too soft. It's salty but then I can also taste the black dye. Whenever I put it on first thing in the morning the thumb's so hard and pricky that its tip is all pointy but jagged like a tiny witch's hat. I have to begin slowly working it over, gnawing at it, to loosen it up.

I'M AT HOME and we're getting ready to go skating. Mum picks my mitten up out of the mitten basket and holds it up while I'm putting on my parka. The thumb's hardened into a spike and the leather's all gnawed up around it. "You're like a dog," Mum says to me. She looks at me, then back at my mitten. "It looks like the dog did this," she says. I don't like it when she calls Sparky "the dog" but I smile because it does look like Sparky did it. "You've got to stop," Mum tells me, "they're good. They're good mittens." She looks at the spiky thumb and then touches its tip with her finger like she's touching the tip of a needle. "Huh," she says, looking at it, "it looks like the Matterhorn," then she throws it back down into the mitten basket.

"The what?" I ask her.

"Nothing."

"The what, Mum? What does it look like?"

"A mountain," she says. "A great huge mountain."

"What?" I laugh. Mum's walking down the hall away from me to go start the car and let it warm up. I'm calling after her. "A mountain, Mum?" It's funny because it makes no sense. "My mitten, Mum? But it's a mitten!"

THEN THE BUS CAME. When I got on I felt relieved to see everyone else was on there. I sat down with Caleb Cryer in our usual seat near the front. Caleb let me go sit by the window because he was drawing on the back of the seat in front of him and he didn't want to move in. Caleb was drawing a little face so that the eyes would look like boobs and he was drawing the nose so it would hang down and look like a penis.

ONCE IN MY CLOSET in my room my friend Lulu and I climbed up onto the shelf that's above the stuff hanging and we drew naked people and people on top of each other humping. We drew close-ups of vaginas. We drew penises and big huge balls and wrote down definitions from the dictionary. I looked up "hard" to see if "hard-on" was in there and it wasn't. We wrote swear words.

Then the people were coming to take off my wallpaper and paint the room white.

I didn't think about it until later when I was at school—they'll paint the closet too. I thought of someone seeing all the dirty graffiti that Lulu and I drew and I'm sitting in class. Thinking about someone seeing it all made my legs want to bounce up and down. It made them want to run.

When I get home I go up to see. "It's still wet," Mum calls after me. I'm running up the stairs. She's not mad so they must've not seen it. The room's empty and white. I go to the closet and it smells like wet paint. I touch the round pole where my dresses usually hang and it's wet. I think of the people who painted it. I'm embarrassed but I'm glad they didn't tell Mum.

I go back down to the kitchen. Mum's chopping up onions. I'm close to her and the counter so I'm watching her fingers hold them, then slice, then turn them in another direction to hold them again, then slice. I can feel the onions on my eyeballs and up my nose. "But Mum who were they?" I ask. I mean the people who painted over our dirty drawings.

"I don't know, honey. Just some guys."

"How many?" I watch her fingers. She has a Band-Aid on her pinkie.

"Two. No. Move over." I'm in the way between her and the stove. "Three. Move." I feel her elbow.

"Did they say anything?" That was the wrong thing to ask but I said it out loud without meaning to.

Mum's not really listening. She's scraping the onions off into the frying pan so it's hissing. "Did they. Say anything. Mmmm." Mum scrapes the huge knife along the cutting board a few times even after it's clean. It's like another version of whittling. Again she's talking slowly. "They did not say. Anything in particular. No."

ON THE BUS Caleb stopped drawing on the seat in front of him for a second. "Hey," he said to me, "smell my finger."

"What? I said.

"Smell it," Caleb said. He was sticking his pointer finger out for me to smell. "It smells like cherries," he told me.

I sniffed it. It did. "Oh yeah," I said.

"It's from Erica's Bonne Bell," he told me, then he went back to drawing all over the seat. Erica's in the grade above us in the fifth grade and she waits at the same bus stop as Caleb.

But most of the ride on the bus I just looked out the window. It's a short ride. The cars whished past us. I thought of how I'd like to be in one of them, low down at the window with the radio on, going somewhere. Some people were driving alone. Some people were driving with other people. It made me think of a long drive we were on once when I was littler.

WE'RE ON THE WAY home from skiing in New Hampshire. I'm little and in the way back seat.

The gerbils are in their cage next to me. It's not a cage. It's glass like what fish are put in but instead we have lots of shavings that smell and Magenta and Mazurka. They dig into the ground and sometimes I can see them through the glass all under the shavings like they're under snow. It was just a weekend trip so we brought them instead of all the cats. "Just don't touch them while you're back there," Mum said when we were getting in. At home we feed them mini–carrot sticks. They suck the sticks in with little jerks like Baby Alive.

"Here," Pete says. He's holding something.

"What is it?"

"It's some Fruit Roll-Up," Pete says. "You can have it."

"Where's the rest?"

"I ate it."

I'm taking it. It's bite size. It looks different. "What flavor?" I ask him.

"It's a new one," he tells me. "No flavor."

"Just plain?" I ask. That's interesting. I put it in my mouth. It tastes like nothing. It's salty. It's rubbery.

Pete's laughing. "Do you like it?"

"Not really. I don't know." I swallow it.

"It's part of my foot."

"What?"

"It's skin from my foot." He points to his heel where he's picked some dead skin off. "Right here."

"Gross," I say. But I laugh. I don't care. I eat skin all the time.

Mum's flipping through something. She's up in front next to Dad. Her head's tilted forward reading. I look at the bone like a round stone on the back of her neck under her ponytail. She looks up and the bone gets swallowed in. I look around too. There are hills that go far and houses where no one seems to be home. Mum looks into the back seat at us and smiles in a drifty way. Cy twirls a single hair like dental floss around his nose as he looks out the window. Pete's looking at a catalog or something. I watch Pete bite at a hangnail on his thumb. I look back at Mum and I see her looking at Dad.

"Reading's making me feel a little sick," Mum says.

We hum. The car hums. The hills are broad and dark green, thick and low. We pass old barns like faded blue jeans. We pass the store in the shape of a giant Indian chief. My room would be up in the feather. I can't even see Magenta and Mazurka. It's just a lot of shavings and that's it.

The Tiny One

I ask, "Where's Marly?"

Mum tells me, "You know where she is." She doesn't turn around.

I don't.

"Can't you remember?" says Mum.

I can't.

"You're like a senile woman sometimes. On the airplane with Aunt Catherine. Probably just about home."

Then I remember. Marly's throat hurt her so much that she was spitting into a glass so she wouldn't have to swallow. Her medicine was dark purple inside a brown bottle and it looked good. On the bottle was a sticker with a big cartoon eye that looked like it was winking. I tapped Mum and pointed to it, "He's winking," I pointed.

She looked. "He's drowsy," Mum said.

We drive. Mum touches the back of Dad's neck. "You hungry, Dad?"

"We'll stop soon."

"We don't have to yet. I'm just—"

I hear the blinker tick on. Dad winks at me in the rearview mirror. But I can't see myself. Up where Mum and Dad are the radio's playing that song "Rocket Man."

"Let's go to Burger King, though," says Pete. I like Burger King better too. No ketchup, no nothing. I take the burger out of the bun and eat just the round brown meat like a giant coin.

After we eat Mum comes back from across the parking lot with a bag of saltwater taffy. In the car Cy sifts through for the pink and orange and yellow ones. Pete likes the black-and-white-striped ones or the green ones. I don't know which ones I like. I just like them. "Why're they called *salt*water taffy?" Cy asks.

"Why do you think," says Pete.

"I don't know. Dad, why?" says Cy.

"Yeah, Dad, why?" I ask.

"Because they're made with salt water," says Pete.

"Ocean water?" I ask, but no one hears me.

"Exactly," says Dad, but he's not really talking to us. He's look-ing over his shoulder out the window, not at us, while the blinker blinks. Pete and Cy aren't really talking to him either. We're all just sucking on soft candy and talking out loud.

"I thought you couldn't drink ocean water," I say.

"You can't," Pete tells me.

"But you can make things with it?"

"Right."

"I love the saltwater taffy," I say. I'm holding my waxy wrapper smoothed out up against the window. It looks cool with the light coming through the crinkles. "Look." I nudge Pete's shoulder with my elbow. He turns his head around to look at my wrapper that I've smoothed against the window and I expect him to just look away. "Oh yeah," he says, "cool. Like batik," then he looks back down at his catalog.

"Okay," says Cy, "everyone try to suck on a piece as long as they can without biting it." For a second it frightens me because I know I'll lose. "I'll give you a dollar if you beat me," Cy tells me.

Cy tells Pete to pinch his hand as hard as he can. I get up to see.

"Why?" asks Pete.

"We'll see who can stand it longest. I'll pinch yours after."

"No thanks," says Pete. He's looking at his catalog or magazine or whatever it is.

"Okay, Via, you do it," Cy tells me. He looks back at me. "You do it with me."

"You're bigger," I tell him. We've done this before.

"I won't do it as hard," says Cy.

"Okay." I dangle my arm over the seat so he can pinch me. "Go," I tell him.

He sticks his hand up toward my face. "You do me first."

" 'Kay," I say. I start pinching below his knuckles. "Harder?" I ask.

"Yeah."

I pinch harder. "Harder?" I'm biting my teeth together to try to do it harder. "Does it"—I wish I was stronger—"does it hurt?"

Cy shakes his head. "It feels like a mosquito." He's smiling.

I try harder. I try to move my fingers around so my fingernails will slice. Cy's face is plain and then he makes a face like saying, *Ow! Ow! Ow!* but joking. We laugh. We look at the imprints of my fingernails on his hand. They're clear lines like dashes, like the way Dad's back looks after Mum goes at it for blackheads.

"My turn," Cy says.

I give Cy my hand. He squeezes and I smile saying, *Ow ooh ow ah,* softly. Then it kills really short and fast like a bite. I scream. I feel the noise of my scream scare me and rise from my toes to my stomach. It's like I'm ringing. I'm screaming.

Dad yells, "Christ!" The car shakes and we're over at the side of the road. Dad's reached back behind him. The door next to Cy's open. Dad's twisted around so he can look at me.

"But what about him?" I say. I'm pointing at Cy. "Look what he did!" I hold my hand up and I wish that the two little nail indents that Cy left on my hand were bleeding.

Dad doesn't care. He says to me, "Get out of the car."

"But—"

"You scream like that and we could all die in a crash. Do you hear me?"

It's scary with the door open. I don't think I've ever stopped on a highway before. Bigfoot woods. Dad doesn't say anything. He stares at me. I hate it. I can see Cy's breath. I feel hot on my back. My hand doesn't even hurt; it just feels a little warm. It just scared me.

"*Okay,*" I say. I'm pretending like I might start to cry.

"Say you're sorry," Dad tells me.

"I'm sorry."

"Say you know it's, it's dangerous. Long drive. Dangerous."

"It's dangerous."

"Don't whine, Via," says Dad.

"But he's the one who—"

"Via."

"But Cy—"

"I don't care," says Dad. "You're the screamer."

"Sorry."

"You can shut the door now, Cyrus," says Dad.

We're moving again. Cy leans on the window's edge. He leans his head against the back of Dad's seat. He sucks his thumb and looks out the window. He still sucks it in his sleep and sometimes when he just feels like it.

Cy looks over at me and does a face with his eyebrows like Mum does when she's in a bad mood. He's pretending to be mad that I wanted him to take the blame but he's also kidding. He takes his thumb out of his mouth and lifts a nostril at me, then pokes his thumb back in. I move close enough that I can smell him.

We're moving and when I listen for the engine it grows louder. I pretend we're in a boat. I'm up in a bunk. The engine hums along nicely. I'm in my bunk and people are up on deck steering and stuff.

Mum turns around. She puts her chin on the back of the seat to look at us. "Look kids," she says. She sticks her tongue out. On the tip of her tongue's a thin film of white taffy like Communion.

Cy pops his thumb out of his mouth. "Mum!" he gasps, smiling. I arch up to look closer. My mum. Then she sticks her tongue out at Dad to show him.

Dad pats her knee. "Good work, sweetheart," he says.

I wake up later when my head edges up against the seat so I feel crooked. We've slowed way down. "An accident," says Dad. We stop. I sit up. My cheeks feel puffy. Something smells bad. It's coming from the grocery bags that are here in the way back with me.

Farther away behind us I can see people waving on the side of the road to tell people to slow down. Where we are the highway's like a small town of cars. Cars are stopped and people are walking around. They hold their collars close to their necks since it's cold. A guy smoking a cigarette looks at me through the back window. We're in our car and we're not moving.

"Fabulous," groans Mum.

We stay there. Dad flicks the radio around. A crowd cheers. I watch the people in the car next to us decide to get out. They're a blond couple and they slam their doors and lock them and walk away. I look at the family in a yellow bug behind them. A little boy throws up and his dad gets mad at him for not opening the door.

Dad decides to go see what's going on. Mum says we'll wait but then we all get out and follow Dad. Farther ahead people are looking at something. We can see all of their backs in rows.

We come around some people. "A deer!" I cry.

"It's a moose, honey." Mum picks me up and props me on the hood of a car so I can see. The moose is standing still sideways in the middle of the highway. He's looking into the woods. His antlers are like a tree on his head.

Mum says to Dad, "Are we too close?"

Cy's got his hands in his pockets. He left his coat in the car. Cy doesn't need a jacket because he's bigger; that's what Mum says when I'm running out the door after him to go play Wiffle ball and Mum yanks me back. I'm not watching the moose; I'm watching Cy. He's standing near Dad and he's staring so hard he looks like he's an animal too. Cy sometimes looks like he has a secret and he looks that way now. He's biting his lip. He says, "Dad," and takes a few steps forward. The moose starts to snort. It paws the ground. Cy starts saying, "Excellent! It's so big!" He starts walking toward it.

"Not so fast," Mum says to him. She tugs him back toward us by the hood of his sweatshirt. Cy comes back and leans against Mum. I'm leaning against Mum too but I'm standing up on the hood of the car. When I look at Mum's face I notice that I'm fiddling with the pom-pom on her hat and I didn't know I was.

"It must be sick or something," says Mum.

"Come on," Dad tells us. He puts his hand on my shoulder. There's a policeman who's got a walkie-talkie and he's wearing a bright orange cape with a silver stripe across it.

Then someone, over near the side, says, "It's hurt!" There's a worried sound together. I look closer and I can't see anything.

The moose starts snorting. It lowers its big head. Its body starts twitching in sharp jerks. It's the same thing like what Sparky does before he throws up.

"It *is* hurt," a woman says. "Officer?" she says. "Officer, do you see?"

"We're aware of it, ma'am."

"Oh no," Mum whispers. The moose starts to get down on his knees like what circus animals do for a trick but then he tries to get up again. When his antlers are in front of the trees behind him they all look like the same thing. Then he falls down on his knees. His head crumples to the side. He starts shaking and then a guy in a tan uniform walks near him. The man holds a small gun out like on TV and shoots.

Cy starts crying. He's crying really hard. It scares me more than the gun. Mum pushes me aside and gets him. She holds on to the hood of his sweatshirt and pulls him back and hugs him. Cy's really crying so everyone's looking at him. Cy's crying head's on Mum's shoulder so I can see his face. He's crying and he looks afraid. His eyes are looking at me but it's like he doesn't even see me. "It's all right," Mum tells him, "shhh."

The Fire

⸺᧯ T H E B U S A L W A Y S drops us off across from the pond down in the school parking lot next to the bike rack. So it did that. We stopped there. I followed Caleb while we got off and then we walked together up the runt hill to the main green grass circle with the huge flagpole spiked in the middle.

The whole picture of my school Bayside looks like a fairy-tale castle or something, a huge mansion up on the hill, and it's excellent because it's my school. Sometimes when I walk to school when it's not winter I go through the shortcut path with the red sumac and the tall grass filled with burrs and those other sticky black things that look like black insect wings or helicoptered bobby pins that stick to my kneesocks. When I come out of the brambly shortcut path onto the boys' soccer field that's there green and flat like a giant palm of a hand, I look up and see Bayside sprawled across the hill before me. All the different mini–red roofs over the windows upstairs are gabled like Disney World or Snow White times. The building where our classrooms are used to be old stables for some really rich guy who lived farther up the hill in a humongous house that burned down a long time ago. Lots of times in class I'll try to make up what sort of horses lived in our classroom which was their stable. I think of show champion horses, some girl's favorite little pony, or like a wide tired old guy with big hairy ankles who'd pull all the carts around.

When me and Caleb came up from the bus from the parking lot the playground looked weird because we saw lots of people running around so it looked like recess only it looked weird because school hadn't really started yet and usually at recess it's just, like, my class and a few other classes. But this looked like the whole school was out there.

Miss Hunt our homeroom teacher was standing at our door. "Stay outside," she told us. We looked at her. She continued, "Or run in and drop your stuff off and then come back out." Miss Hunt's breath was rising in puffs. She had a round Band-Aid on her chin and I wondered why.

"Why?" asked Caleb.

"Something with the heat. It smells bad in there. I don't know."

I looked next to me and Lulu was standing beside me. She smiled like a hello kiss. With her smile I realized that this would be fun to have recess now. Lulu smiled more. "There was a fire," Lulu told us.

"No way," said Caleb.

"Yes way," said Lulu.

"Why didn't Miss Hunt say?" asked Caleb.

Lulu shrugged.

We watched Miss Hunt open the door to let us inside. A warm waft of contaminated smell came at us and then surrounded our heads. It smelled like burning rubber in the car. "Sick," said Caleb. He put his sleeve to his nose to filter the smell. "It smells like pollution." We dropped our bags on the floor underneath the coat hooks and went back outside. Lulu stood waiting for us.

"Where was it?" I asked.

"What?" said Lulu.

"The fire."

"Under like the first-grade room or something," said Lulu. "Down in a basement or somewhere."

"There's a basement at school?" The idea was cool but it kind of scared me. There's the Sloyd room, but that's different.

Lulu shrugged again. "I guess," she said.

Caleb was looking around, imagining. "Fire trucks and everything? Awesome!" he said. He looked at me. "I wish it happened while we were in school."

We've had lots of fire drills at school but never real fires.

ONE OF THE FIRST nightmares I ever had was after Pete told me about Pompeii and showed me pictures of the people all frozen into rock from the lava and everything. A few nights later I dreamed it was dark and I was far away like on a mountain but there were people hurrying around because we had to deal with these rivers of red-orange lava that were flowing everywhere. Everything was a disaster and I remember standing on the edge of the lava flow, my little ground space getting swallowed up by the lava, and I was standing on the edge like I was standing on a dock, looking down at my red sneakers with the red rubber at the toes—I was wearing my red-and-white-striped T-shirt and I knew I had to jump, we all had to jump.

AT HOME me and Cy talk about what we'd take if the house was burning down. I say my baby pillow and the cats. And Sparky. But Sparky would probably get out on his own. Cy says the cats and some of the paintings in the living room. "Why?" I ask him.

He looks at me like I'm hopeless. "Do you know how much those paintings are worth?" He snorts.

"No."

"Well. A lot."

Dad's fixing the doorknob on the door behind us. He laughs. "Sure they are," laughs Dad.

Cy turns to him. "What would you take, Dad? What would you take if the house was sinking?"

"Sinking?" says Dad. "Is that what we're on? A sinking ship?" Dad twings a screw or something out of the doorknob while he talks and when it falls to the ground he cups his hand over it so it won't bounce away.

"I mean burning, Dad," says Cy. "Burning down. What would you take with you, Dad?"

"Hmm," says Dad. He's on his knees looking at the little screw that he just twinged out of the doorknob. "Your mother," Dad says, "I'd get Mum."

"Mum?" says Cy. "What about *us,* Dad? Just Mum? What about your kids?"

Now Dad's screwing the screw back in. "What about my kids, huh? Those kids. Sure, I guess I could come back in for my kids once your mother's safe and sound."

ONLY ONCE there was kind of a real fire in the house. It was the Christmas the pipes burst so the cellar was flooded and there wasn't any heat. The oil truck or repair guy couldn't get up the driveway because it was frozen solid like a toboggan run. I didn't know what they were going to do once they got up the hill but I knew that we really wanted them to make it. I liked it, though. We could see our breath in the living room.

We're wearing hats and parkas over our nightgowns while we unwrap our presents. I'm sitting on my green inchworm with the yellow seat and horns which was the first thing I saw when I came in and the thing I wanted most. Cy's out in the front hall setting up a plastic racetrack for my cars that I got but we're all sitting close to the fire and listening to Christmas carols. Pete's eating malted-milk balls out of a carton that he got in his stocking. Marly's drinking tea and it steams up in long fast swirls from her mug. Mum's only wearing her light blue terry-cloth bathrobe at first but then she puts a hat on. She's staying really close to the fireplace since she isn't dressed that warm.

Mum's leaning against the mantelpiece to warm her back when the fire catches the bottom of her robe. No one notices until Dad does when the flames are right up near Mum's hair. Dad tears her bathrobe off of her—it's like he's being rough and going crazy like he's losing his mind out of the blue because we don't know what he's doing—and throws it into the fireplace. Mum stands there naked for a second, looking at the fire, then Dad hugs her, then she runs upstairs freezing to get some clothes. I look at her lumpy robe smoldering in the fireplace and it looks like the wicked witch, melting.

ME AND CALEB and Lulu stood outside the door and watched Miss Hunt go back in the door to school. Caleb looked at me and Lulu. "Let's go look at our room," he said. He meant our classroom. We knew it probably didn't get burned or look any different, but still it was a good idea.

At the window there's a ledge at the bottom of the wall that you can stand on and peer up to look in. We looked in. It all looked the same. Miss Hunt was in there putting papers in piles on her desk. She heard Lulu tap on the glass. When she looked up at us she smiled but shooed us away. We laughed before we jumped down. We laughed and jumped. See, this was the way it was the day before yesterday. It was still just school and jumping down. It was all recess and running around. It was Valentine's Day.

SEVEN

Reading

AFTER THE WEIRD early recess we had reading. We had the divider open since reading's a class we do all together. For most of the day the divider is closed. I'm on Miss Hunt's side. The other side's Mrs. Crockel. The divider's like a big cardboard accordion that opens and closes in the middle. When everyone's all riled up and hyper at the end of the day or after recess and the divider's closed usually people get pushed into it and it comes pushing out like a stiff curtain. It hurts when you get pushed into it and someone's right there on the other side that you couldn't have known was there. Me and Derek banged heads that way, through the cardboard. Another time I rammed into Angus and got my wind knocked out. I wheezed like an old man on the ground. Cy and Pete knock my wind out all the time but every time it happens I can't believe the way it feels. Same thing with a déjà vu. Mrs. Crockel helped me up after Angus knocked my wind out. "There," she said. "Much better." But she was too close to my face and I could smell her gross breath.

Mrs. Crockel's breath smells like broccoli when it's cooked too long but with a sting to it. I know everyone else knows it but we always forget to talk about it. Her name sounds like "broccoli" and the smell too. Her head always looks like there's stuff going on all over it. Her hair's dark and curly, her eyes are wrinkly, and then she has stuff all over like her earrings are big and her glasses and then on her glasses is like a necklace that dangles around her neck so she can let them hang down. But she never does. They're always on. Her skirt or hips are always knocking things like the Kleenex off of her desk or she can never get the window opened or closed. Sometimes when she reads out loud she'll be sitting at her desk reading reading away, out loud, and then she'll stop talking but keep reading to herself. She forgets she's reading to us. We try to stay really quiet so she won't wake up out of it, to see how long she'll stay quiet reading to us just in her head.

Miss Hunt handed out cool rubber triangle things to put onto your pencil, grips, so you hold the pencil the right way. I chose green. It was see-through when I held it up against the light from the window and it looked like sour-apple candy so I tried chewing on it. I tried to use it as an eraser but it didn't really work.

Mrs. Crockel started reading to us a story about pioneers and this time she was standing up so her going silent probably wouldn't happen. The pioneer mom in the story dyed the girl's dress blue with indigo. Mrs. Crockel told everyone to look at Honor's dress for an example. It was flannel and its blue was the color of the sky but a little darker with little yellow flowers on it.

The desk in front of me was empty because it's Bethany's and Bethany was out sick again. Her chair was tucked cleanly into her desk like she definitely wouldn't be coming. Bethany's sort of my friend. She's always tired but when she's funny I like it. I've never had her over or anything except for one birthday party but she sits right in front of me so I always see the back of her head. Usually she wears her hair in braids and straight ahead of me I see her straight part slicing through her dark hair on the back of her scalp like some kind of map.

I wasn't listening to the pioneer story anymore. It was dumb. I like the pioneers but this one was about nothing. I took the cool pencil grip off of my pencil and held it up toward the window to see the color it makes when the light goes through it. It was snowing. Lightly, but it was snowing. The flakes were those tiny dusty ones that don't even look like flakes. They're like little swarming bugs. They're like a big version of dust whirling around in sunlight. Snowflakes always look like they're coming at you, like they're coming at the window. Except for those big fat nice ones that fall so slowly it's like you're in a dream or a movie or walking across a stage.

I held the pencil grip out in front of my face and winked at it through both my eyes so I could see it move from one side of the window to the other. The walls in the classroom are orange so when I looked through the green grip at the wall it made brown. Mum would always say that the orange walls were cozy, that on a rainy day that it was a nice cozy day for school. I'd know what she meant but I'd pretend I didn't. It is cozy at school, even outside of our classroom. The hallway down to the bathroom is long and one whole side to the right is a window the length of the hall and as high as the ceiling, and on the other left side is all doors to classrooms. In the rain it looks dark outside. The window's all wet. You walk in the warm hallway with the lights on, dry, and the rain's right there streaming down on the other side of the wet glass. You can hear teachers' voices and the rooms all look yellow with their lights on. The hallway's so long and thin that you want to run down it like running down a tube. We're not allowed. But sometimes you just book it anyway and try to run on your toes so your feet don't make noise.

We could hear the second-graders next door singing. First they were singing *with a knick-knack paddywhack give the dog a bone. . . .* I never sang in that classroom when I was in it. We never all sang together in that classroom when I was in it. Then they were singing

The Tiny One

My Bonnie lies over the ocean,
My Bonnie lies over the sea.

We could hear it muffling through the wall:

Oh, bring back, bring back,
Bring back my Bonnie to me, to me.

But I never sang in that classroom. Mrs. Winston the second-grade
teacher never sang with us.

When I was in first grade me and Billy Hoolihan would go up
to the second grade for math and reading with Mrs. Winston who
was the second-grade teacher. Then when me and Billy were in
second grade we'd go up to the third grade with Mrs. Mifflin, then
when we were in the third grade we went up to the fourth grade
for math and reading with Miss Hunt. But now we're here, so we
just do our own better math and reading on our own and we have
little sections for the more advanced kids. The kids in my class have
always been older than me because Mum put me in nursery school
a year early.

But first grade was when Billy and me started bumping up to
the grade above for math and reading. That was when Pete was still
around and not away at school yet. That was when I'd blink all the
time. I was pretty little when Pete was still at home. I remember it
though. The kitchen was more lively in the morning before school.
He'd tease me and I'd laugh sometimes but sometimes he'd make
me so mad I'd want to kill him with a gun. That was when I'd blink
all the time in rapid blinks. I couldn't help it. It was like I had to
hold the water back in my eyes. My eyeballs would sting if I didn't
blink. Or they'd water up.

PETE WOULD SIT across from me. The kitchen's yellow and
Pete wouldn't care about opening up the Advent calendar doors so
he'd let me open his for him. Cy told me about some calendars that

you open and there's a little candy inside. Ours are always just flat paper. We're eating breakfast and Pete's talking to me. He asks me, "How come you swallow all your food before you take another bite?" I'm opening the number 6 door on the Advent calendar. It's an orange king with a blue background. He's holding a red gift.

I turn around to look at Pete.

Pete's having Cap'n Crunch with the eggnog. It's the other Cap'n Crunch with the pink berries that we usually never get. "You should eat like this," Pete tells me. He shows me by shoveling a spoonful into his mouth. He chews just a couple of bites, then shovels another bite in. His mouth is full. "Much faster."

"I guess."

"And you get more." He's holding his spoon in a loose fist, thumb first with the knuckles along the handle like a backhand grip.

I try holding my spoon that way with my next bite of cereal. It takes a second to coordinate which way's which. I like it. I feel like a boy. I feel like someone who goes out into the woods a lot.

"Don't look at me," Pete tells me.

I look down.

"Why you blink so much?" Pete says. His mouth is full. I can see the eggnog in there in his mouth while he talks. He has to hold his head back a little bit while he talks so it doesn't spill out. "And you know what else you do? Sometimes you hold your breath a little when you're breathing. I can hear it. You go—" He swallows all of his food to show me. Pete holds a breath in for a couple of seconds before releasing it with a little puff of noise like people do when they're giving something big a push or picking up something heavy. "You do that," Pete tells me. "And you blink all the time. Why?"

BACK WHEN I'd blink all the time was when I was in first grade. Me and Billy Hoolihan would go up to the second grade for reading, spelling, and math and the kids were much bigger because

already I was small and a year younger in my own grade from starting nursery school early. I'm still small. My friend Lenny calls me
Midge from "midget." When it was time for us to go Mrs. Bird our
first-grade teacher would nod to me and Billy and we'd get up and
go around the corner to Mrs. Winston's room.

MRS. WINSTON'S ROOM'S taller than our usual Mrs. Bird's
room. It's on a point so there are windows on every wall except for
the one with the blackboard. Mrs. Winston smiles at us when we
come in. She nods too, jerks her head toward our desks like telling
us to come in and sit down. She smiles at everyone a lot and speaks
really softly. When Dad went to the hospital once to get a bump
taken off his Adam's apple, Mrs. Winston had us all make him cards.
Some of the kids didn't even really know who he was because they
hardly knew who I was since I wasn't even in their grade. Mrs.
Winston's the only person I know who's written a book. Marly
says it's about a big black dog and a witch and a little boy on a
marsh. The cover looks scary but it's for kids. Bigger kids.

I make a book called *The Book About Me* for Mrs. Winston to
show her I can write a book too. I tell a few stories about me and
then everyone has a different page in it and on Mum's page at the
end I write "She's almost the best mother in the whole world."
Mum reads it and then looks at me with a face that says, *Thanks a
lot*, since I wrote "almost." I'm thinking of Caleb's mom as maybe
the best mom. Caleb's mom gives us French fries then sundaes for
breakfast at Brigham's while she smokes cigarettes with her sunglasses on. For dinner she takes us downtown to Lorraine's sub
shop for cheese steaks or Italian subs. She swears in front of us and
then says "Sorry" with a serious but funny face. One morning she
watches *Roadrunner* with us. She's slouched down low on the couch
with her knees pointing out to the sides. She really watches without talking or anything. Then we look and she's fallen asleep. Caleb
puts a blanket on her and we turn the TV off and quietly go outside
to his rope swing. In Caleb's family it's just him and his mom.

ONE TIME WHEN we came into Caleb's house from the bus, Caleb's mom was in front of the TV with the blow-dryer on. She was blow-drying something fluffy like a kitten in her lap. It was white.

"What are you doing, Mom?" Caleb's standing beside her looking down at her busy hands. "Mom, what *is* that?"

Caleb's mom looks up at the ceiling. "Oh for heaven's sake," she says, not to us.

"What? What is that, Mom? What is that fluffy thing?"

"I think I'm losing my mind," she says.

"What? Mom, what is that?" says Caleb.

"Our dear dog Humphrey got to the Murphys' guinea pig."

"What? The Murphys?"

"Who're the Murphys?" I ask.

Caleb's mom's looking at her lap. The white fur's almost all dry. "The new neighbors," she tells me, jerking her head toward the window, toward the Murphys' house.

Caleb's pointing to the ball of fluff in his mom's lap. "You mean that's *Churchill,* Mom? That's Angela's white guinea pig?"

"If Churchill's the name then Churchill it is," she says. "Humphrey brought him over here. Filthy. Covered in dirt."

"But Mom, what are you doing?" asks Caleb. He's excited. He says, "Humphrey killed Angela's guinea pig? I don't get what you're doing, Mom."

"I cleaned him up. Now I'm drying him."

"But, Mom. Churchill's dead, Mom?"

"Caleb. Shhh. This'll be our little secret. I'm going to put him back in his pen out there and pretend Humphrey didn't do anything."

"Put him back dead?" cries Caleb.

I ask, "Who's Angela?"

"Put him back dead, Mom?" Then Caleb looks at me. His lips are wet because he's excited. He sprays some spit while he tells me who Angela is. He's almost shrieking. "She's the one it's her guinea pig. Instead of a big pet her dad gave it to her a little one. I don't know her really. She looks like a wuss."

Caleb's mom looks at me. The blow-dryer is whirring and Caleb's voice is swerving around. "Angela's a sweet girl," Caleb's Mom says to me, almost mouthing it, through the other two sounds: Caleb's talking and the blow-dryer's going.

"You're not gonna tell them, Mom?" Caleb's loud. "They probably wonder where Churchill is right *now*, Mom. They're probably really wondering. Hey, Mom. Mom, where's Humphrey? Where did Humphrey go?"

"They're not home. I checked," she says.

"Huh? Where's Humphrey?"

"At the kennel being groomed," she says.

"Huh? Wait. Mom, you're not going to tell them?"

Caleb's mom turns the blow-dryer off. "I don't want Humphrey to get in trouble. This way they'll never know."

"Mom!" cries Caleb.

She looks at me and rolls her eyes. "Can you keep a secret, Via?" I smile. I nod.

Caleb's mom whispers, "Won't even tell your mom?"

I shake my head while I reach down and touch the fur. "Soft," I say.

"I know," says his mom, "very very soft."

I'm there when Mrs. Murphy comes on the weekend. Me and Caleb are on the couch playing Crazy Eights. Through the cracked door we can hear the cars down on the street. Each one that passes sounds like a sheet of paper being crumpled fast into a ball. We hear Caleb's mom on the stoop saying, "Oh thank you, Mrs. Murphy. Yes. Yes, he's new. Cute, but shy."

Me and Caleb crane up to see Mrs. Murphy a little better. Mrs. Murphy's at the front door and she nods at us. She has a pinched-up face. Her dark hair's like a hat on her head because her hairline comes down onto her forehead. "Well. How new do you have to be?" Mrs. Murphy's saying to Caleb's mom. "Mailman's job's to read mailboxes." She talks so fast it's like she's trying to win a contest at it.

Caleb's mom takes an armful of mail from Mrs. Murphy. "I suppose you're right. Hopefully it won't happen again. Thanks, Mrs. Murphy," says Caleb's mom. Then she asks, "Is all well next door?"

Mrs. Murphy's sentences fly out like cards from a quick dealer. Her eyelids flutter as though the speed of her sentences were windy in them. "Someone's up to dirty tricks," Mrs. Murphy says. "Some welcome mat in this town. Poor Angela's guinea pig froze. Dying for a pet. Something her own in a new place, maybe. I don't know. Well, she ignored the ratty thing after a couple days anyway but anyhow. Froze to death. That early frost. We buried it back near the magnolia. Hard ground. Then just the other morning, Walter out there emptying the trash, the guinea pig's back in its cage. Curled up in the corner. Clean as driven snow."

Caleb's mom says, "Wow. Alive?" Me and Caleb giggle.

Mrs. Murphy says, "What, dear?"

"The guinea pig," says Caleb's mom. "Did it not die?"

Mrs. Murphy shivers her head impatiently with a frown. "No, dear. Dead. We buried it. Someone put it *back*. Dug it up, put it back in the cage. Dead for us to find it. Now who on earth would put so much thought—and time—into a strange prank like that? I'm not so sure it's not a threat. Of some kind. Walter doesn't think so. Me, I'm not so sure."

When Mrs. Murphy leaves, Caleb's mom closes the door and collapses laughing to the ground right there at the door. The mail in her hand slips in a fan across the floor. "Oh boy," she says, laughing, "oh boy oh boy oh boy." Me and Caleb are on the floor too. Caleb's laughing so hard that he's thumping his foot up and down. I keep thinking of Mrs. Murphy's face when she says "No, dear. Dead" to Caleb's mom and I can't laugh hard enough.

MRS. WINSTON'S EYES are blue but watery and reddened a lot of the time. Her eyelashes look like the tips were cut off with a pair of scissors. They don't curl. Mum says that's what happens when you cut your eyelashes. They never go back. Mum says Mrs. Winston probably cut them stubby when she was a foolish young girl and now look.

I SLEEP with gum in my mouth to see if it's true that it gets in your hair and it does. Mum has to cut the gobs out so then I have bangs and weird ones over on the side sort of. It's all over my blanket too so it's still there and later it hardens like matted tar.

MUM TAKES ME to the doctor to see what's wrong with my eyes. I pretend I don't want to go but I almost always like going. It's not my normal doctor, Dr. Hooper. It's an eye doctor. His office has lots of little signs with letters and *E*'s pointing up and down and sideways and backward. He turns the lights out in the office and shines a big light at me, comes closer. I squint. He's squinting too. I can see his cheek all wrinkled up. He holds a little stick teetering above his head. He says, "Look at this up here," like he's playing with a puppet. He wheels around a machine that looks like a Martian and then pulls its head down so it looks like it's about to lick me.

"Stay still," he tells me. On his forehead is a lightbulb that makes it feel like we're underground. I've only seen doctors in cartoons wear those lights on their foreheads. His face is close but he's not looking at me; he's looking at my eye. His eyebrows are long and he has long hair just like it coming out of his ear. He leans forward. "You like school?" The light is like a planet in my face.

"Uh-huh."

"I hear you're very good at it," he says.

"Oh."

"Like to be an eye doctor?" he asks.

"No."

"Look up at that corner over there. An acrobat?"

"Um. No."

"How about a teacher?"

"No."

"What then?" He stands back to look at me.

"Maybe. Maybe a nurse," I tell him.

"Yes. Help people."

"Yeah. Wear white tights."

YOU BUNCH the tights all up and stick your foot in, then pull them up bit by bit instead of trying to put them on like pants. Mum shows me. We're on my bed. She does one leg to show me. Her ring gets caught. Then I do the other. "You'll remember this," she says, "because you'll put tights on this way for the rest of your life. When you're a woman."

ON THE WAY home from the eye doctor me and Mum stop at Howard Johnson's. The counter is bright blue like pool paint. The leather seats are padded round like drums. Mum has a bowl of mocha-chip ice cream. The chips are so small that they look like jimmies mixed in. I have a malted-milk shake. I dent the straw with my teeth and bend it while I suck so I have to suck hard. The straw splits like a piece of grass so it makes a whizzing noise and doesn't work. Mum asks for another one. She holds up my frayed one to show the waitress. "She mangled it," Mum tells her.

Mum says to me, "When you're thinking of different things all at once, try to just think of one thing."

"Oh."

"When you think about being very busy, then your body gets all busy too," Mum says.

"Oh."

"Like with hiccups. Once you forget about them, they go

away." Usually when I have the hiccups Mum tells me she'll give me twenty-five cents for the next hiccup, and then I can't do it. When I fake it and say "See?" Mum always knows I'm lying.

Mum takes a bite of her ice cream by tracing her mouth over the spoon and leaving a mound behind. "No," she says, "that was a bad example. Or—well, just pick one thing you like and always think of that when you're thinking of too many other things."

"For blinking?"

"Right."

"Oh." I can feel my eyes starting up.

"Try thinking of Sparky. Or Cinder. Something like that."

Cinder's our dog before Sparky. I think of that. Me and Cy are walking home from school and we come to the railroad tracks and there's a black lump on it. We get close and it's Cinder on her side. Her tongue's out like she's panting but it's frozen stuck in a big lick and her fur on her side looks like it was wet and then dried clumpy. Cy starts crying. The top of Cinder's head looks dented and there's shiny gunk like dark Vaseline near her ear which is flipped up like when it blows inside out in the wind or when I'd hold her ears up together like a bow on the top of her head. I start to cry too. Cy's farther down the road and he calls back to me crying telling me to hurry up. I want to stay and look closer at Cinder. Cy calls to me again and means it so much that he bends his knees while he yells my name. I want to look more at Cinder but I run away to catch up to Cy.

It's not a nice thing to think about. It makes me feel thin and wobbly. Pete says there's Cinder's ghost flying around the lawn and the woods and along the railroad tracks. He says sometimes when you hear a dog bark at night and it sounds like her, it probably is, barking while she's flying. I can't remember what she sounds like but I like thinking of a dog floating in the air. I like thinking of Cinder flying, her little ears out flapping like Dumbo's, her legs moving slowly through nothing like carousel horses or the flying reindeer.

I look at Mum. She's holding her ice-cream spoon up in the air near her head and reading a little frame that's next to the ketchup.

It has pictures of different meals on it. Behind her through the Howard Johnson's window I see an old lady with a walker trying to get in the door. "Mum?" I say.

"Mmm?" She puts the frame back where it belongs.

"Do dogs blink, Mum?" I ask her.

"Of course." She's tipping her bowl to finish it. "Everything does."

"Oh yeah," I say.

Mum's spoon clinks the bowl like a bell. "You forget?" she asks.

"Yeah."

MARLY'S BRAIDING my hair in little braids. We're on the porch and Cy's a step down. Cy starts crying. Marly stops braiding. She touches Cy's shoulders. Cy's crying about Cinder. The air isn't blue anymore. It's sort of black and white. The trees are drooping looming on the other side of the shed. They look like giant wilty ferns. The house is behind us. No one's turned a light on yet so it falls back in the darkness. Cy's crying. We sit still and the air grows darker. All the outlines blend into one soft space to where night is like charcoal on paper smudged behind glass or like rain washing over what's been left behind.

MY WEIRD RAPID BLINKING just stops one day. We're in the TV room and I'm sitting on the floor in front of the fire in my flannel nightgown with wet hair. I'm brushing it. Mum's reading a magazine on the couch. "Hey Blinky," Mum says to me. "Guess who hasn't been blinking." I look at her and then I look at the fire. I try to blink fast and it doesn't feel right. I try at school and my eyes are just regular eyes that don't water or itch.

CY GETS PINKEYE sometimes and Mum says not to touch the red towel but I always do. I always want to remember what it's like to have pinkeye but then I hate it. The only good part is waking up in the morning and picking the crust off. It feels like the tight stitching of a football is holding my eyelids sewn together. The crust feels huge. It's like a thick stripe of stale pizza crust. Then I pick it off and it's these little tiny pieces of crust like yellow sugar or dried grainy honey. The rest of the time it itches and it's almost like when I had the blinking problem all over again.

The pinkeye's pretty much gone now but I'm playing it up like it's not because I'm supposed to read in church. It's for Sunday school. It's for before First Communion. Half of the other kids have already done it. It's just a psalm or something. It's short. It's short but you have to walk all the way up there after they call your name and then stand on a little box and read into the microphone. I don't want to do it at all.

"I can't because of my pinkeye," I say to Mum.

Mum knows it's gone. Even if it wasn't, I could still read. Mum's mad.

"It's hard to see," I whine. It never is. Sometimes it's foggy around the edges but you can always see. "It is, Mum," I lie.

Her face is red and she doesn't get mad at me like this very often. It's like she's not even my friend.

"My pinkeye," I say again. I even kind of shrug. I want Mum to tell Father Kelly that I can't do it.

"You'll never be an actress," Mum tells me. I don't understand what she means really but she's very cross.

WE'RE IN OUR PEW. It's just me and Mum since it's not Sunday. It's Saturday morning and it's time for me to go up there and read my psalm. Father Kelly calls my name for me to come up and read my little piece. I don't move. I see Father Kelly scan the congregation and then land where he knows we usually are. He looks at me but he doesn't look at me long. He looks at me long enough to see that I look back at him and then look away. He waits. Mum doesn't say anything. I look at her but she just looks straight ahead. The muscle at the corner of her jaw balls up and then lets go.

One of the altar boys goes up to read it instead of me. All I hear him read is "There is no fear in love."

Mum doesn't say anything in the car on the way home. I try to get her to laugh. "I certainly sense your displeasure," I say. Mr. Emerson said it to an angry man whose car was stuck.

IT WAS WHEN me and Mr. Emerson came walking over the bump of a hill by our driveway and on the other side there was a man standing beside his metally green car.

The car's tilted into a ditch, nose first. The man thumps his hands on the roof. "Damn!" he's saying, banging the roof. Then the man kicks the side of the door. "Piece of shit," he says. He looks at us walking toward him. He puts his hands out in front of himself like he's holding a tray. He moves his arms as he yells, "This car and crap are the same thing," yelling.

We stop near him. Mr. Emerson stands still but leans the top of his body forward a little bit as though he's talking to a cat that's on the ground. "I beg your pardon," Mr. Emerson says.

We're right there but the guy still yells. "I said *this* car. *This* car and crap are the same thing."

Mr. Emerson tries to talk to him. He says, "My word. May we assist you?" but the man isn't paying attention.

He yells some more. "I'm stuck!" He isn't talking to us, just talking like a fountain squirting water in spurts straight up into the air. "Fuck! I'm stuck!"

"So we see," says Mr. Emerson.

"Piece-of-shit tin can won't even fucking start!" The muscle strands in the man's neck are stretching like rubber bands holding his head on.

"I understand," says Mr. Emerson. "Would a telephone be of assistance?"

"I called already. Fuck!"

Mr. Emerson stands back and looks at the general situation. He looks at the car in the ditch way over on the side. "Good Lord," Mr. Emerson chortles, "how on earth did your car get all the way over there?"

"What?" The guy is rubbing his head, squinting. "Whoa, man—it was all way out of hand, man. Fuck! It's not even my car." His tone's like he's arguing with Mr. Emerson, but he's not. "It's her frigging thing. Shit! It's not even mine. This sucks!" He kicks it. "This sucks so badly you don't even know." He kicks, then slams. "You don't even know how much this *sucks!*"

"I see. Yes. Well. I certainly sense your displeasure," Mr. Emerson says.

I SAY TO MUM, "I certainly sense your displeasure." I'm not sure if it fits but Mum acts as though she doesn't hear it anyway. She's driving and I'm looking at her. She rolls her window down. The air comes in and it smells sweet like grass and wet dirt mixed with the ocean. Mum's biting her lip. She's mad. The radio's on and it's that song about someone knocking at the door, somebody ringing a bell. I always mix it up with that other one that has someone knocking on the ceiling three times. I guess it's the knocks. But the music doesn't sound good since Mum's mad. She's biting her lip and not looking at me. It's like other times when it's practically like I'm not hers and I can't get to her. Like once when she's bent over getting things out of the hamper. I sneak up behind her—"Boo!" I scream. Mum's body sticks up rigid and she drops all of the clothes. She turns around. I expect to see her nice face in a smile. Instead it doesn't look like her. Her face is red. She yells without really opening her mouth, "Don't you *ever* do that again! Ever!"

I FEEL LIKE a brat sometimes. Sometimes when I tattletale Mum tells me I'm being a brat. But sometimes I do things that make me feel like a brat. Like when Mum brought some sneakers home for me once. I wanted running sneakers but these ones were gross. They didn't even have a name. I wanted Adidas or Puma like Pete. Adidas. All Day I Dream about Sex. These ones Mum got me are queer. They're lightish blue suede with a kind of plastic stripe. The soles are tan. They're dorky. I sneak them out to the edge of the lawn after dinner. They're still tied together by their laces. I throw them as hard as I can over the edge and it feels nice. They fall down the hill and I hear them land in the bushes. I turn around. No one sees me. I go back inside. No one saw.

Then it's hot summer. Pete and his friend Jay come in sweating from clearing the sides of our hill. They've been out there whacking the sumac with machetes all day. I'm on the floor on my stomach in the front hall coloring in *Curious George*. A chain saw's purring steady then revving down the street. The screen door slams behind them. Pete comes over to me. He holds something down in front of my face. The pair of blue sneakers are dangling hooked on Pete's two fingers. "Oh," I say. They're still brand-new but dusted with dirt on the suede like that fancy chocolate powder that's on mousse cakes.

Mum's coming down the stairs. My stomach ripples. Pete turns around and holds the sneakers up to her. "Oh well look," Mum says. She walks over to us and kind of looks down at me. "The sneakers that you left on the bus."

I'm looking at their bare feet while Pete talks. "Left on the bus?" Pete says. "I thought they'd be V's. They were right smack in the middle out there."

I look up. Mum's glaring down at me.

"They're so geeky," I tell her.

She's looking down at me. She nudges me with a light kick but it hurts. "Ow," I say.

"You spoiled brat," Mum says to me, flat, and I can tell like she really means it.

———

The Tiny One

WE LEARNED last year that Eskimos eat mostly blubber. It's a big happy time when they have a new whale's blubber to eat. The kids fight over who gets to eat the eyeballs because they love them so much. Eskimos tie things together with sinew which is like the thread that comes out of meat. Mr. Emerson says if you use a word three times then it becomes your own like you finally know it. You have to use it in a sentence, not just say it. *Sinew.* A *sinew* from the blubber is caught in my teeth. Mum chews her meat and then spits it out when there are too many *sinews* in it. On the side of Mum's plate is a pile of chewed pieces of meat that had too many *sinews*.

Mum. I think of different things to try to remember. If you tell yourself to remember things usually you can. I tell myself every once in a while. Right now I looked at Mrs. Crockel. I looked at the way her head was tilted and the blackboard was behind her with "loom" written above her shoulder. By her hand was the back of Angus's big head. I told myself remember this. Remember this and this is fourth grade.

I HAVE a dead grandfather Pa. It's the only other person who's dead. I didn't think I remembered it very well but I remember it now. I don't remember what I felt like but I remember what I saw. I remember what I watched.

THERE WAS Marly braiding some rope over by the terrace since she wishes she could have long hair. Pete's behind the shed, and Cy's digging a hole on the edge of the driveway where the Big Wheel's turned crashed on its side. We all know that my grandfather Pa's sleeping fully clothed and with no covers over him on Marly's bed upstairs since he was watching us from her room and then decided to lie down for a little bit and told us so through the window. Pa leaned over and called to us outside through the screen like it was a microphone. "I'm gonna lie down just a short minute."

"Some timing," said Mum. Pa's her dad. She was unloading the things in boxes onto the card tables they had set up on the lawn. We were having a yard sale.

"I'll be up before anyone comes," Pa said, and turned from the window. He was saying something but we couldn't hear him since it was muffled and indoors. Then Pa came back to the window and called through it again. "Via you go nap too." I was sitting next to Mum and hoping they'd forget. My naps were getting more forgotten. I looked at Mum. She said to me just a short one. She said I could lie on the couch in the living room instead of my room upstairs since no one was inside downstairs.

I'm on the couch and Marly's running around the house in an arc and then she keeps going. I put my nose to the crack in the window so when she comes rounding my corner I can hear her breathing and laughing to herself. I can hear her skirt swishing around her knees.

"Marly!" It's from the other side of the house where the porch is. It's Mum. "Can we please get a move on it here? It'll all get ruined. We've got to bring the blankets in too." Then I can see Mum. She's by a table. She picks up a garbage bag and stuffs some of the clothes on the table into it. When I was still outside, the plastic of the garbage bags smelled damp already. Mum stands up straight. "And Marly!" she calls. "The laundry! Tell Pa there's the laundry out back."

Marly's on the step. "He's sleeping," she says. Her voice is high. The blankets in her arms touch the ground.

The sky grumbles loudly and the wind flutters the price-tag signs taped to each table. "See, it's saying hurry it up!" Mum means the wind. She means the rain that's about to come.

Pete comes around the shed. His gray shirt blends into the shingles. Mum has her chin tucked in to fold an old quilt. Pete walks toward her. "Here, take that bag and do that table," Mum says to him.

"I told you this was going to happen," Pete says. He means rain.

Mum's folding a stroller. "Where'd Cy go?"

"Nobody even came," Pete says.

"Well they didn't have much time to," says Mum.

"I told you," Pete says.

"Well. Here. Will you get that stuff into this bag?" Mum hands him a garbage bag.

"The worst that'll happen is everything will get wet," Pete says.

"And then mildew," Mum says. "Marly!" she yells.

Marly makes a high-pitched noise which makes Mum and Pete laugh. Mum stands still so she can hear and yells, "The laundry!" She hears a response but can't hear it enough.

I can hear it because it's right next to me. I hear Marly's feet go padding through the kitchen and out the back door. Then she comes running around outside from the back of the house and stops where I can see her. Marly brushes the hair out of her face. "I can't reach it!" she yells. She's excited. She can't reach the laundry. Mum answers okay. Marly turns to look at me in the window as she walks away. She smiles.

Cy's hitting a tennis ball against the side of the shed. The shingles make the ball go sideways or dart up if it hits an edge. I can't see him but I can see the other side of the shed and I can hear it. He gets close to the wall so it's fast sounding *bhap bhap bhap bhap bhap*. Mum hears it. She calls out to him. "Cy! Everyone's doing something but you over there picking your nose."

"I'm not picking my nose," Cy calls back. The ball's going *bhap-bhap-bhop-bhap-bhop*.

"Well come help," says Mum.

Bhap-bhap-bhack and then I hear the ball go bouncing down the driveway.

Cy comes into the frame of my window. I see Mum touch his head. "Over there," she says.

"You think really people will buy it all?" Cy likes it. He and his friend Liam with the minibike set up lemonade and things like that and try to sell them on the street.

"Probably some," Mum says, "but not today."

The trees are blowing like they're being shaken and I can see the backs of their leaves pale green against the dark gray sky when they blow. The gray shingles on the shed look purple. There's thunder again. Mum laughs with Cy as they hurry. Pete laughs a little too.

In the window in the hall I see something pale pink waving like a bird or my tutu. I lean so I can see more. Marly's arm clutches it and then tosses it to the ground. She has a chair from the kitchen. She's pulling down the clothes without undoing the laundry pins. She's talking to herself. I can see her mouth moving when she's squatted down to pick up the clothes. The window's shut. The glass is wavy so she and the colors look wavy through it. While she's bent over she yells, "I got the laundry!" Then through the other ear I hear Mum and my brothers laugh. Pa coughs in Marly's room upstairs. "I did it," Marly yells again.

The thunder sounds again but it doesn't scare me because I can hear all of my people outside. The couch's material feels warm and damp and my skin feels soft like the way the trees look outside, the way the sky looks, the way Marly's arm looked holding the pale pink shirt in front of the bright trees and the dark, warm sky.

I can hear Mum putting the trash bags on the porch. "If it's quick we can just put everything back out again," she says.

Pete's still on the lawn. "It doesn't look like it'll be quick," he says.

Mum's going back down the steps. "Well if," she says. The air looks like some of the green in the clouds has come down to us.

Then Marly's beside me on the couch. When I look at her she says "Shhh. Lie down."

"But."

"Something's wrong with Pa," Marly whispers. I look out the window to see where Mum is so Marly will go do something. "I can't tell if he's sleeping," she whispers.

"He's upstairs," I say. I take Snoopy by the neck and put him on my lap.

"I know but I can't tell," says Marly.

"Go tell her," I say.

"You come with me," Marly says. She lifts me from the bed even though she barely can and then takes my hand. "I tried to wake him," Marly says.

At the porch door the rain's pouring over the roof and Mum and Pete are shaking the water in their hair and watching Cy come running toward the steps with a garbage bag held over his head. When Cy comes up Mum rubs his head and says, "Listen." We all listen. We listen to the rain. "It's like people clapping, isn't it?" says Mum. And it is like that. Mum points to the gutter where the water's coming down in a stream just beyond Pete's head. It's bigger than a hose. "Look at that," says Mum. She's sitting on the railing. The water's coming off of the roof. All around us it's loud water falling and loud singing rain. Mum turns around and looks out. "I love this," Mum says. "Don't we love this?"

I hold on to Marly's hand. Mum looks at us. Mum smiles. Her face is all wet like a washed fruit. Then she sees I'm out of my nap on the couch. "Did Marly get you to watch the rain? Aren't you lucky to have a sister like that?"

I look to see where Marly's looking and she's looking at the driveway. Marly grips my hand a little tighter. "I don't know if Pa's sleeping," Marly says.

"I hope he's watching," Mum says. "Pa!" she calls. She calls him Pa too.

"No—I tried to wake him," says Marly.

"He's sleeping?" Mum says. Mum isn't looking at the rain anymore. She's looking at Marly.

Marly tosses my hand and then grips it. "You better go see," Marly says to Mum.

Mum walks in the door beside us. She calls up the stairs. I hear her going up the stairs and then Marly pulls me inside with her. We stand at the bottom of the stairs. The rain sounds everywhere since the windows are all wide open. My feet are wet. Then we hear Mum start to yell. She's yelling. She comes running down the stairs. "Kids!" she yells. She steps on my foot as she runs toward the corner of the room. "All of you, get up there!" She has the telephone at her ear and the rain's coming down in sheets over the open window behind her, splattering in. "Peter bring water or something!" calls Mum.

Marly pulls me running up the stairs and in the room Cy's hitting Pa's face with his hand and Pete's trying to pour water over his head. Then Pete tries to pull Pa out of the bed and put him on the floor to do something to him. We're all saying his name, even me—"Pa Pa Pa"—and Pa's not answering and then Mum's in the doorway biting her lip with her forehead hard against the frame and when I see her face I start to cry and she picks me up so my nose is against the round skin of her shoulder and I can see her free arm in the doorknob. She kisses me on my ear and holds my head very tightly with her hand.

EIGHT

10:00 Art Class

AFTER READING we had art. I love art class. Always. I do drawings and stuff at home too. Like when it's raining or just when I'm bored. Like I'll be on the floor on my stomach in the TV room drawing, kicking my feet together in the air up behind my head. Mum's on the couch sewing something. "Look—Mum," I tell her. "Mum, look."

Finally she looks. She tilts her head sideways so she can see my drawing. "Mmm. Interesting. Why's the water purple?"

"What?"

"The boat's pretty," says Mum. "Why's the ocean not blue?"

"What?"

"You heard me."

"What?"

"Why's the ocean purple?"

I look at my drawing. "Water's purple sometimes," I tell her.

"Fair enough," she says.

It was Valentine's Day so we were making hearts and stuff for Valentine cards in art class. Everyone made them for their parents. We folded the construction paper and then cut the half heart and then open it like a book and then there's the full heart. It made me want to make snowflakes instead. My metal scissors were sticky because there was glue matted in the joint. They were bruising my fingers. I could feel it. The left-handed scissors have orange rubber handles so you know they're the left-handed ones. I wish they all had rubber handles because then they might not bruise so much.

Miss Gracie put a shoe box down on our table. I sat up on my stool to look inside. "Excellent!" I said. Brendan leaned up to see. The box was full of tinfoil hearts. They were red and silver but like metal. I saw some gold ones too. I took a couple out. "Will they glue on?" I asked.

Miss Gracie heard me even though she was across the room putting some construction paper away behind the sliding-door cabinet. "They should," Miss Gracie said. I held up a red one. It folded like thick Reynolds Wrap when I bent it. I wrapped it around my finger like a Band-Aid. It made me think of me and Mum.

MUM'S SQUATTING DOWN digging for clams in the mud. We're at Caulkins Cove. I'm standing beside her. I'm in my bathing suit bottoms with only my sneakers on. The mud inside of my sneakers feels like warm cream around my toes. No one else is with us since we're not on a picnic. We went on a picnic today already to Reunion. Me and Mum came here just to get clams for supper.

Mum's squatted down in the mud with her boots on raking up clams with a little hoe. Mum has a peach-colored handkerchief on her head. The wind flips it so it flaps down onto her forehead into her eyes like bangs. She flips it back over with the back of her wrist because her fingers are covered in dark gray-green mud.

The Tiny One

"It's clay," Mum says.

"I know," I tell her.

She wipes her hand on my calf so the mud's like finger paint on me. "Hey!" I yell.

"Is for horses," Mum says. "It's good for your skin," she tells me. She means the mud.

My legs feel firm in the wind. My wet hair's blowing around like in a giant blow-dryer of the day and I like it. I get a cramp in my side and say, "Ow!" It goes away. Then it flashes there again. "Ow!"

"What?" asks Mum.

It goes away. "Nothing," I tell her. Then it's back again in a sharp stab. I touch my side. "Ow!" I cry.

"Heavens!" cries Mum. She's raking with the little spade or hoe or trowel or whatever it is.

"Did one bite you?" I ask. They leave a little black mark on her fingernail. One bit her earlier in the summer and the black nick is just beginning to fade on the fingernail of her pointer finger.

"No. I'm saying 'heavens' to you with all of your ows. You gonna help me?"

"What?"

"Are you planning on helping me?"

I'm walking toward the water. "In a sec." I like my squishy feet with the mud in my shoes.

"Come here," Mum calls.

"What?"

"Why do you always say 'what' when you hear what I say? Come look at this."

I walk back. "What."

"Come down here," she says.

I squat down next to her. She's holding something in her muddy hand. I think of the girl's tooth in *One Morning in Maine* all covered in grainy mud like tar. It overlaps in my head with when Babar's shoe comes off in the mud on the other planet when he steps out of his spaceship.

"Look," says Mum. She's holding something.

"What is it?"

"I don't know," says Mum. "I thought it was a shell but I think it's a—" There's a bucket of water beside her. "Wait, let's see when—" Mum dips her hand into the bucket of water. I look at her head. She's watching her hand swish back and forth in the water. Her hair's blowing in the wind. The sun glitters on the ocean behind her. It's like flocks of tiny birds that never stop lighting along the surface of the water. I watch the sun glitter on the hairs flickering around Mum's face. The wind feels soft. I like it when it's just me and Mum. I look at her lips. They're smiling smooth halfway. Where the red lip part meets her skin is a smooth soft line and I want to touch it. Mum's lips. "It's not a shell," she says. "I think it's a—" and Mum lifts her wet hand out of the bucket. She holds it up. It's jewelry. It's a heart-shaped thing about the size of a quarter that goes on a necklace. It's red like a stop sign, a little shimmery like that. Mum looks at me. She smiles.

"In the mud?" I say. I can't believe it. "Right there in the mud? Like a treasure?"

"I guess so," Mum says. "Our very own treasure."

"How?"

"Beats me," says Mum.

"It's a necklace thing," I say. It's sparkly but flat.

"Isn't that strange," says Mum. She turns it in the sunlight so we can see the reflecting shine. It glints. "It's quite pretty," Mum says.

WHILE WE WERE making our Valentines in art class we were talking about what Miss Hunt would do for Valentine's Day for us.

Brendan said she'd probably give us those little pastel hearts like thick Necco Wafers that say I'M YOURS or BE MINE in red print. That's what Mrs. Mifflin did last year.

"Red cake," Timmy said. One of Timmy Avon's legs is smaller and shorter than the other one so he has a special sole on his smaller shoe that's thick like a brick to catch him up. Sometimes he'll use his big shoe like to kick someone or pin their leg down when they're on the ground. He uses the kind of crutches that have a circle around the arm. When he's just going across the room he doesn't need them, just when he's going all the way down the hall or running around at recess. When I run past him sometimes I feel like a show-off.

Honor said she thought that last year when her sister Jennifer was in Miss Hunt's class they got cupcakes with red-hot hearts on top. That would be good. I thought of red-hot dollars. Fireballs. I can make myself handle them now. They used to be too hot. I suck then I hold the fireball between my teeth for a rest. Then my lips burn. I get a little glass of water from the kitchen and plop the fireball in. It rolls around. I can see the red swirl off of it up into the water. The water's sweet and when I put the ball cold in my mouth it's perfect and pale pale pink. Mum would chew cinnamon gum. I'd always want pieces of hers but I'd have to take it out of my mouth all the time for breaks because it would sting. It's the same with Slim Jims. Pete always has them and I want one but I have to take it out and wait before I put it back in again.

At home on Valentine's Mum puts a little heart of chocolates at the foot of my bed. None of us are wild about chocolate in my family but it's the thing to do. Mum crushes them with her thumb to find the caramel and coconut ones. The jellyish ones are so bogus they make me shiver.

Honor was talking about getting a solid chocolate kiss the size of a softball. It's a real Hershey's Kiss just like the little ones, wrapped in silver, but huge. I've never seen one. I wondered how you'd bite it but I didn't ask because I was smearing Elmer's glue all over my palm in a thin layer and I was thinking more about that. Once it dries I peel it off and it looks like skin. Glue's made from horse hooves. Then I glued more hearts onto my Valentine. I had a stripe of gold hearts, then a red stripe, then a silver stripe. The construction paper behind was black and I was leaving a space in the middle that was shaped like a heart.

———

THEN WHILE Honor was talking a girl with boobs from the upper school came in and rushed past our table. She's an eighth-grader. She had a light blue ribbon in her ponytail. I don't know her name but I've seen her before. I've seen her wear a peasant blouse that I like. The embroidery around the neck isn't colored like most of them. It's just white. The ties at the neck hang loose with a couple black beads. She walked right over to Miss Gracie who was sitting at the desk at the other end of the room. It's a big wide-open room, the art room, like a gym or something but it's not that big. I watched the girl. She sat down at the other side of the desk so she was across from Miss Gracie. Miss Gracie looked up at her. They were both sort of hunched forward talking to each other. The eighth-grader looked so grown-up and to be talking with Miss Gracie like that she seemed even more grown-up. I thought of myself when I'm in eighth grade and it's a picture of someone who doesn't even look like me. It looks like Marcia Brady or someone. I can't imagine my forearms ever growing up so you can see the muscles or my hands so you can really see the bones and joints. It's like my eyes will change color to blue by then.

Then the eighth-grade girl stood up. "Well I can't!" she said. Miss Gracie looked over at us to see if we were noticing. No one was except for me. Everyone else was listening to Honor talk. She was talking about a boat or something. I could tell Brendan wasn't listening. He was shredding the hearts to make shiny threads.

"Yes you can," Miss Gracie told the girl.

The girl was upset. "No," she cried. "Just tell him I don't want to." She started to cry and Miss Gracie touched her.

"Look," Miss Gracie said to the girl, "in the end it's up to Dad anyway."

"I know," said the girl. She was wiping at her eyes with her sleeve. "I just wish it didn't happen."

The Tiny One

Miss Gracie hugged her. Their dad. Miss Gracie said, "Tell Dad I'll come over around dinnertime."

The girl pulled herself together. "Okay," she said. She was still crying though. "I just wish it didn't happen," she said again.

"We all wish that," said Miss Gracie.

Then the girl left. Miss Gracie saw me looking and raised her eyebrows up at me. "My sister," she told me, sort of mouthing it. Like Mum and Sasha.

SASHA'S HERE VISITING and she hasn't been here for a long time. I look at her. She's standing in the corner of our kitchen over where the potato chips and stuff are up on the shelf. She's eating peanuts out of the jar while she talks. I watch her. She's wearing cutoffs like mine and a black T-shirt that scoops down in the front. Her hair is pulled back but pieces are falling down. She looks tired but her face is so friendly and pretty. I stand up on my yellow chair. "Look at her!" I say. "Don't we like her?" I yell.

Mum laughs. "Certainly we do."

I can't stop smiling when I look at her.

Sasha smiles a big wide smile at me while she's chewing the peanuts. She keeps talking. She's talking to Mum. "I mean, I'd like to like work for a magazine or something and write articles but I don't want to have a deadline."

Mum's head is in the oven pouring something onto something else. It hisses. She speaks from the oven. "That's good, honey," Mum tells Sasha. "Tell them that at the job interview."

Sasha laughs. "That's not what I meant." She puts the peanuts back and goes over to the door to the porch and opens it. She stands outside and lights a cigarette. She smokes and talks to Mum through the open door. I finish my soup. I'm not really listening to Sasha and Mum but I'm watching them. They're having dinner later. Sasha leans on one leg and puts her hand on her hip while she smokes. She has a piece of leather tied around her ankle. It has a blue glass bead on it that's the color of a blue bottle we have in the bathroom upstairs.

O N C E W E W E N T to go see Sasha in a play. I was pretty little but I remember. Mum carries me into the dark. It's not on a stage. It's a big room with black walls and no windows. We all sit on the floor around the edges and the play's in the center. It's the first thing I've been to like this. They sing and dance. The girls all have leotards on top and flowy skirts on the bottom. When the man gets shot his friends carry him away. His shirt's unbuttoned a ways and his neck is hanging back so his Adam's apple is poking out. He's dead. It's so sad. His girlfriend is so upset and the music sweeps long and low while they slowly sing. I look at his big Adam's apple and I feel like that's what's going on in my own throat. It's lumped up because it's sad. It's like being on the ferry leaving Sky Island at the end of the summer.

I've never felt like hollow in my throat from a play or something before. I look at Mum. I can see her face in the dark watching them. I want to tell her about my throat but I don't know what to tell.

When the play's over I go with Pete to Sasha's house to pick up her bag for her. I'm on his back, piggybacked. When we get there a lot of other girls who look like Sasha with their long hair are out in the living room. They smile at me and want me to come sit on their laps. They smoke cigarettes. The smoke twirls up into the air in violet squiggles. They sing along with the music. It's some lady singing who sounds like a bird. I hear her sing the word "shampoo." In Sasha's room where we get her bag there's a tapestry on the wall. It's white with purple and green prints on it. On the way home I ask for one like it for Christmas to put in my room. Mum laughs but she doesn't forget because I get it and it's on my wall.

———

The Tiny One

WHILE SASHA'S SMOKING out on the porch and talking to
Mum I put my soup bowl up on the counter and then run to my
room to put my new ballet skirt on because I want to show it to
Sasha. It's just like a tutu but only the bottom so I can wear it with
normal T-shirts or over a leotard. It's a skirt that shoots out like
petals to a flower. It's lavender. While I run up the stairs the music's
coming out of the living room that deep-voiced guy deep singing
"Equal Rights." When I come back into the kitchen wearing my
new lavender tutu skirt, no one's in there. The kitchen's empty. The
frying pan's crackling softly. The door where Sasha was smoking is
still open. I come around the table. There they are. They're right
there on the porch. I stop. Mum's hugging Sasha and Sasha's shaking. Sasha's crying. I can hear Mum saying, "Shhh." Sasha's crying
so hard that I can hear her voice in it. Mum says "I know," gently.
I'm scared to go nearer but I don't want to go the other way either.
I put my hand on the corner of the table and stay there. I think to
go under the table.

"I just wish it didn't happen," Sasha says. She sniffles.

"I know," Mum says. She's rubbing her hand back and forth on
Sasha's back. Mum's voice sounds quivery like she might be crying
too.

"I just really really wish it never happened," Sasha says again.
Then she sobs. She's shaking.

"I know," Mum says. "I think we all wish that."

USUALLY WE'D LEAVE our art things in our cubbyholes in
the art room but since the cards were for Valentine's Day and it
was Valentine's Day we carried them like banners as we walked
through the halls on our way back to our homeroom. Lulu held
mine when we went into the bathroom and while I went into the
stall to pee. The bathroom was empty except for us. Lulu was saying something.

"What?" I held my pee in a second to hear what Lulu was
saying.

"Bzzzzzzzz" was all she was saying. She was imitating my pee because it was buzzing out I had to go so bad. Then we laughed.

When I flushed the toilet I thought of Mal leaning back on Cy's bed. "You're sure?" he's asking. He and Cy want to know if I see blood in the toilets in the girls' bathroom at school.

"Uh-huh," I say.

They're both paying attention to me. "See," Cy says to him, "I told you."

"A lot?" asks Mal.

"A lot of blood?" I ask.

"No. Do you see it a lot?"

I shrug. "Sort of. I guess."

Jill and I went into the boys' bathroom once with Brendan. Jill looked at the urinals on the wall. "No fair!" she said. "How come you guys get such big sinks?"

I came out of the stall and Lulu was sitting on the sink with her butt dipped into it. She jumped down. Out in the hall we skipped because we're not allowed to run. We were in time with each other like we could have been racing in a three-legged race. My shoelace was loose and it whipped around my calf like a tangling piece of grass, then undid, then whipped again. "Can you spend the night Friday?" Lulu asked.

"I'll ask," I said. I had my sleeves pulled over my hands so one of my sleeves was stretched long like an elephant's trunk. I whacked Lulu with it in her face and we laughed.

WHEN WE GOT BACK from art class the snack tray was there in homeroom so we could have snack before history. Jeanette from the cafeteria is the one who delivers it. Jeanette's always dressed like a nurse. She has silent shoes with thick white soles. When she comes while we're in class she opens the door and quietly slides the tray onto the short table by the door and then leaves while we're in the middle of class. It's a brown tray with yellow and orange Dixie cups. Along one side's a white napkin with cookies on it. You have juice or milk depending on what you asked for back at the first day of school. It's all juice—everyone gets juice—except for two or three milks for new kids who don't know any better at the beginning or whose moms make them get milk. People spit in the milk and you can't see it. It's almost always orange juice but sometimes it's red or purple bug juice. The green juice is Martian juice. The cookies are usually boring graham crackers or the sugar cookies I hate. I like the vanilla wafers with yellow in the middle. When it's Oreos it's like we've won a prize. Some kids call them Hydrox. I eat the vanilla wafers by going around and around, nibbling, so the cookie stays the same shape only smaller. That's how Cy eats his Snickers—he goes around and around, then eats the chocolate on top, then the nougat on bottom, and saves the caramel-and-peanut combo for last. I don't even really like the chocolate part of the Oreo cookie but I take the top off and suck on it like Communion.

The homeroom snack was gross sugar cookies so I gave mine to Brendan Furey. Brendan looks tough and real like he might have a big scar on his face but he doesn't. But he also looks pretty. I like looking at his face. His hair is light but his eyes are dark. Things like his jean jacket are perfectly worn in. He doesn't live near Masconomo so it's hard to go over to his house. He and his brother Trevor had me and Stephanie over for dinner once. Just for dinner. Brendan had me. Trevor had Stephanie. Trevor and Stephanie are in the sixth grade. Trevor looks like Brendan but Trevor's head is bigger and more square. His hair's darker.

We all dressed up. I wore my navy-blue dress with the white collar. Brendan and Trevor's mom closed the door to the kitchen and we sat out in their dining room with a white tablecloth and candles. Their mom served us like we were in a restaurant. There were candles on the table and a silver vase full of snapdragons. It was nice. Before dinner Brendan gave me a present. It was a bead necklace that he beaded himself, blue and black and green. We were like different people. Brendan had a tie on. The candles flickered on our faces and hands. Every time their mom came out to take our plates or give us something she had a funny smile. She made real Shirley Temples for us and put them in wineglasses practically as big as my head. We had artichokes, French fries, and steak. Stephanie's lips looked glossy in the candlelight from the butter for the artichokes. For dessert we had butterscotch sundaes. Me and Brendan had butterscotch because that's what we like. Trevor and Stephanie had chocolate.

After dinner me and Brendan went up to his room while we waited for Mum to come pick me up. We played a little Nerf basketball with the hoop on his door. We touched each other's eyeballs with our tongues. It felt soft and weird but nice and warm like warm grapes without their skin.

At school the next Monday me and Brendan were back to normal. I come down the slide and Brendan's kicking Lulu in the shins and then he pushes her onto the ground. Her wind's knocked out. I come jumping off of the swing and run over. I push Brendan and he pushes me back. Then we're wrestling on the ground. I can feel the wet grass under my thighs. He's on top of me. It's like when I'm so mad at Cy and I want to hurt him but it's not really like that because it's Brendan. It's Brendan with his bangs like brown-goldy straw that fringe on his face. It's Brendan with his freckles that I want to lick off. Our faces are right up close. I grab Brendan's middle finger. It's bending back. I bend his finger backward as hard as I can. I hear the noise and I feel its dull sound in my hand. The next day he has a metal splint on it with a little cushion at the tip but he's not mad.

NINE

History With Mr. Waring

⎯ AFTER WE ATE our snack Mr. Waring from the Upper
School came down for our history class to talk to us about the
Boston Tea Party because we're going on a field trip to see *Old Iron
Sides* in a couple of weeks. I was drawing on my sneakers. They're
white leather with green suede stripes. Adidas. We don't use ball-
point pens in school usually but I brought that one from Mum's
desk at home. The sole is tan rubber zigzag and I trace the pen
inside the zigzagging lines. The pen moves smooth on the rubber
so it feels good. We're waiting for a couple of people to sharpen
their pencils. They're waiting in line.

IN KINDERGARTEN ONCE I sharpened my pencil and then
went running after Lenny. Matt tripped me by mistake and Jamie
Pauling was standing there with his pencil just sharpened and sticking straight out and it went jabbing into the side of my neck just

under and behind my ear. Jamie Pauling's as little as me but he's a boy. He's probably even littler. His lips are thin and when he smiles it's like a little tight elastic being stretched. At the hospital Mum held my hand while the doctors pricked metal needles around to see if anything was in there because they thought they could see some pencil lead. I couldn't see it because of where it was. There was nothing in there but still even now years later there's a little gray mark that's still there like a gray freckle. "It's a tattoo," Mum says.

"No it's not!" I say.

"Yes it is. That's what a tattoo is."

"But Mum, I don't want a tattoo behind my ear."

"Honey, it's so tiny. It's so tiny you hardly see it when you look for it."

D A D H A S a tattoo on the back of his shoulder. It's nothing. It's like half of a circle or a *C*. It's dark blue. I like to touch it because there it is but I can't feel it. I touch it with my lips while he sits on the edge of our terrace after a swim over in the Emersons' pool. "But what is it, Dad? Dad, what *is* it?" I ask.

"I don't know," he says. "A birthmark."

"Blue!"

"Mmm."

I press it. "But what is it?"

"A birthmark," he says. He'll never tell me. "I was born with it," he says. I'll never get an answer.

And I'll never get an answer about Mother Nature either. We're going skiing for the weekend. We're passing the Old Man on the Mountain. You have to look up at the right time because otherwise it just looks like a pile of rocks up there making a cliff. At the right time it's perfect. It's a huge profile of a man in the cliff on the mountain. I used to never be able to see it and I thought everyone was playing a joke on me. Then I could. "But who made it?" I ask. Cy's asleep in the way back. His thumb's poked loosely in his open mouth. He sucks it in his sleep still sometimes. "Who made it?" I ask. It's like a kaleidoscope the way it just merges from a man's head into rocky cliffs as we pass.

Mum turns around and looks at me in the backseat. Dad's driving. "Mother Nature," she says. She's smiling because I always ask and she always answers the same way.

"I know. But who really *really* made it, Mum?"

"Really. I do not lie."

"Come on," I say.

"Nature, sweet pea. Mother Nature."

And mostly I understand but still I feel like I'll never get an answer. There's an Indian profile too along the same road on the side of a different cliff. He's not as good but you can still see him. The pine trees poke up and look like a mohawk on the top of his head. And then there's a waterfall called the Flume which sounds like a carnival ride but it isn't.

MR. WARING WAS there from the Upper School for our history class to tell us about the Boston Tea Party and the Redcoats. Miss Hunt stepped to the side of the room and listened and then she left him alone with us. Mr. Waring's sleeves were rolled up and his tie was green. He took his glasses off and chewed on the tip of the ear thing while he listened to questions. When he wrote on the board it wasn't in neat prissy cursive. He just scribbled something on. We could read it. He leaned against the blackboard and tossed the chalk up and down while he talked. Robby Gruen had his head down on his desk in the back row and was falling asleep. Mr. Waring didn't say anything. He just threw a chalkboard eraser at him. We laughed. He's funny, Mr. Waring. He made us laugh when he imitated the British during the Revolution being all prim and proper. He told us about "Don't shoot until you see the whites of their eyes." It was like we were older. It made me excited to be in the Upper School one day. All of the teachers down with us in the

Lower School are ladies and girls and everything's neat. We don't have anyone like Mr. Waring.

Mr. Waring was talking and standing in front of Bethany's empty desk in the first row in front of me. He put his foot up on the desk and bent his knee like he was about to tie his shoe but his shoe was tied already. He was just standing that way, resting his leg there, while he talked. He twirled his pencil on his knee. I couldn't stop looking at his crotch. It was right in front of me and I could see the round of his balls through his tan pants. I looked down at my desk but I couldn't help it. I kept looking back up. I saw him see me looking but he didn't move and change his position. I felt my face wash hot up from the neck and then go cool. Mr. Waring looked at me looking again but still he stayed standing that way with his legs apart. It made me feel like embarrassed.

THE FIRST TIME I was ever embarrassed I didn't know what being embarrassed was yet really. I have a clean dress on but I can still smell the ocean and seaweed on my fingers. It's Maine at the end of the summer. The hill's mowed green behind the man who's talking up at the award table. I smell that too. I can hear someone mowing somewhere else far away. I hear it through the wind. Summer's ending. The ocean behind the white fence is as blue as Mum's ring and it looks full like it's breathing up wind. The award table's between two tall trees. The white tablecloth is lapping in the wind. On the award table the cups are silver and twinkling. There are little ones like short glasses, but silver. There are big ones like salad bowls and platters that look like puddles of light in the sun so I squint. There are miniature models of boats. I don't know who the man is behind the table but he looks nice standing behind all the prizes. His short-sleeved shirt's the color of watermelon. His arms are tan. Everyone's sitting on the grass. Some people are on benches. They all listen to the man in the watermelon shirt and laugh together at certain things. Everyone laughing together under the trees outdoors sounds quiet even though it's not. They all clap when a person goes up to the table to win a silver thing and shake the man's hand. Marly's sitting Indian style and I'm on her lap in the pit of it. She laughs too at some things. I'm watching her hand tear up little pieces of grass.

The year before Cy had already gone home with Dad so when they called his name Mum told me to go up to get his prize. It was for the Midget Sailing races. They called Cy's name. I ran up. The award-giver man handed me the silver cup. The cup was almost round like a ball but then the top of it was open like an ordinary cup. Mum said it had Cy's name on it. There was a little blue flag scratched in above the writing. I held it like a tennis ball and ran back to Mum. Everyone was clapping and laughing. I sat back down on Mum's lap with Cy's prize in my hand. Mum kissed me and her legs felt prickly from the prickly hairs she needed to shave. Everyone was clapping. I put my head near her boob. Everyone was clapping and smiling. I liked it, but I didn't like it. I wanted them to stop but I didn't. They clapped and clapped until it lopped off into bits like rain.

But the year I got embarrassed the same boy keeps getting up to get prizes. He's Eddie Greenough. He never takes off his hat. It's dark green felt like his name. Mum says that's how you get lice, by never taking your hat off. Eddie hangs his head down plus with the hat you can hardly ever see his face. Marly's laughing because Eddie's winning so many prizes. Marly laughs and throws all of the little pieces of grass she's picked up in the air with her palm and then catches them with the back of her hand like you do with jacks—flip—then catches them with her palm again, flip, back of her hand, back and forth, back and forth, until all the pieces have fallen.

I can't stop looking at the award table. It's like a fairy palace. It's like my tutu. There's a tall thing that looks like a silver crown and it's gleaming. There's a model boat that looks just like the sailboats out in front of our house that race. It looks just like them. It even has little strings and cleats and little pulleys. There's a number 4 on the sail. I want to hold it. I want to pull the little strings so the sail will get pulled in. Cy's not here today either. I think Mum forgot to tell me to do it. I think maybe Mum forgot to tell me to get Cy's award like last year so I get up out of Marly's lap. Marly asks me where I'm going but she's not paying attention.

I walk around the people and go up toward the table on its side. I want to get closer. When I get there I can see everything better. It's all shiny mirrors. It's like a queen's party. There are silver teacups and teapots. There are big tall things like vases. The white cloth looks smooth and cool like a milk shake tastes. When the award man calls Cy's name, I'll be ready. I move closer. Already I can tell I won't be able to get close enough to everything even when I'm right there.

I'm at the edge of the table and all I see are the shapes shimmering and then I hear it. It sounds like clapping. It's laughter. I turn around. It's loud. My hands are on the tablecloth and I turn around. All of the people are laughing. Everyone I look at is smiling. All the smiling faces are like a good dream, but it's bad. They're looking at me. I look up at the award-giver man behind the table and I'm surprised at how close I am to him. He stoops over toward me. He's smiling too. I look up at him. He's supposed to give me the cup. He smiles. "Yes?" he says. Everyone's laughing. He bows forward toward me—"May I help you?" he asks me.

I don't even look for Marly or Mum. I run along the grass like I did before but this time I don't have the cup in my hand and I don't know where Mum is. I run away to the white fence. I can hear the laughter fading behind me. I run through a little clump of tall grass and I grab some with my hand and I can feel some of that spit that the bugs leave come off between my fingers. I wipe it off on my dress. The gate's unlatched. I jump over the tiny stream there and get down the road far enough that I'm home. I walk down the steps to the house. The screen door slams behind me and I go into the living room and lie down on the window seat. No one's home.

I'm crying. The boats out on the water are all pointing toward the sunset on water that's as smooth as painted wood. I feel like I don't want anyone to see me.

When Mum comes home I guess I don't look any different to her. "Hungry, pumpkin?" she asks. "Or just sleepy, maybe?" Then she goes into the kitchen. I'm on the window seat still. I'm doing two things. I'm playing with the tiddlywinks and I'm putting a deck of cards in order so I can teach myself how to shuffle with a bridge. I'd forgotten but now I remember again. Thinking of all of the audience laughing at me makes me want to put my head down on a pillow. So I do.

Mum comes back in and picks up towels left on the floor from swimming earlier. "A dress like that deserves a brighter face," she says. I know she was there but I wonder if she was paying attention.

The next morning we go down to the ferry landing to see someone off and in the parking lot I see the award-giver man in the watermelon shirt only today his shirt's red like a fire engine. I feel that feeling inside of me again of wanting to hide and I try to stay out of his view so he doesn't see me. Mum's saying good-bye to people but she can tell I'm hiding behind her. She's talking to people. I keep getting in her way down by her legs. "What is with you?" she asks.

MR. WARING STEPPED his leg down from Bethany's desk. "Are you with me, people?" he asked. Robby Gruen was talking in class behind me and giggling. I thought he probably was giggling at the way we could all see Mr. Waring's crotch. Mr. Waring went to the blackboard and started drawing diagrams of names connected with lines. It looked like a drawing of the tree houses I think of while I'm falling asleep.

WHEN I GET in bed I bring Sparky sometimes to protect me and keep lookout. Sometimes when Sparky sleeps with me I wake up and I've got my arms around him holding his paws with my hands like he's my husband. While I fall asleep I think about connecting all of the trees by planks and making a different tree house in each tree. I could make one tree a store, another tree a TV room. It would be all pulleys and planks but then I'd look down and Sparky would be way down there looking up at me, wagging his tail.

I'M UP in the tree house but then I get down to go get one of the planks from the cellar to prop it up to the first level of the tree house so it's like a ramp. I get on the ramp. "Come on, Spark," I call him. He's wagging his tail but he doesn't want to get on. I pull him by the collar and his fleshy fur rolls up around his head because he's pulling back.

Dad's walking back to the house from the garden. "What are you doing?" he asks.

"I want Spark to see the tree house," I tell him.

Dad laughs. "Leave the dog alone." I hate it when he calls him "the dog."

"He wants to," I tell Dad.

"He wants to what?"

"He wants to see the tree house."

"Dogs aren't meant to go up in trees," says Dad.

"I know," I say.

SOMETIMES DAD FAKES throwing the tennis ball so Sparky takes off to go get it then stops on rigid legs when he doesn't see it falling anywhere. Dad throws the ball straight up into the air so Sparky doesn't see it. Spark looks so stupid when he doesn't know where the ball is. He turns around and looks at us, ready. He's so ready it's like he's about to bounce off of the ground. His ears are up tight and he's got a big dog smile on his face. Spark's face is so funny, looking left, looking right, then—*boink*—the ball beans him on the top of his head and bounces right off. I laugh so hard on the ground that I'm silent and Dad looks concerned.

MR. WARING TOLD US to copy down what he had written on the board. Robby Gruen was still snickering in the back of class. "All right," said Mr. Waring. "I've heard enough out of you, Gruen." Mr. Waring's voice was prickly like it made me sit up a little straighter. "Down to the office," he said.

I turned around to look at Robby. He was sitting still. "Me?" he said.

Mr. Waring pointed at the door. "Pronto," he said.

I'd never heard that word before. It sounded like "Poncho" and Speedy Gonzales. Pronto, I said in my head. I couldn't wait until class was over when I could say it loud and crisp. I liked it. It sounded like "Tonto" or a pet pony.

TEN

Recess

⟋⟋ AFTER MR. WARING'S HISTORY we went out to go have real recess like normal, not like the weird one earlier in the morning. Out in the hall someone threw up. "It reeks!" says Caleb. They always put wood chips all over it like at a restaurant like the Ground Round when you can throw popcorn on the floor or spill your soda and it doesn't matter. The chips smell like peppermint. I don't know why they don't clean up the throwup instead of putting those chips on it. It smells so bad. I gag. I hardly ever throw up but I gag a lot.

ONE TIME I threw up. I got Cy's Big Wheel and I got on. I go toward the hill of the back driveway. I coast down and the pedals start turning so fast that I have to lift my feet off of them. I keep going. I try to drag my feet to slow down but it's too fast. I turn to stay on the road and I can feel the wheels raise up on the side like I'm tipping and then it goes back down. I'm low down and little sticks fly up when I go over them. I'm heading for the Byrons' wall. It's brick with ivy on it. I think to tip over to stop but then I'd fall on the tar. I stick my hands out to try to grab the ground so my palms scrape on the pavement and then I hit. My head hits and then I'm on my side on the grass.

The Big Wheel's still parked up like it should be with its nose against the Byrons' wall but I'm on the ground next to it. It's like a car crash. I touch my forehead. It feels wet but when I look at my hand there's no blood. I whimper. No one saw. I'm hurt. My head's like someone's squeezing it. I stand up and I feel like I might fall. I touch my head again and there are little pebbles stuck into my skinned palm like my palm's made of butter and the pebbles are like toast crumbs in it. I kind of start to cry but I stop. It's like little grunts. Then I get up and I walk up the driveway. It's long. My head feels hot. There's a bump like a Ping-Pong ball way up at the top of my forehead half in the hair. I can feel it but I hardly touch it with my hand. I just kind of feel around it like a crystal ball.

I walk down the porch and into the kitchen. Mum's at the kitchen table with papers spread out in front of her like giant white cards being shuffled. "Hello, love," she says. Then she looks up.

I begin to cry. "I fell," I cry.

"From where?" Her glasses make her look more concerned.

"I hit the wall."

"Hit the wall?" She's looking at where I'm pointing to on my forehead. "What a bump!" she says.

Mum brings me so I'm on the couch in the TV room. My head's on a pillow. Ice in a dish towel is on my forehead. The dish towel smells like grease. Mum has to tuck the edges in behind my head so it won't slide off. The things I think of in my head are like someone else is thinking them and they don't make sense. I keep thinking of trying to figure out how to bake a knife with a knife and I don't even care. I stay thinking about it too long. I don't even know how to bake. I can't explain it to Mum.

Sparky's lying on the rug sleeping on his side with his legs straight out like someone pushed him and he tipped over. I see his feet twitch.

Later on Dad comes in. He's in his suit. He's getting a book from the coffee table and he's surprised to see me. "Hm," he says. He looks at me lounged out with the ice pack on my head. "What's happened here?" he asks.

"I ran into the Byrons' wall."

"Ran into it?"

"Yeah."

"You were running along and—charge—ran right into it?"

I laugh and it makes my head feel stiff and hard like it's full of wet clay that's drying into a block. "Dad I was on the Big Wheel, Dad!"

"Aha, the Big Wheel," Dad says. He sits down on the couch by my stomach and puts the book on his lap. He lifts the ice up and looks underneath at my forehead. "Ouch," he says. He touches the bump really softly and when he does I can't help it, it's like he's pressed a button to make me do it and I throw up potato chips and grape juice all over his arm on his white shirt.

Later when I wake up Dad's standing in front of the TV watching golf. The look of the green grass on the golf course feels good in my head. The announcer whispers things like "It's a tough shot out of the rough" and "Bogey birdie." Dad's standing in front of the TV watching while he sands a small block of wood in his hands. I hear it, the sanding, like a baby saw. The noise sounds like a dog panting. The noise stops while he watches the guy putt. The tan golfer's tufts of hair wisping out from under his visor blow in the wind. He's thinking hard, squinting. An airplane hums in the background sky like the sound of distance and missing someone. The announcer's voice is a patient whisper. The golfer taps it and the ball coils into the hole. The clapping sounds like whispering too, a flutter saying *shhhh*. I close my eyes and listen to Dad's sanding again. It says, *Vee-ah-Vee-ah shhh shhh shhh. Vee-ah-Vee-ah shhh shhh shhh.*

WHILE WE WERE putting our coats on to go outside to recess after history, Brendan was telling Angus that he'd give him his snack for the rest of the week if Angus would put one of the wood chips in his mouth. Brendan was telling Angus that it had to be one of the wood chips with a little bit of throwup on it. Angus bit his lip and then looked at Brendan. "Do I have to eat it?" Angus asked. He meant the wood chip with the throwup, not the snack.

"Um," Brendan thought about it. "No. You just have to put it in. And hold it in for a sec."

I wouldn't do it for anything. Nothing. Angus picked up a chip that had a little bit of like pale pink tuna-fish barf on the corner. He looked at it. He put it in his mouth and someone yelled "Bogus!" and when Angus started to make a face I pushed the door open to run out to recess and breathe the air. I wriggled around in the fresh air. I couldn't stop twisting my shoulders and sticking my tongue out it was so gross. I couldn't stand it. I felt like doing a back flip on the pavement to get it out of my mind.

Lulu came running out behind me. The air felt warmer than it had in a long time. We ran to the tunnels. They're part of the playground. They're two cement tubes that are long enough to fit about three kids in. We huddled together even though it wasn't so cold out anymore. Lulu gave me a present. It was a Smurf holding a red heart for Valentine's Day. Then she gave me a piece of gum. It was grape Bubble Yum but it smelled too strong for us to be able to keep chewing it once we'd have to go back in. We're not allowed to chew gum at school. I eat paper in class sometimes and pretend it's gum.

Someone stuck his head upside down into the tunnel. He was on top of the tunnel looking down in at me and Lulu. It was Robby Gruen and he didn't have his hat on so upside down his hair floated out of his head like a cheerleader's pom-pom, then blew in the wind. He was laughing hysterically at something. He was snorting and his eyes were sealed shut from his smile. "God," I said. I looked at Lulu. "Cool your jets," I told him. But Robby was laughing so hard he didn't hear me. It looked like someone was pulling him and then they pulled him away. Robby gets really hyperactive a lot and spazzes out.

THERE ARE other kids who are a certain way a lot. Bethany's always tired. She yawns. She even falls asleep on her desk and the teachers don't really get mad. Her eyes look droopy a lot of the time and she doesn't say very much so when she does say something and it's funny it's even funnier because it's coming from her. Angus Baker almost always has tips of boogers snailing out of the edge of his nostrils.

Some of the new kids who are on Mrs. Crockel's side I don't really know. There was one boy who was only here until Christmas who was like a busy head. He didn't talk much but he'd laugh out loud at nothing or suddenly look worried out of the blue. Once we looked out the window and he was running straight out into one of the playing fields, laughing all by himself. "Jacob!" one of the teachers was calling after him because we'd already all come in. His blond head looked fuzzy as he smiled around out there in the distance. "Jacob!" she called again. He kept running and then ran in a sort of arc as he turned around to come back in.

ME AND LULU TOOK our jackets and mittens off and left them in the tunnels. It wasn't that warm out but it was warm enough. It was warmer than it's been in a long time. I was cold without my coat but I zipped my sweater all the way up so it was a turtleneck and when the sun was out it was okay and no one was telling us to put them back on so we stayed that way. Me and Lulu went to climb on the steep rock by the pond. Then I fell sliding down and skinned my elbow through my sweater so Lulu and I rolled my sleeve up to look at it better. Bits of the moss were in the blood like bugs.

"How did dirt get in there if your sleeve was down?" asked Lulu.

It was a good question. "I don't know," I said.

It didn't hurt. I picked the flecks of dirty moss out but there was a little too much blood so I dabbed it with my skirt. I looked at Lulu. "Whoops," I said. The blood got all on my blue-jean skirt. The blue jean was light enough that you could kind of see it but dark enough that the blood just looked brownish and part of the dark jean when I rubbed it in.

"Use your tights," Lulu said. She meant to dab the cut onto my tights because my tights were dark red already so it wouldn't really show up. I tried it. Then I didn't care. I just used my skirt. We looked at the cut some more. I could tell it would be a good scab to pick because it wasn't deep, just thin. It didn't hurt but it kept on bleeding.

Then me and Lulu both looked up because right near us a huddle of girls was following Abby Bowditch who was carrying something. All of their voices were high and soft like they were looking at something cute. They were coming toward us. There's a little shelf in the rock that Abby put something down on. They're two grades ahead of us in Lulu's brother's class. I looked at their legs in their tights and they looked grown-up. Their ponytails looked grown-up.

Me and Lulu got up to go see. We peered through them. It was a chick. I couldn't really see. We edged a little closer. It was a little yellow chick. He was tweeting like crazy and he was really cute. The wind blew on his fuzzy fur. I think he was from the science room. The eighth-graders watch them hatch or something in the incubator. "Incubator" sounds like "Incubus" the cat. These girls weren't eighth-graders, though.

I forgot about my arm and then I remembered. I looked and it was still bleeding. I pressed it to my skirt again since it was dirty already anyway. I watched Abby. She saw that me and Lulu were trying to look and she told her friends to make room for us like she was our baby-sitter or something, like she likes being the older person directing around. Abby has a crush on Cy and he's older than her. Lots of the girls do, so then they're nice to me like maybe I'll tell Cy how nice they are. Abby's weird though. I bet she pushed Deidre off of the slide.

The chick was really cute. It looked like it was wearing a tiny fur coat. The wind blew on it so it made a teeny bald spot in all its fuzz and it tweeted and closed its eyes then opened them again. It was all fluffy like a kitten. Abby picked it up. "It's so soft," she said. All of the other girls were going "Oh it's so cute, oh. . . ."

Abby was wearing her jacket but it wasn't zipped up. She put the chick up to her face and rubbed it against her rosy cheek. Abby's cheeks are always rosy. She's taller than the other girls and even though her face is kind of pretty it looks rubbery and, like, itchy or something. Abby brought the chick down from her face and held it in one hand. The little guy was chirping like crazy. "Shhh," she told it. "It's so cute isn't it?" she said. Everyone was humming yeah. "I just want to"—Abby was staring at it in her hand—"hug it but it's so small." She laughed. I thought maybe it was chirping so much because Abby was holding it too tight. "I just want to—" and then I saw Abby's hand flex really tight around the chick and the chick looked stunned and stopped chirping. Then it started to chirp a little again and then Abby squeezed it again and then it stopped limp. It didn't look cute and puffy anymore. It looked like a little dead bird. I looked at Abby's face. She was smiling still but she looked weird, like a little scared or excited. Everyone else was all quiet. I looked at Lulu and Lulu's mouth was parted open. I nudged her but she kept staring at Abby. I looked back at Abby. Abby was smiling still and she touched her face with the chick again but this time the chick was just a limp fluffy blob.

I tried to edge away and I backed up my arm all over Abby's white parka. Then I saw there were imprints of my bloody elbow stamped in swipes all over the side of Abby's white parka. Abby looked down at herself and then looked at me. Her nostrils opened up. "Oh my God!" Abby said. She was still holding the dead chick in her fist. "Disgusting!" Abby said, looking down, looking at me. "You got blood all *on* me!"

We ran away. Me and Lulu ran away. We ran up the hill. "She squoze it!" Lulu was saying. We were laughing because it was so creepy. We were running toward school and the tunnels with our jackets. "I mean, she just squeezed!" Lulu cried. I took Lulu's hand and we ran around the swing set toward the tunnels.

When me and Lulu got to the tunnels we turned to look at a car coming around the circle. It was a brown UPS truck with its door wide open the way they are and music was blaring out of it. It was a song that me and Cy used to sing on Mum and Dad's bed. The UPS guy kept rounding the circle and went toward the office so we couldn't hear it anymore. Lulu and I kept on singing anyway—*Ooooh you're a pretty pretty pretty pretty pretty girl. Pretty pretty such a pretty pretty girl.*—while we put our jackets on and went back inside because the teachers were yelling "All in." Me and Lulu skipped singing toward school and the door. I was holding her hand and we ran through some slushy ice and then there was some ice and I slipped a little but didn't fall but it rang through my whole body up to the top of my head and we laughed.

AT HOME on the steps of the porch Dad always chips the ice off, kicking it with his boot or the little rake that's in the car for the windshield. He lets the car warm up. He's in his suit with shaving cream still in his ears. He's not wearing the suit's jacket. His black pants match his head of hair and his white shirt matches the snow outside. He leaves his tie around his neck like a scarf but doesn't tie it on yet. The car lets up smoke into the cold air. Dad lets out smoke from his mouth while he scrapes off the windows. His shoes are shiny. I watch him polish them in his room. I help him rub the stuff off. The polish in the can looks like a hockey puck but like you could eat it like black butter. When he comes home change jingles in his pockets. Upstairs before he takes a shower he does push-ups on the rug in his socks and boxers.

Once he comes home so early. I'm lying on the floor in my room with Sparky. I hear the door down there rattling shut. I go halfway down the stairs to see who it is and it's Dad. He's standing at the brown thing sifting through the mail. His briefcase and tan overcoat are looped through his arm in a bunch at his side. I ask, "Why are you home so early?"

He keeps his head down looking through the mail. "I was fired," he says.

I run upstairs and cry on my bed. Sparky comes to the edge and wags his tail. I kick him in the chest and then hug his neck and then kick him again. What will happen? Where will we go? I can't imagine. We'll be poor and live in a dirty place. Maybe we'll all have to go on our own ways. What did Dad do that made them so mad? Mum comes in much later because of dinner and asks what's wrong. I'm lying on my side looking away but I roll onto my back so I can see her face. The way my head's turned I feel like I have a double chin. The hair by my cheek feels damp from crying. I tell her what Dad said.

Mum's smiling. She tucks a few pieces of my hair behind my ear. "Honey, I think he was kidding," she says.

I look at Mum's face while she rubs my hair back behind my ear and I can hear the dryer down the hall. I'm wearing Cy's pajama bottoms. He never wears them. I'm wearing one of my favorite shirts. It's a white baseball T-shirt with red sleeves that stop halfway between my elbows and my wrists. I have a postcard of the pope tacked on top of my wall hanging. I look at it. I look at it and feel Mum's hand on my forehead while I listen to the dryer down the hall. It's a warm sound like the purr of a motorboat or a chain saw steady. Mum's hand's on my forehead and I hear the dryer and I think of me and Mum in the laundry room down the hall.

I think of sitting on top of the washing machine. When I swing my feet out and bang them in against it the sound is like a drum but

The Tiny One

I can't do it too hard or I'll dent it. Mum's squatting down taking things out of the dryer. She hands the lint thing up to me because she knows I like to clean it off and roll all the lint into a ball. I'm peeling the lint out of the lint tray and I look at Mum. I say, "I'm thirsty."

"They should have named you Thirsty Revere," says Mum.

"I feel like an orange," I tell her.

Mum's head is practically inside of the machine down there. It says, "You don't look like one."

I don't get it. Then I do.

THE DRYER SOUNDS LIKE the feel of something I think of a lot. I don't know why I think of it, but my head drifts there like before I fall asleep or when I'm riding my bike home from school. It's a familiar place. It's a space of sea that I think of a lot. It's in Maine. It's near Juniper Point and the Spindle. It's just an area of dark blue Atlantic water. If it were land it would be a field I think with wildflowers on it, Queen Anne's lace all over it. It has that same worn-in freshness and light. I don't know why I think of it. It's not that near anywhere we go for picnics. We just pass it. It's a round of ocean. Sky Island is there on the shore. From this distance the rocks on its beach look like beads. The green field, stretching down to the water, smooths out like a woman's neck or a thigh to a knee. It's like I'm a little above the water looking over and down at it. The waves spoon up and down, glinting tipped flecks of sunlight like everywhere else. I'm suspended up. I keep thinking of it. It's a closed-in space of pretty water and I feel like I'm hovering beside it, trying to see. It's like that's where rain is born. It's like that's where I could be, or like that's where I've been.

PART III

Afternoon

ELEVEN

Lunch

⟞⟝ AFTER RECESS we went to lunch. We always walk in a line through the halls. On the way to the cafeteria the tiled floors are speckled like that other kind of bologna that Mum never buys with the big white circles in it. When we get to the cafeteria we still wait in line. The cinder-block walls are painted yellow and when I run my finger along the track between each block it's smooth and fits perfectly like I've made the line with my finger on frosting. Along the windowed wall on the side where we line up is like a counter with radiator vents on top so we lean on them. They're never too hot. Out the window is the back of the school. It's a gravelly parking lot that we never go to.

While we waited in line I looked out at that parking lot. There was only a red van parked back there. It looked like winter. All at once I felt it all in my stomach, round gray winter with a van parked in an empty parking lot. I told Lulu I didn't feel good and she just looked at me. I thought of Abby sitting out there in the red van squeezing the poor chick. Then I thought of being out in the red van by myself, and I wanted to be. At the same time I was glad to be with people. I couldn't decide. Sometimes that happens.

Most of our lunch trays are mint green colored. Other ones are light orange like the color of St. Joseph's baby aspirin. Our lunch trays have compartments for each food like a TV dinner. There's a rectangle for the main thing. It was Welsh rarebit. It's cheese sauce poured over a couple of saltine crackers. There's a round thing for soup but on days we don't have soup it's either got the dessert or nothing in it. There's a little square for peas or lima beans or something like cooked carrots in cubes like dice. Sometimes we have some iceberg lettuce or slices of cucumbers. There's a square for dessert—Jell-O, usually, or some kind of whipped stuff with whipped cream on top. There's another little square that you can put your milk carton on. You go in one door into the kitchen and slide along the metal railing where you can see through the glass to whatever we're having steaming in a metal square. Bernice passes you a tray with everything on it, and then you come out another door and go sit down.

Wednesday's always Soup and Sandwich Day. The best sandwich is grilled cheese but we always have it with tomato soup and I don't like tomato soup. Sometimes they give us Fluffernutters which is fluff and peanut butter sandwiches which is too sweet and I can't really handle bread on sandwiches, that's why I like grilled cheese because it's not really bread. On Fridays we don't have meat ever so we have fish sticks or pizza since Bernice doesn't cook meat on Friday. You can't eat meat on Friday if you're Catholic. I know that's why because of Mum and us but other people probably don't know why. Everyone always wants pizza. I like the fish sticks better but I pretend I like the pizza as much as everyone else does.

W E H A V E fish sticks at home but we never have real fish because either Mum or Dad doesn't like it. I can't remember which one. We have clams and lobster and stuff but only during the summer. I don't know why. We never go to the fish store in town. It has a big red lobster painted on the window. Under the window and inside are lots of different fish on ice like someone just threw a lot of dead fish on a snowbank. Me and Caleb look at the lobsters in the tank. His mom's buying three of them to have for dinner with a friend. In the tank down on the ground we can look down at lots of shrimps. Lots of them are floating up on the surface of the water. They're swimming the doggy paddle with all of their eyelash legs. Some of them can't swim right so they're on their sides going in loops. If they'd slow down their little hair legs they probably wouldn't spin so much and they'd be able to get someplace.

Afterward we go down to the harbor because that's where Caleb's mom's friend works and she has to tell him something. He's inside the offices by the railroad tracks. Caleb and I go down on one of the docks to look around. It's weird to be in my school clothes and on a dock and not barefoot and in Maine. I don't know the ocean in Masconomo like in Sky Island. I only know it like from looking at it out the windows at home. Me and Caleb stand there and watch the boats come in and out of Masconomo Harbor. The seagulls arc and caw above us. Some of the lobster boats are unloading their pots. A crowd of them bob up and down against the seawall and they look like the shrimps in the tank at the fish store, but grown giant, motoring head-on, bumping up into the wall.

AT LOW TIDE in Maine me and Amanda and Ethan catch crabs sometimes from the dock. We hook periwinkles or mussels onto the end of the line and then hang them over and wait. We use bacon too. You can feel a tug. When you pull them up first it's just the dark green water and then you can see the crab, hanging on bony with all of its sharp edges. They look like giant hard bugs. They look like they're straining to hold on. A lot of the time you get the crab on the line all the way up right to the surface of the water and then it lets go. Its claw arms go out and it floats falling down into the dark like a tiny umbrella or heavy leaf. When we do get them, we put the crabs all in a bucket and then once we have a lot we take them up to the top of the dock's ramp and dump the bucket over so the crabs all scrapple down the ramp in a race. Some of them fall over the edge before they get to the bottom. The little ones are always the fastest but the biggest ones are the best to watch. They walk around and then stand still with their big muscle arm claws raised a little bit, standing there like they're posing or ready to fight. When they get flipped over onto their backs their stomachs look like a bodybuilder's stomach.

ETHAN'S FRIEND Jared is visiting him from home. We're crabbing quietly and then Ethan's friend Jared starts laughing and taking the crabs apart that we've got in the bucket. You have to hold the crabs from behind otherwise they can pinch you. Jared tears a little leg off, then a big claw. "Don't," Amanda tells him. The other claw's still moving around. Sometimes we catch them deformed like that.

"Why not?" Jared's laughing. He plucks one of the extra-thin little claws in the back. It looks like the wing of some bug like a dragonfly. "We can use them as bait." Jared laughs.

Ethan's quiet. It's his friend.

"We can't use them as bait," Amanda says. "They won't eat each other."

Jared's still laughing. "They're crabs!"

We've smashed them with rocks to look at their insides before. It was different, though, taking them apart. I hoped one would pinch Jared and then a big one did and I felt like a witch. It left a mark that turned black on his thumbnail like Mum gets when she goes clamming and they nip her.

IN THE LIVING ROOM we catch the flies and then rip their wings off. I pluck out a hair from my head and Ethan ties it around the fly's neck. It sharpens its front legs like a little bad guy dreaming up an evil plan. It doesn't have any wings so it walks around the window seat on our leash like a black spot with nothing so it kind of looks like the ticks we get off of Sparky and then burn with a match on the porch in Masconomo. Sometimes when the ticks get really full of Sparky's blood you can step on them with your shoe and the blood squirts all over the place when the tick pops. There are some splatter stains of blood on the wall on the porch in Masconomo from doing that.

PETE AND STEVEN who used to live down the road blew up a toad with a firecracker underneath a bowl on the driveway at home once. When Pete turned the bowl over to see what it did I looked fast and it looked like spaghetti sauce. They were laughing. Pete didn't want to have to clean it up. They were laughing but not wanting to look at it because it was so gross.

"Why didn't the bowl blow up?" Cy asks. They're all laughing.

"You're such an ignoramus," Steven tells him.

"Shut up, Steven," says Cy. Cy's littler than them.

"Dufus," says Steven.

"Well why didn't it?" asks Cy.

"The bowl," laughs Steven, "firecracker. Doy."

"Well why didn't it?" Cy asks. "It's not such a heavy bowl."

Pete's laughing. "It's weird," he's laughing, "it's weird that it didn't."

Cy smiles at me. He won against Steven.

PETE AND CY fish at the end of the dock in Maine because the whaler's busted and it's getting fixed. They've been out fishing all day but they can't get enough. They come up with a dogfish. It looks like a little shark. When they cut into its stomach there are babies inside. Most of them swim away but they get two in the bucket. They're like tiny sharks. I watch them. They'd be good in the bathtub with Barbie they could eat her.

Pete throws one back in. "No wait!" I say.

"What?" He's thrown it already.

I say it really fast—"Don'throwthotherone."

"Why not?"

"I want to keep it." My pet.

Gabriel from up the hill and his little sister are looking at it before I bring the bucket into the house. "It was right inside the mother's stomach," I tell them. Gabriel's little sister's scared of it. She leans on Gabriel's leg and hides behind him. Her hair's so blond and fluffy that she looks like she might float up off of the ground. She smells like frosting.

"I thought fish came from eggs," Gabriel says.

"Duh," says Ethan. Then later when we're inside Ethan says, "Fish do come from eggs. Don't they?"

I shrug. I don't care. Ethan does, though. "Like caviar," he says. I shrug again. I'm carrying the bucket past the kitchen. It jiggles the water and some water jumps out with the sloshing.

"It stinks," Mum says from the kitchen. She doesn't see the water lap out onto the floor.

"It's a baby," I tell her.

"I guess so," says Mum.

As I carry the bucket up the stairs I can hear Ethan go into the kitchen and ask Mum, "How do crabs get born?"

I keep the bucket in my room overnight. When I wake up the baby dogfish looks ugly and small and mean. It's sick. It floats and then slithers. I bring the bucket down to the dock and tip it all swirling over the edge back into the dark water.

THERE'S A MAN named Goldie who lives out on Dogfish Is-land and he's got scars all over his palms from fishing with just a rope and not a rod. He likes Mum. His face is so wrinkled that the wrinkles are like deep lines that I bet if I put pieces of grass in them they'd stay. They're not saggy so his face doesn't look droopy, just wrinkly. He walks down the pier in little steps like he's stepping around mussels and barnacles to find soft patches of sand to step on. He has a gold tooth too, right up front, and when I ask Mum if that's why his name's Goldie she says, "No, love." She says, "He wasn't born with a gold tooth."

I know that. "I know," I say, "but maybe it's a nickname."

"Fair enough," she says. She's rolling something, dough or something, up on the counter. Thinking of Goldie being born is hard for me. I look up at Mum. It's not dough. It's chicken that she's rolling in flour. The flour on her hands looks like the talc at gymnastics.

Mum takes the flyswatter off of the hook to go after a fly that's bugging her and the chicken. Her hand that's holding the red swatter is all floury from the flour. Mum waits for the fly to land. We watch it land on the door frame. Mum steps into her swat like a volley and gets it. "You might be right," Mum says.

"What?" I forget what we're talking about.

"It might be from his tooth," says Mum. "I never thought about it. We'll ask."

Goldie comes by on his way back from the boatyard downtown. Mum gives him some potato chips or oatmeal cookies with tea. They smile with each other. They look like they have a secret like they're both witches. Mum's a witch. That's what Dad says. When I ask Mum if she is, she just raises her eyebrows and smiles. It's the same face she makes when I ask her "But how did you know?" when she knows something that I haven't told her yet. I ask, "How did you know?"

She makes the face. "A little bird told me," she says.

LIKE WHEN MUM squats down and looks at my stomach when she gets home to see what I had for dinner with the baby-sitter. Her eyes are at my eyes since she's squatted down. I look into them. They're close. They're not blue and they're not green; they're right in between. There's a freckle in one of them. For a second it strikes me. They're *her* eyes. They're *Mum's* eyes. I'm glad she's home. She lifts my shirt up. "Hmmm, what's in here," she says. She's looking at my stomach. "Let's see. I see a . . . minute steak. Some peas. And a . . . what is that? It's a . . . I think, mmm-hmm, it's a Creamsicle," she says. The baby-sitter couldn't have told her because I'm the first one to meet her at the door. How does she know?

"How do you know?"

"X-ray vision."

"How do you know?" I ask again. I want to know.

That face, then: "A little bird told me."

So, WEDNESDAY's Soup and Sandwich Day; Friday's always fish sticks or pizza. All of the other days it just depends. Sometimes it's chicken à la king or chop suey. Sometimes it's rice with some meat in a brown gravy. The best is when we have tacos. We can smell them from down the hall before we get to the cafeteria. Everyone starts going "Yes! Tacos!" pushing each other about it and smiling while we're walking in line. We just started having them this year. When the door opens for seconds there's a scramble and everyone runs to get more like when we have pizza.

I DIDN'T KNOW what a taco was until this year. Ethan de-scribed it to me last summer up in Maine. "It's like a big Frito shaped like a"—Ethan's using his hands to explain—"like a, um, like a . . . I don't know. It's like a sandwich but instead of bread it's a big Frito and inside of it's ground-up meat. That meat like how Pete makes it when he crumbles it up with A-1."

Pete makes it and I love it. "You mean the crumbly hamburger with A-1?" I ask. I can't believe this combination. I love Fritos too, and no bread in sight.

"Yeah. That hamburger," says Ethan, "and then it's got a little bit of stringy lettuce and chopped-up tomatoes. And cheese that's like shredded." He pauses. "But you don't *have* to have the tomatoes."

Ethan knows I don't like tomatoes all the time. But he knows too that I like them in Italian subs so that maybe they'd go over okay with me in a taco.

"You can fill them with other stuff too," Ethan tells me. "They're shaped like a U so you can fill them up." Shaped like a U throws me, but it's okay. I get the idea.

I FOLLOWED CALEB to a table. Lulu followed me. Caleb's head is cute and his haircut made me think he was wearing a hockey helmet and was about to go skating around. We sat down. Caleb spilled part of his milk into his Welsh rarebit square. Pierre came to sit next to Caleb. Caleb stuck his hand out over on the empty seat. "I'm saving it," he told Pierre.

"I know," said Pierre, but he didn't, then pretended he was sitting down at the table next to us anyway.

"Dork," Caleb said.

Patrick Curley came and sat down next to Caleb. Patrick Curley has lots of brothers and sisters. His brother Michael Curley is friends with Pete. His sister Megan is friends with Marly.

Hugh Putnam sat down next to Lulu. Hugh's from the grade above us but he eats lunch with us sometimes because he falls back to our class for reading. I gave Caleb my Welsh rarebit and my red Valentine's cake because I didn't want it. Caleb showed us how loose his tooth was. He flicked it around with his tongue. It was to the side on the top. He tugged at it. He let me try. I grabbed hold of it and was kind of scared to hurt him but I wanted to pull it. "Do it," Caleb told me, but he couldn't talk very well with my hand in his mouth. I wiggled it back and forth and then pulled hard. I felt the root go. It was like pulling up a strong little dandelion. Caleb went "Ahhw" like a grunt but it was out.

I had it in my hand. It looked smaller than it looked in his mouth. Caleb smiled and there was blood on his other teeth.

"You have blood all over," Lulu told him. He put a napkin in his mouth.

The Tiny One

I polished Caleb's tooth with my napkin. "Look," I said. I held it up. "It's Caleb's little tooth," I said, and our table laughed.

M U M   H A S a whale's tooth with a drawing of a woman dancing on it. It's black like ink but it's carved in. When I turn the tooth over and look into the inside of it, it looks like veins in dripped wax. They make perfume from whale oil.

One Sunday afternoon I bring Mum's carved whale tooth over to Mr. Emerson next door to show it to him. He's in his basement where he has table saws and woodworking stuff like we have at school. He's building a cradle for his granddaughter. To me it looks like a tiny boat. Mr. Emerson brushes the sawdust off of his hands and then takes the big whale's tooth from me so he can look at it. He looks at the carving of the lady doing her jig. "Scrimshaw," he says. He studies it for a second. He looks at me, holding it out to give it back. "Coveted ambergris comes from whales."

I   A S K   M U M about each thing on the mantelpiece. Next to the piece of scrimshaw there's a marble egg on the wooden holder. Mum says it's a dinosaur egg that turned to rock.

"But it's so small," I say. It looks like a normal egg size.

"Dinosaurs were small once," Mum says.

"I know but." I hold it in my hand. It's smooth and cool. It's the perfect weight to throw it through the glass in the window. "Is it really a dinosaur egg?"

Mum's spraying Windex on the glass table. "It really is," she says. She looks up at me with the face she has when she's kidding but also when something's highly impressive so I can't tell.

I ask Mum about the scrimshaw. She tells me Aunt Nellie gave it to her.

"Who's Aunt Nellie?" I whine.

Mum gives me a look that tells me she's not going to answer.

I KNOW WHO Aunt Nellie is. I always mix her up with Aunt Catherine. I think they must look alike but I'm not sure. Aunt Nellie's not our real aunt. We park at her house in Masconomo when we go to Moaning Beach so we don't have to deal with the main parking lot. Her house is tall and beige cement with a green metal roof that comes down a little like a cap to a Christmas-tree ornament like the houses in the *Madeleine* books. It's got iron railings on the bottom half of the tall windows that are like baby balconies. We never go in. We walk past it across the sloping lawn and down a short path that I always wish was longer with its cool roots and turns that comes out on a shoulder of rock where then you can see the swipe of beach right there. It's called Moaning Beach because when you walk on the sand it makes a moaning sound like a person or a dog. It sort of sounds like a person who's buried way under is trying to speak. I get shivers when I think of it that way.

Anyway, we go to Moaning Beach for walks in the winter or for days in the summer before we go up to Maine. Mum loves any beach. I love it too. Sometimes in the spring or fall she brings us there after school. Cy brings Uncle Terry's yellow surfboard. I do handstands and cartwheels on the hard sand near the water for Mum. She's brought a camera.

"Okay, Nadia," Mum says to me, "don't show off too much."

I stand up from my handstand. "I'm not," I tell her. Sometimes I do but this time I really wasn't.

Mum has the camera up at her face. "Come on," she tells me. "Do your stuff."

I walk toward the water.

"Oh," says Mum, "don't be a lemon."

"I'm not a lemon," I say. Now I want to keep doing handstands and stuff but I don't want to be showing off either. I stand there. She ruined it.

The Tiny One

USUALLY AT THE BEACH Mum reads or does needlepoint. Sometimes she just lies on her stomach like someone shot her in the back and she's dead. She's lying that way, flat, face away, her arms raised like she was frisked. I think she's sleeping. I go over to her. I sit down straddling her back gently. I want to ask her who discovered music. I want to ask her why I'm a girl. Her skin's warm on my legs. I'm straddling her back, looking down at the top of her back and her undone bathing-suit strap. I feel her shake. It's little shakes like right before a big laughing fit. But something doesn't feel so funny. "Mum?" I say.

There's no answer. Then she sniffles. "Not now, loveboat," she says. I look down over to the side at her face. Her eyes are closed but she's frowning. I look closer. "Shhhh," she says to herself. She's crying. "Shhhh, shhhh," she's saying to herself, crying to herself. It scares me. I'm scared to look at her face all the way until dinner. In the car on the way home she talks to Cy and she sounds normal but I don't look. I look out the window. I look at the brushy felt where the window rises up out of the car door.

At dinner that night I brace myself. I look up at her. The pot of rice is steaming up toward her face. Her hair's wet and brushed back. She's smiling at something Dad said. "That's very true." She's smiling. Something warm pours through me.

"You were crying," I say.

"Yes I was," says Mum.

"On the beach," I say. I'm eating my lip.

"That's right," Mum says. Dad touches her hand while she serves him some rice. "I was tired," she says.

WE GO TO STAY at Aunt Nellie's house in Bermuda. Or maybe it's Aunt Catherine's. She isn't there. It's just us. Most of the houses are light pink. The roofs are white. Our Easter baskets have candy in them that I've never seen before. I recognize the Butterfinger so I eat that first while I check out the other stuff. The grass on the lawn is prickly. It looks like drying string beans. I see a big crab crawl across it and go into a hole. Pete plays lacrosse on the beach with a guy he knows and Mum laughs with a lady who's her old friend who I've never seen before.

Marly brings me down to the end of the beach and we sit in a cave where the water comes rushing in. The cave has arches looking out to the water. We look through the big arches. I sit on a rock that's like a dark gumdrop on the wet sand and when the bigger waves come skidding in their water skims over my feet like clear syrup. "Listen," Marly says. The waves are tumbling. When they roll into a crash it sounds like they're saying *hereIamhereIam*. It's the same noise as at home but here the waves look like smiling dolphins in the sun and at home most of the time they look like animals that keep their heads low down under the water. We listen. "Hear it?" Marly asks. We listen. "It's like being in a shell," she says.

After dinner me and Mum walk along the beach again. The air is warm and soft. The air's like cream, smooth as I walk through it, smooth as I breathe it in. We hear the waves like a crowd. The water's glowing in the dark all along its edges. I run to it. It's glowing. "Via!" Mum calls after me. I get near the edge. It's slurping up against the sand and it's glowing in the dark. It glows in the dark as much as my Silly Putty or that yo-yo. When I press my foot into the wet sand it glitters all around where I press like it's being lit up by a light underneath the beach. I press my feet all over. I'm excited. My feet go up and down like tapping fingers. "Why?" I yell. I pick up a handful of wet sand to try to see but the little lights shiver onto my palm so I can't see any one of them and then they disappear. Mum's walking toward me. She's walking quickly and then when she gets on the wet sand I can see each of her steps light up underneath her feet like she's in a dance show. "Why?" I yell again. The waves behind her are crashing with light green foam in the dark.

Mum's laughing. Her teeth sort of look like they're glowing in the dark too but with blue glow instead of green. "It's phosphorescence," she says. "They're eensy-weensy bugs."

"Bugs!" I laugh. I do a cartwheel. "Bugs?" I do a cartwheel and when my hands press the sand it glows. The waves are roaring. The warm dark and the roar.

"Like how fireflies do it," Mum says. I can see the wind in the dark blow at her hair. She thinks for a second. "I think they're bugs," she says. "We'll ask Dad."

I run and kick the water. "I love it!" I say. I kick it with each leg in hops. I throw my arm up in the air because there's nothing else to do with it. "Ya!" I yell. The wind blows spray onto our faces.

"Come back here," Mum calls. "Let me at you."

I run curvy over to her, bouncing, watching my feet. "I love it!" I say.

Mum's squatting down next to me. She squeezes my hips and the warm wind is blowing at us. "And I love *you*," she says. I nuzzle in. "Mmmmm," she says, hugging me, and I say it too. I get my nose close in to her neck. I hear the waves from in there. I want to get into her neck. I feel glad and like the glowy bugs are squirmy inside of me and it will all last forever.

SOMETIMES MUM GRITS her teeth when she hugs me. Sometimes she squeezes me too hard. "Ow!" I cry. "You're hurting me," and she might be squeezing so hard that I can hardly squeak the sound out to say so. I try to squeeze her back. Her arms are limp at her sides while I try. "Harder," Mum says. I try. "Harder," she says again, and I'm too little to do it hard enough.

IN BERMUDA we eat lunch on a terrace a few steps up from the beach. Mum lets me skip it and keep playing making rivers in the sand with my new friend Jackson who's so cute he looks like a puppy. I go up to Mum anyway. Lunch is over but she's sitting having an iced coffee with the lady who makes her laugh all the time. Mum's sitting down and I flop onto her lap on my stomach with my feet still on the ground. The skin of her legs smells like warm sun. She's talking to her friend then she rubs my bare back. "I love this little back," she says. "You're brown as a berry, pint size." I'm looking at the stones on the walkway by her feet. They're different in Bermuda. They're gray but they have little airholes like Choco Lite chocolate bars. Mum's smoothing my back with her hand. She smooths it over and back, back and forth. Then she blows her lips on my skin in the middle to make a fart noise. I laugh. I laugh while she squeezes me. She flips me over and is kissing me all over. I'm laughing. She's gripped onto my knee so I can't go anywhere. I'm laughing and wiggling. She's inside my ear. "I want to eat you all up," she says, and in my ear it tickles and makes my back curl. I'm laughing. She's everything everywhere like she's more me than I am.

I TRIED TO PRETEND my milk was strawberry Quik milk but it tasted way plain and I didn't want any more. I was done eating my lunch. I didn't really have anything but I wasn't hungry. Sometimes I'm just not hungry. But sometimes I want Oreos before bed and I'll sneak them up to my room in my underwear.

ONE TIME I snuck some food up to Uncle Terry. He was hungry.

It was this one time when I was upstairs in the spare room looking for some glue in the bureau. The glue downstairs was frozen solid through. Mum said there was some up there. She was down in the TV room with Dad. Then I hear something behind me. I turn around and look at the bed. It seemed like it jerked. I back up to the doorway because it frightens me. Before I go back to where I was I squat down to check under the bed from my safe distance. I see the sole of a boot, a hand. It's a body. There's a man. He's looking back at me. It's Uncle Terry. I'm scared and relieved all at once. He puts his finger to his lips like *shhh*. It's Uncle Terry under the bed. I stay where I am. I can't decide whether it's fun or not. I stay squatting and stick my head out into the hall. No one's there. I look back at Uncle Terry. Mum says Uncle Terry has his own agenda and I don't know what an agenda is. It sounds like a special kind of camping kit or car. I get up and walk over to him. I squat down by the bed and Uncle Terry brings his head out so I can see his face. He's grown a beard.

"Hi," he whispers.

"Hi."

"Did I scare you?"

"What are you doing?" I ask.

"Shhh, quiet. I scared you a little. Didn't I?"

"No. A little." It's weird. A man under the bed. "What are you doing?" I ask him.

"Hiding."

I whisper, "From me?"

"Not anymore."

I ask it again, whispering, "What are you doing?"

"Hiding."

"Why?"

He smiles. "From your mom. And dad."

"Then will you come downstairs?"

"I'm gonna sleep here. As a secret."

He smells like kitty litter. I don't know what to say. "Why?" I ask.

"It's just easier," he says.

"To make it a secret?"

"Right."

"Why?"

He shrugs. "It's a grown-up thing," he says. I hate it when grown-ups say that but somehow I don't care this time because it's like he's a kid. He's under a bed. "Will you keep a secret?" he says.

There's a dark green knapsack behind the door. "Is that yours?" I ask.

He doesn't answer. He's crawling out from underneath. He sits up and leans against the wall. One leg's still under the bed. There's dust in webs on the leg that's sticking out. He asks me, "What did you have for supper?" It's his breath. It smells like kitty litter with everything dirty still in it.

"Um. I can't remember."

"Think."

I gave Cy most of my circles of hot dog. I asked out loud to the table, "Are baked beans called Boston baked beans everywhere?"

Dad answered, "Yup. And Boston's called Beantown sometimes."

"Oh yeah," I said. And we live right here.

"Maine lobster's called Maine lobster too," said Mum. She saw what was cool about it.

"Everywhere?"

"Even in Paris. They send them over on ice."

Uncle Terry touches my arm. "Think," he says again.

I look at him. "Hot dogs and baked beans."

"Great. Any left?"

I don't answer. I don't know.

"Go see, okay? And if there is, just take the plate from the fridge and bring the whole thing up. And a fork."

I'd bring them to him. I wanted to bring them inside of a flashlight where the batteries go like Bobby Brady brought them to the Indian boy in the Grand Canyon. I love camp things like that. Like in runaway stories or Davy Crockett Daniel Boone when they list the food supply they've brought with them in their satchel like—two biscuits, a can of black-eyed peas, half a loaf of stale bread, a jug of water, and three squares of chocolate.

Uncle Terry takes my wrist before I go. "You won't say anything, right? Cross your heart, hope to die?"

I nod. "Stick a needle in my eye." I'd like to tell Cy. "Cy?" I ask.

"No. Is Pete home?"

"No."

"Marly's at school too?"

"Yeah. No."

"Right. She here?"

"She's at a slumber party."

"Your dad's here, right?"

"Yeah."

"Okay," he says. "Do your stuff." He lets go of my wrist and pats it while I get up. "Hey," he says. I'm at the door so I turn around.

"What?" I whisper. I'm excited.

"Nice hat," he tells me.

I forgot I had it on so I touch the visor. It's a Bruins hat but it's a baseball hat. I like it but I wasn't that sure because I'm always not sure about the bumblebee colors. "Thanks."

In the fridge there's a whole bowl of dinner. It's pretty big. It's down low and behind things where it will fit. I take out stuff to make room. The bowl's white and cold and drops of water are under the Saran Wrap like in a terrarium. I lift it out. Uncle Terry's up in that room and it's like he's my pet in a cage.

I hear Mum coming down the hall toward me in the kitchen. I put the bowl back in the fridge but jam it on the top shelf. Mum comes in. "What on earth are you doing?" She puts her glass in the sink. She's not looking at me.

"Nothing."

"What's all the racket?" she asks, but she's not paying attention.

"I was, um, going to make fairy bananas but I don't want to anymore," I tell her. After I say it I realize I don't need anything out of the fridge for fairy bananas. Just bananas and jimmies. She doesn't notice. I look over at the fruit bowl. We don't even have any bananas.

"Did you find some glue?" she asks.

"What glue?"

Mum's walking out again. "Elmer's glue," she says, walking away.

"Yeah. No. I don't need it anymore."

She talks to me from out in the hall. "Don't forget about all your stuff on the floor." She means in the TV room.

I call after her. "I'll clean it up!"

I get the bowl back out of the fridge and then take a fork from the drawer. The drawer squeals shut like you're hurting it whenever you close it again. I put the fork on top of the clear wrap. I pass Mum and Dad in the TV room and walk right up the stairs. They're laughing at something. I can hear Cy on the phone in Mum and Dad's room upstairs. I get down the hall and push the door open with my foot. Uncle Terry's not under the bed anymore. He's lying on the bed, sitting up. His shirt's red. "There she is," he whispers. I bring the bowl to him. He smacks his lips and wiggles his tongue around in the air like he's hungry. He crosses his ankles. His feet look long and his socks are gray.

I sit on the bed while he eats. He looks hungry. "Delicious," he says. The bowl doesn't look as big when he's holding it. At first he doesn't take the Saran Wrap all the way off. He just folds it over so there's a little hole on the side where he can stick the fork in. He looks at me. "You probably shouldn't hang out in here," he says. His mouth's full. "Someone will come looking. Or, wait. Wait until I finish this and then you can bring it back down." I watch him eat.

When Uncle Terry's done I take the bowl to bring it back downstairs. When I'm walking down the hall upstairs I hear Mum coming up the stairs so I jump into my room. I put the empty bowl on the floor by my bed.

Mum's standing in the doorway of my room. "Time for bed," she says. "But first you've got to go clean that stuff up downstairs."

I'm sitting on my bed. "Okay," I say.

"Now," she says. I don't want to leave the bowl here. It's around the corner at the foot of my bed on the floor.

"Okay," I say again.

"Right *now*, Via," she says.

"Okay."

"What are you up to?"

I say it too fast. "Nothing."

"Well hut two," she says. I stand up. Mum walks across my room to do something with the window or over at my bureau.

I go down the stairs into the TV room. Dad's reading the newspaper so all I see are his crossed legs. When I was littler I could sit on Dad's foot that sticks out when he's got his legs crossed. I'd sit on his foot and he'd bounce me up and down on it while he read the paper.

My things are all over the floor. I push them all together into a pile. They're those paper things that are costumes that you fold onto paper dolls. I was coloring them in. I wanted to glue the costumes on instead of just folding them on with those little flaps because they never stay.

Mum comes in. She's holding the big white bowl. The fork rattles in it when she looks down at me and holds it out. "You ate all the beans?" she asks.

Dad thinks she's talking to him so he flicks the paper down and looks. He sees Mum holding the bowl out to me. "What's going on?" she asks me.

"Cy did," I say. "No he didn't."

Mum explains to Dad. "This was in her room next to her bed."

Dad keeps his eyes still but moves his head sideways like it doesn't make sense. They both sort of laugh quietly so I smile too. Then Mum looks at me.

"I gave it to Sparky," I say.

"With a fork?"

"I don't know."

"What do you mean you don't know?"

"I ate some and then I threw some out."

"Threw some out? Where?"

"Down the toilet."

"The toilet?"

There's nothing to do. "No. I ate it all," I tell her.

"You don't even like them. You hate baked beans."

"Not anymore," I tell her.

"Since dinner you've come to love them?"

"I don't know," I say. I can feel my voice getting higher.

Mum's voice starts to sound cross. She hates liars. Each word of hers is clear. "What do you mean you don't know?" When I don't answer she says it again even clearer. And louder. "What do you mean you don't know?"

She's standing above me and she's serious. I start to cry. "I ate the baked beans." I'm crying. "Why? Why are you so mad?" I'm crying. "All I did was eat them."

"Okay, okay," Mum says, "just relax." She comes down to me. "Shhhh. Relax, relax." She touches my back. "Did you pick up your stuff?"

"I'm trying to," I say. "I'm trying to right now." I'm crying. Watery I can see Mum and Dad making funny faces at each other. "Stop it," I tell them. They're laughing kind of and trying not to laugh. "It's not funny," I cry.

EVERYONE WAS EATING their weird red Valentine cake. I wasn't hungry. I gave mine to Caleb. Before Patrick put his red spoonful in his mouth he looked at it and said, "It looks like guts." It was bright red.

"Ew," said Lulu, "it does. Bloody."

Patrick spooned it in. "Mmm." He smiled. "But the guts taste yummy in my tummy."

AT THE BICENTENNIAL there was red, white, and blue cake. Me and Charlotte's pieces were blue. It made our lips turn blue and they stayed that way overnight. In the Masconomo park downtown there was a bonfire on the edge of the harbor that was so big that it burned for three days. Pieces of the big logs fell into the harbor. "Like a funeral pyre," Mr. Emerson said. He didn't go but I described it to him. He said he saw it from the road in the distance.

"A what?" I ask.

"A funeral pyre," says Mr. Emerson.

"What's that?"

"A cremation of sorts."

"A cremation?" I knew what that was because Nodoby our cat was cremated after he had cat leukemia.

FIRST NODOBY'S under the chaise longue in Mum and Dad's room and won't move. He has just his head sticking out and his paws splayed out to the sides like a wishbone in a way that they never would do normally. His eyes are glassy and cross-eyed and his chin is flat on the ground so he looks like one of those stuffed, flattened foxes with a stuffed head and then the rest of them's a scarf.

Puddle sits crouched in a hunched-box position a few feet away from him. So does Jezebel, but on the other side. They don't look at Nodoby but they sit in there, close by.

"They're worried for him," Mum says about Jezebel and Puddle while she picks Nodoby up. "Just like people," she says.

Me and Mum bring Nodoby to the vet. I hold him on my lap in the car. His head with the cross-eyes goes to the right while his two front paws go to the left like straight knobby sticks.

The vet's tall with long fingers. He has suspenders. He looks like a farmer. He speaks to Nodoby softly. "That's it," he says to Nodoby. He opens up Nodoby's mouth gently with his hands. The inside of Nodoby's mouth is scary looking. It's not pink. It's waxy and almost white. Then the vet speaks to us. "See that?" the vet says. "Hardly any red blood cells." He holds Nodoby's mouth open and I look some more but I wish I didn't. For a while I can't get my mind away from it. It's a mouth as empty as it gets.

TWELVE

Homeroom

~~ WHEN YOU FINISH your lunch you bring your tray up to a little window where you chuck the silverware into a steel bucket filled with sudsy water and you pass your tray to Leo who's dressed all in khaki. Leo uses a spatula to scrape your leftover food down a hole into I guess a big garbage can underneath. Then we all walk in a line back to homeroom. So we did that.

Miss Hunt had left little bunches of candy inside cellophane wrapped up with a red ribbon inside of our desks. There were those hearts with the writing on them, little red-hot hearts, heart-shaped Sweetarts, kisses, and gummy-looking things that I've never had before. There were some envelopes in my desk too. Some were red and some were white. A couple were pink. The one on top was from Lulu I could tell from the writing. I forgot about my Valentine's cards. I left them at home. They were mostly all Charlie Brown ones, little ones the size of baseball cards. I knew right where I left them. They were right on top of the brown thing in the front hall in a red stack like cards but puffing up like an accordion. Now I didn't have any. I held the top of my desk up and stared into my desk. I felt like crying.

Honor Pruett was walking around the classroom carrying a brown box like what doughnuts come in. I knew that inside her box was probably the same thing that she always has for bake sales and birthdays and everything. They're good but she always brings the same thing. Her mom makes them. They're chocolate cupcakes with white frosting with a Blow Pop stuck into them like a flag on the moon. They always get all bought at bake sales but they're expensive because of the Blow Pops. At the bake sales people go crazy over the brownies and the peanut butter things. My favorite things are the Rice Krispies Treats or the meringues. I like zucchini bread. I like the penuche fudge but not the chocolate fudge. I like the caramel apples. I also like it when someone has the oranges or lemons with a candy cane sticking into them. It's the perfect sweet and sour. The best was when Billy had tons of blueberries with Cool Whip and he'd give it to you in a white paper cup with a white plastic spoon. It was like ice cream in your mouth kind of but then a fresh blueberry would burst open. Mum always makes elephant ears for the bake sales. They're just really big chocolate-chip cookies that are kind of brittle and delicate. I like the name better than I like the cookies but the cookies are all right.

I was still looking inside my desk because I thought I might cry so I didn't want to look up. I looked at the bundle of candy Miss Hunt left in there and right then candy seemed gross like it might be filled with worms or maggots. Honor started passing out red napkins so I had to put the top of my desk back down so she could give me one. Then she passed out the cupcakes and they all had red hearts on the frosting and a Blow Pop. I gave my cupcake to Lulu and she split it with Robby. They were laughing. I felt like I'd fallen down and no one knew. Like everyone was running to run around the flagpole and I'd twisted my ankle in the ditch and no one's even noticing that I'm not coming running.

I THOUGHT OF HOW I really went falling once when I was littler and Mum jumping in the water to get me.

We're on Sky Island. We're on the ramp that goes from the float
up to the wharf. The ramp's tilted because the tide's so low. I'm
following Pete and it's really steep up the ramp like we're walking
up a steep hill but with the wood slats for traction. The tide's lower
than usual so everything down there underneath us—the rocks and
mucky planks—looks dirty. We're home from a picnic and I'm following Pete. I can see the fringe of his cutoffs and the back of his
tan legs. At the top of the ramp I see that the space is pretty big
between the ramp and the wharf. I try to step and I do but at the
same time I'm looking out, through the space, because there's no
railing for a second and I like it, the drop-off down and no railing.
I'm looking and then all of a sudden I'm there—I'm out in the air.
I'm out in the air and then falling and then I'm in and under the
cold water and it's dark green and loud around my head. Then it's
not loud at all. When I come up in the water I see Mum running
the last couple of steps down the float before she jumps in next to
me. I'm small enough that she just pulls me toward her with the
string at the neck of my life jacket like I'm a little boat. I drift
toward her and she holds me with one arm.

At the float a lot of grown-ups are standing on the corner so
their weight makes the float dip down. A man with white hair pulls
me up. Dad's coming. He's carrying a picnic basket. He puts it
down and picks me up. Another man helps Mum. When Mum gets
out all her clothes are wet. On the side of her stomach her white
shirt's red like paint and then I see it's blood and it scares me. Dad's
carrying me and he's walking quickly so we're bobbing up and
down. Dad's rubbing my leg with a towel and then I see that it's
from me. I'm bleeding. It's at the place where my leg meets my
body but I can't see it because my life jacket's in the way and my
legs are around Dad's waist and his arm's in the way too.

The Tiny One

In the kitchen Dad puts me on the counter. He sits me on the edge of the sink so my feet are in it. He leaves and then he's back again. He takes my life jacket off and then Mum's there and then Pete's there too. It doesn't hurt but it scares me. I look down at my leg and it's like three long scratches like stripes at the top going across. Then Dad covers it. He presses. He lifts up the towel and they're not there anymore. Then they're like little scratches, then the red blood grows up out of them, then they fill up so it's one big swipe of red war paint. Dad puts the towel back down and presses. "They're not deep," he says.

Mum's chewing the side of her cheek. "But why are they bleeding so much?"

"It's just that kind of thing," Dad says. He looks at me. "You okay?"

I don't answer. Mum says, "Look at her. She's like shell-shocked."

"Yeah well that was quite a fall," Dad says. He wipes my leg with a paper towel this time. "It's a long drop for such a little person." On the paper towel I can see how red blood is. My blood.

The man with the white hair who picked me up out of the water pokes his head into the kitchen. "Anything we can do?" he asks.

Dad turns around to see who it is and then he's back to me. "No, Tom. Everything seems to be fine," says Dad. Then Dad remembers to say it. "Thank you," calls Dad, aiming it over his shoulder behind him.

"I don't know what was so sharp," says Mum. "It doesn't look banged up like bruised."

"She bounced on the line that ties the float to the wharf," says Dad.

Pete looks at me and smiles. "She did?"

"I think it was probably the barnacles on the rope," says Dad. "Scraped like that."

I want Mum to be closer and it's like she hears me think it because she comes and smooths some hair away from my face.

"You all right in there?" she asks. Mum takes the wet towel that's around me and wraps a dry one around. "You're being very brave," she tells me. Her hands feel nice rubbing me through the towel.

And I like watching Dad's hands. He's talking to Mum and looking at me but it's like they have a life of their own. He has a pile of things on the other side of the sink. A tube of something that he rubs on when the bleeding slows down enough so the slices look like red leaks. He's got a few of those big Band-Aids. He puts one on and it almost fits all the way across my thigh. He puts another one on so it kind of overlaps. You can't see any of the cuts. The Band-Aids almost look like diapers. I can see seeped blood coming through the Band-Aid's tiny pockmarks.

Mum carries me into the living room. She's got my blanket with her. She props me up on some pillows on the window seat and tucks my blanket in all around me. I put my knees up and she pushes them down. I put them up again and she leaves them. Out the window I can see the ramp that I fell from. I can see the rope lines that Dad was talking about. They're crisscrossed in an X way down underneath the ramp. I sort of remember the feeling of a bouncing tug before I hit the water.

Mum puts a white plate of lace cookies on the glass table near me. She holds one out to me. I don't want one. She puts her mug of tea down beside them and then leaves the room. I watch the glass of the table steam up under the mug.

Marly comes in to eat the cookies. She's been on the mainland all day with Isabelle. She has a new T-shirt on. It's a purple Indian print. She wants to see my Band-Aids but I don't want to show her. The blanket's all tucked in. She's mad I'm not letting her see. "Well can you still talk?" Marly says. Because I haven't said anything. Marly's in a bad mood. I could tell just by the look on her face when she walked in. "Well *can* you?" Marly asks. Then she sees someone outside through the window and goes running out the door to see them. I try to see who it is but I can't. I hear the screen door slam as she goes out, then I hear her trailing away saying something. I lean my head against the window. It's open down near my hand and the air feels like the sun looks on the water, soft and quick.

PETE FELL OFF the wharf once too. It was nighttime and he was playing Kick the Can or German Spotlight or something and William Leverett went to tag Pete's hand while Pete was dangling hanging over the edge of the wharf and Pete let go so he wouldn't get tagged and he fell down onto the rocks.

Cy came and woke me up. I could see the outline of his head in the dark in front of me. I felt the bed sag down when he leaned against it.

"Pete might have broken his back," says Cy.

"What?" I ask. I squint. It's dark but the door's partly open so there's a rectangle of bright light with a triangle of the linen closet door out there.

"Pete might be paralyzed," says Cy. His voice is filled with it. He reaches for my hand. "Come on."

I don't know why he's waking me but it's exciting. We go into the bathroom. Pete's in the bathtub. Mum's sitting on the toilet seat holding Pete's hand. Cy's holding my hand. It feels nice. Mum's joking with the doctor so I don't think it's that serious. Dad's in Masconomo. Marly's in Martha's Vineyard with her boyfriend Stuart. We watch Pete wiggle his toes and bend his knees. He's okay. The doctor looks at Mum and says Pete's fine. I look around. The bathroom's small and white. I like being in the bathroom with everyone in the middle of the night. It's like we're hiding together. It makes me think of coughing and Mum bringing me in for the steam in the winter.

I COUGH and cough. Mum comes into my room in the dark and lifts me out of bed. She carries me down the hall to the bathroom with the shower. The shower's streaming down steaming and when she opens the door and we go in it's like bright, hot fog. I cough some more. Mum sits me on the counter next to the sink and takes off my nightgown and I feel like I'm dreaming. She rubs Vicks on my chest and some of it gets on the side of my eye and in my eye so it burns. She rubs some on my back and when I cough the muscles in my stomach hurt. The shower's loud and no one's in it. The mirrors are steamed over. Then I sit down on the floor. The place on my chest and back where the Vicks is feels like it's invisible and I could reach my hand through it. Mum sits on the toilet and rests her head in her hand. I fall asleep on the cotton rug and when I wake up Mum's asleep with her head leaning against the sink. The shower's still going. It's like we're in a cloud. The window's black on the other side. My underwear's so damp it's wet. I go to Mum and tap her shoulder. I jiggle it. Mum looks at me with one eye and then jerks up. "Small fry," she says. She's sitting up. "I fell asleep."

When Mum brings me back to bed I want to go with her and she lets me. Their bed's big and I lie in between them but closer to Mum. Now that I'm out of all that warm wet air I want to cough all the time. My stomach's sore from coughing over and over. There's a big tickle back there in the dark of me but I hold it in. I don't want to wake them. Dad's snoring. I know if I cough Mum will leave and go sleep somewhere else because of me coughing and Dad snoring. I lie there trying not to cough. It tickles but I clench my toes up and it passes before it starts tickling again. When I wake up Mum's gone. I go back into my room and Mum's in my bed. She tells me I was kicking her in my sleep. She says it was like I was riding a bicycle kicking her in the stomach and legs over and over.

"Sorry," I say.

Mum tells me again what I was doing, how I was kicking her, but she's sort of talking in her sleep. It's like she's mad about it.

"YOU DIDN'T WANT yours?" It was Honor.

I looked up. "What?"

"You didn't want yours?" She meant the cupcake with the Valentine's hearts and the Blow Pop stuck into it.

"No."

"Did you read my Valentine?'

"No," I told her. I wished she would go away. She was big and wide in front of my desk.

"I didn't get one from you," she said.

"My mother left them all in Boston."

"Oh."

To our right Lulu was laughing with Robby. I glanced over at her and caught her eye and then she stopped laughing. I could tell she thought I was ignoring her. She looked down and then looked up at me like a dog. "Are you still coming over?" she asked. She meant that on Friday was I still going to spend the night.

"Yeah," I said. "I'll ask." I opened my desk again because I felt like I was going to cry. I felt like I was going to do something but I didn't know what, like maybe scream or burst into tears or run out of the room and keep going. I thought of teetering along the railing on the wharf in Maine, balancing.

Jamie Pauling came over to my desk. He's on Mrs. Crockel's side but he came over to Miss Hunt's side. "This is from Brendan," he told me, then he handed me something. It was one of those little bears that hug your finger.

"What?" I asked.

"Brendan told me to give it to you," said Jamie.

It was one of those little bears that hug your finger like a clip. You can clip them onto things and they hang on. If you squeeze his back his arms open wide and then when you let go they close. It's better than candy but it reminds me that I stole a few just like them from Tessa next door. They were on a white shelf way down low in the Emersons' downstairs bathroom, all lined up, little ones—a koala bear, a black bear, a polar bear, a panda bear, a brown bear, and even a couple more—and I took two of them. The one that Brendan gave me is fuzzy. It's a nice color. It's the color of my corduroys that have faded so they're almost white but they're still tan.

I looked up at the classroom. Miss Hunt was out of the room and she left the door open. Robby was having a hysterical laughing

fit on the ground. Pierre and Darren were drawing like war diagrams in the lower corner of the blackboard. Caleb had Patrick in
a headlock to try to give him a wedgie but they were laughing.
Lenny was chasing Timmy because Timmy took Lenny's Blow Pop.
They tipped over a desk and the crash was loud and it scared me. I
put my head down. I felt scared. Like something might happen.
Like something in Boston that time with Sasha.

SASHA'S BRINGING ME to the Ice Capades. I have one of
those flashlights that's like a blue police siren. It's not a flashlight.
You turn it on like a flashlight and then the flashing light spins
around on top. In the rink they're cool in the dark with all of the
other people's waving around like they're writing things in the air.
Once I'm out of the rink in daylight it looks dumb. I flick it on. It
spins. Big thrill. Sasha sees me looking at it letdown like that and
she laughs. We're about to cross the street and Sasha's looking at me
and I'm looking back up at her. I look up and behind Sasha's bright
face a man is coming across the street toward us. He's almost to us.
He's looking down and he looks like he's smiling about something
that he's thinking about. But a car is coming. I slap Sasha's leg so
she'll look. The man is in the way. He's right in the way of the
coming car. Sasha yells at the car coming. She yells against it like it's
a bad dog but it still comes—"No!" She yells again but this time it's
the same yell of "No" that it would be if she'd just let go of a fragile
vase by mistake and it was about to hit the floor—"Oh NO!" I
hear. I hear the thudding smack of the man's head I think on the
hood but maybe the windshield and Sasha pulls my face toward her
stomach. Down on the ground I can see my flashing light thing
smashed and the batteries have fallen out of it like its body has been
ripped open and I don't remember dropping it.

"WHAT'S WRONG?" It was Honor again standing at my desk.
I put my head back down. I didn't want to answer her. She was

clapping two erasers together while she looked at me so they dusted together in a chalky cloud. I could hear the soft *poof* and smell the chalk. "What's wrong?" Honor asked again.

"Stop doing that," I told her. I meant clapping the erasers. It was making the air gritty.

She stopped.

"I don't feel good," I said. My head was resting on my arms and I was looking sideways at the crease in my bent elbow. I had the tiny bear Brendan gave me in there in the crook of my arm.

"Stomachache?"

"Leave me alone," I told Honor. While I said it I heard my voice hum buzzing against my ear that was against the desk and inside my wall of arm.

"Is that why you didn't want a cupcake?"

"Leave me alone," I said again.

Miss Hunt came back in. I wanted it to be quiet. I wanted to go home with my little bear that Brendan gave me. I wanted to go home and look at Mum.

THIRTEEN

Social Studies

~⌒ MRS. CROCKEL OPENED up the divider and then clapped her hands together twice. She told us to double up for social studies. Matt Means sits next to me so we always double up at my desk. On the other side of me is Billy but he's next to Darren Sauer on his other side so they have to double up. They always give us newspapers and then we look at them together. I like social studies but I pretend I don't because everyone else doesn't. We like it when we all read the funnies together.

Mrs. Crockel flattened a newspaper down on my desk for me and Matt. The *Beverly Times*. In the center of the front page was a picture of two men in suits shaking hands on like a stage. There were two men behind them in the background standing up and clapping. The SALT talks—"No it doesn't," said Robby Gruen. We get the newspaper at home. On Sunday mornings Dad's got them all sprawled out at the head of the dining room table. The cats like to get up there on the table and lie on top of the newspapers. The cats always like sitting on paper. I don't get why. I'll be drawing something on a piece of paper on the floor in the front hall. Before I know it some of the kitties have surrounded me, lying on top of scattered spare sheets of paper like they're huge furry paperweights.

KEVIN KNEISLER USED to be the paperboy. He'd leave his canvas bag of papers on the side of the driveway and hang around all the time. His hair was light and he had white peach-fuzz hair on his cheeks. He'd usually eat the pound cake in the fridge or whatever packaged Sara Lee–type cakes were in there. He'd just walk right in. Marly and Pete's friends all just walk right in and hang around but Kevin's no one's friend. He was just on his paper route. He's Marly's age. Or Pete's.

Kevin's jumping on our trampoline. He's out here jumping on our trampoline and I want to get on. I want him to get off and leave. I stand by the edge and watch the springs creak growing big and small like rubber bands being pulled in a slingshot. Kevin jumps into a sit and then stays sitting so he bounces a bit with his legs apart like a big baby and then steadies. He's wearing a sweater that has oblong wooden buttons at the neck. "You want to get on?" he asks me.

I nod.

"Come on," Kevin says.

"I don't want to jump while you're sitting on it," I tell him.

"I'll get off," he tells me.

I climb up. The trampoline is black. Sometimes when the sun shines on it right I can see through it to the grass underneath. One of the cats might be sitting under there because they like the shade. It used to be the Emersons' tramp. Pete and Mr. Emerson set it up over on the Emersons' lawn but then we were all over there bouncing on it so much that after a while Dad and Mr. Emerson carried it over here without taking it apart. I wanted to jump on it while they were carrying it but I knew I couldn't. I love it. I can do a back flip but when I do a forward flip I land on my feet for a second and then go falling forward. Cy double bounces me. When Pete's home he double bounces me so high it scares me a lot but I like it. The springs around the sides scare me. They pinch. I pretend they're a stream around the edge like a moat filled with piranhas. When you jump to the ground from the bouncing it's like your legs are dead.

I stand there next to Kevin and wait for him to get off.

Kevin's pulling something out from a zipper on his sweater. It's a roll of money. He unrolls it and starts counting. I push with my legs to make the trampoline ripple to jiggle him. "Get off," I tell him, but I'm watching the bills. I like looking at money.

Kevin separates the bills into two piles on the trampoline. I sit down and watch him. There are ones and fives. It's like Monopoly but it's real. "Do you want one?" Kevin asks me. I look at him. "I'll give you one if you'll do something," he says.

"Like what?"

He picks up a dollar bill. "I'll give you this if you give me a kiss."

"A kiss?"

"Right here," he says. He points to the middle of his furry cheek.

"A kiss?" I'm wrinkling my face. I can't help it.

"Okay. I'll give you two." Kevin picks another bill up. The air is cool and still. The number "1" printed in the corner looks pretty. They'd be mine.

"Really?" I ask. The bills look so reliable and tidy.

He points again. "Right here." I kiss lots of other people. I could do it. "Right here and it's all yours." I'll put the money up in my jewelry box. When I open it the ballerina twirls slowly on her toes. I'll put it in the safe part underneath the top tray.

"Right now?" I ask.

"Right now." I lean toward him and press my lips together. I bump his cheek with them and make a little noise. It's over. I lean back. "All yours," he says to me. He hands them to me. I uncurl them and smooth them on my knees to look at them. My pants are blue corduroy and they've faded nicely so they're grayed on the outer layer. I smooth the bills on the soft material. "You're very pretty," Kevin says. I look up at him. I don't like it. I look back down. I have two dollars like a grown-up.

ME AND CY MAKE bets for money but I never get any. Like me and Cy are in the front hall lying on the floor with the cats. "We're not having SpaghettiOs. We're having TV dinners," I tell him. I'm lying down but I've got lots of energy because that streamy Rolling Stones song is playing in the living room the one that sounds streamy and up high and like they're shouting it flowing along about love being a kiss away. Cy told me that's what they were yelling because I could hardly hear what they're saying, but now I can. It's off of that album with the cover that I like to look at because it has a cake with plastic little band guys stuck into it like birthday candles and the cake's stacked on top of records on a record player. It's the same album that has that song where Mick says "Boston" through the twangy guitars. I like hearing "Boston" when Mick's saying it. He says it in another lilty song too but I don't remember which song it is but in the song there's a pickup truck that's painted green and blue.

"I know I'm right," I tell Cy. "We're having TV dinners."

Cy says back to me, "You want to bet?"

"Okay."

"SpaghettiOs or TV dinners," says Cy. "Take your pick."

"It's TV dinners," I tell him. "I told you." I get up off the floor because I can't help it the music makes me want to get up.

"I'll bet you a doll hair," says Cy.

"You're saying 'doll hair,' " I tell him. I know the trick. Cy says it instead of "dollar" and then when I win the bet Cy plucks a hair from my doll or from me and gives it to me saying "Here's your one doll hair." The other trick's "I'll bet you two bucks." Then when Cy loses the bet he goes "One buck," and bumps me with his hip, "two bucks," and bumps me again.

"Okay. I'll bet you a hundred cents," Cy says to me. I don't know what he means. "That's the same thing as a dollar," he tells me. "You know, like one hundred pennies in a dollar? One hundred cents?"

"Oh yeah," I say. " 'Kay."

"I bet you a hundred cents that we're having SpaghettiOs for dinner," he says. We shake on it.

We ask Mum. It's TV dinners so I'm right. "You owe me a hundred cents," I tell him.

"Okay. Let's see," says Cy. He looks up at the ceiling and touches his chin.

The music's not loud anymore. It's that song that comes after. It's slow and sort of sad with the twanging guitars and the train station. It makes me sway.

Cy's looking up at the ceiling, touching his chin. He says, "There's dog doo, flowers—"

"What?" I ask him. I'm swaying with the music.

Cy looks at me. "I'm giving you a hundred scents," he says. "Get it? Like smells. Um, skunk, onions, pizza—"

"Cy!" I kick him. Cy laughs and hits me back but it's the noogie kind right in my arm so it feels like a bruise even though it hasn't had time to bruise yet.

SPARKY LIES DOWN under the trampoline underneath me and Kevin and groans as he does it. "You want another one?" Kevin asks.

I put the two bills one on top of the other. I fold them in half.

"I'll give you one of these," Kevin says.

I look up. "A five?"

"If you kiss me right here." Kevin points to his fly.

"Gross," I say.

"It'd be over in just a second," he says.

"On your pants?"

"I'll go like this." Kevin looks over at the house to see if anyone's looking. I look too. No one. He unzips his fly but leaves the button done up. It's like a rip. He has white underwear on. Then he moves his underwear around and I can see just an edge of his penis but not the whole thing. "There," he says.

"Kiss you right there?"

He nods.

"Gross," I say again.

"For a fiver."

It would be over in just a second. "Just kind of on your pants?" I ask.

"Sure. Right here. Just like you did on my cheek."

I look at the open crack in his pants. Now I can't see. It looks dark down there. Before I think about it I bend my head down with my lips pressed tight together. He edges toward me with his waist so when I'm there my lips bump up against pink flesh. It's rubbery and I think I feel it twitch but it's over. My head's back up where I was. I smile because it's over. "All yours again," says Kevin. He gives me the five. I can feel my heart beating. Kevin zips up his fly.

"I'm going in," I tell him. I jump down and run across the lawn to the porch. At the door before I go in I look at the money. My money.

I'm in the yellow kitchen. The kitchen table's white with a yellow stripe as thick as the length of my finger around the border like a racetrack. It's sort of like where the springs are around the trampoline. Both are like frames or moats. I say to Cy, "Look what I have," dangling the money.

"Did you take it from Mum?" Cy asks. He doesn't really care. He's getting a glass of ginger ale.

"No."

"Where did you get it?" Cy's not really listening. I watch him fill only half his glass and I watch the ginger ale fizz.

"That's for me to know and you to find out," I say.

"Well la-di-da," he says. He gets the grape juice out from the fridge and fills the rest of his glass for a mixture.

"Kevin gave it to me," I tell him.

"Why?"

"I kissed him."

Then Cy looks at me. "Yikes," he says, making a funny face, smiling. He leaves and then Mum comes in a little bit after.

She asks, "Now, where did you get that?" like Cy already told her but now she wants to hear it from me.

"Nowheres," I tell her.

"Listen to me." She's right in front of me, looking right at me.

"Kevin gave it to me."

"He gave it to you," she says, not like a question.

"Uh-huh."

"And why did he do that?"

"Because he just did."

"Don't lie to your mother, Via."

"Well because I gave him a kiss and he gave it to me."

"A kiss." Mum's face scares me.

"What?" I say.

"What did you say?" Mum asks me.

"Kevin gave it to me."

"Because you kissed him." Her eyes look big.

"Yeah." I say it softly.

"How?" asks Mum.

"What?"

"How and where did you kiss him?"

"On the tramp," I tell her.

"On the lips?"

"On his cheek."

Mum shakes her head. "That damn kid," she says. She comes to me and grabs my wrist hard. She's close to my face. "Don't you ever, ever do that again." She looks right into my eyes. "Do you hear me?" She's squeezing too tight. I can feel her ring digging in to the knob bone on the side of my wrist.

I nod.

"Loud and clear?"

I nod. I think of down by his fly. There was a smell like salt and my hockey gloves.

"Ever," Mum says. Mum picks my money up from the table. "And I really mean it," she says.

"What are you doing?" I ask. Mum doesn't say anything. She's walking out with my money. "Mum!" I call after her. "But it's mine!"

I DON'T REALLY remember social studies that well. I kept looking up from my desk thinking that I'd see the back of Bethany's head with her part down the middle in front of me but she was out sick. I wondered what Bethany's house was like and like what kind of things her mom brings to her while she's sick in bed. I haven't been sick in a while. It's usually a sore throat and fever and stuff that I get. Mum sometimes brings me ginger ale with vanilla ice cream in it or a purple cow which is grape juice with vanilla ice cream.

ONCE MR. EMERSON was really sick and was in the hospital and then me and Mum went to visit him at his house when he came home. I'd never been up in Mr. Emerson's bedroom before. Mum told me that the room we were in wasn't his real bedroom where he usually sleeps with Tessa. Mum said he was staying in the spare room just while he was recovering.

Me and Mum go into his room to see him and he looks up. He isn't doing anything, just sitting up in his bed. Mr. Emerson looks up and smiles at us. He says, " 'And tho' we are not now that strength which in old days moved earth and heaven, that which we are, we are.' " Mum smiles and kisses him on his head and then goes into the bathroom to put the flowers in the vase that Tessa gave us downstairs.

When we leave Mum tells me not to go just pop in and see Mr. Emerson for a while because he needs his rest. Plus, she tells me, he's also taking medicine that might make him say strange things. He might say things that I wouldn't understand.

Partly I forget and partly I remember but anyway I go see Mr. Emerson while he's still sick. I like him too much. Tessa's in the kitchen but I sneak up the back stairs.

Mr. Emerson's in bed. He looks funny without his glasses. His eyes are dark. He looks funny without his normal shirt on. He has a robe on but he's under the covers. The covers are white and his robe is crimson. He reaches for his glasses on the bedside table. He puts them on and looks at me.

"Remember," Mr. Emerson says, "no matter where you are or what you're doing."

"What?" I ask him. He seems normal so far.

"Not all the darkness in the world can put out the tiniest flame."

"What?"

Usually he'd say it again for me until I hear it. This time he looks at me hard. "You're wondering where everyone's gone to," he says.

I nod just because I don't know what else to do. The way he's looking at me it feels important. I stare back at him. My head feels like it's growing bigger, though, because I feel a little frightened. I feel like I'm welling up and I'm not going to be able to control it.

Mr. Emerson reaches out and touches my hand. The smell in the room is gross. Like medicine and stale sheets. "They've gone," he whispers to me, like a secret.

What? I say it. "What?"

"They've all gone," he says.

I want to ask him who. I want to ask him where. "Where?"

"I don't know," he says.

"What?" I say it softly. I don't know whether to be scared of him or to hug him. I don't know whether he looks kind or mean.

He says it again. "I don't know." But then he says, "Nobody knows." Then he says, really loud and fast "Damn it how should I know!" really fast.

I've never heard Mr. Emerson yell. I'm not breathing right. His hand touching mine scares me a little too. I can't breathe. I can't handle it. "I miss it," I manage to say. I mean him being normal. What does he mean? I run home. My face is wet and the air is cold and the long grass on the side of the road pokes up through the crispy snow. I have to slide across some ice. I run up the steps and in the door. The front hall's there waiting and I stick my face into the brown velvet sofa and cry. I want to go tell Mum but she'll get mad that I went to see him in the first place.

I'm on the couch crying and when I close my eyes I'm like a dark roller coaster going down and down and every time I swoop farther down with a breath it's darker. I think of Mum's face. I see Mum's face down by the water somewhere and it shimmers like light, then it's gone. I look up at the window and I see her face in the glass and then it's just glass. I put my head in the cushion and I think of Mum's face. I get it and then I can't keep it. I get it again. The soft velvet on my face makes the dark behind my eyes feel darker. Somewhere down near the kitchen I think Mum's calling me but I'm falling asleep.

When I wake up on the couch a little bit later something feels different. There's movement. Sparky licks my face. Then I look. It's not Sparky. It's some brown, dopey-looking dog. But at least it's a dog. Then I recognize it. It's Sasha's boyfriend's dog. Pogie or something's its name. Something like a pogo stick.

LULU'S BROTHER Brian was sick and got his tonsils out last week. Lulu went to the hospital to visit him one night after school. She said they had strawberry Hoodsie ice creams and that while they ate them with the flat wooden spoons they watched two nurses get into a big argument in the hall. One of them threw her clipboard smack on the ground and started pushing the other one and then the other one went running all the way down the long hall like it was a tunnel.

————

I WAS in the hospital once. I had an operation. I was little and I still did gymnastics then.

After gymnastics I go up to Mum's room with her while she sorts through her desk and I show her things that we did. I pretend there's a balance beam and I'm showing her how the redheaded girl Trish walks on it with her toes all spread apart like tentacles. "She goes like this," I tell Mum, "watch." I do it, walking with my toes all apart but when I look up she's not watching. "Watch," I tell Mum again. This time she does. When I'm done I look at her.

"I like how your hands are like this too." Mum flexes her fingers out like a starfish. I look at my hands. They are like that and I didn't even know it. "Does Trish do that too?"

"No," I tell her. I try to spread just my toes apart without spreading my fingers apart and I can't do it. I try again.

"That's quite a face," Mum tells me. She makes it and her mouth is wide open with her tongue sticking out to the side on her cheek. I stop and I can feel my tongue doing that. I can't do it so I try to do that thing that Pete showed me when you make a V with your four fingers, two on either side. It's like *Star Trek*. I can only do it if I help myself split the fingers apart with my other hand. I stop. I do a cartwheel. I do a little round off.

Mum sits down on the chaise. "Come here," Mum tells me. She's got the brush in her hand. I do another cartwheel and then go stand in front of her between her knees with my back to her. Mum takes my pigtails out. My pigtails have made my hair dented where the elastics were. Mum brushes. I pretend it hurts but it feels good. I look at us in the mirrors. She brushes straight over my head, back, which I hate because then the hair poofs up and it looks like Wolfman Jack.

"It's like a werewolf," I say.

"Beautiful," says Mum. She blows her lips on my shoulder so they make a fart sound. She says, "I could eat you," then bites my shoulder with a nip.

I'm in my leotard still. I love my leotard and Mum calls it a leapotard still since that's what I called it when I was first learning what it was. It's serious looking with maroon stripes and a zipper down the front. Mum's brushing. Then she stops around the back of my head. She's not brushing anymore. She's rubbing my head back there.

"What's this?" Mum says. She's feeling something at the back of my head. I've felt it before and wondered the same thing. She kneads around. "This hurt?" Mum asks.

"No."

"I can't tell if—" She's rubbing around it. "Here," she tells me. "Face this way and whoosh your hair down." I know what she means. She means like before I flip it back—whoosh—out of my face. I do and she fingers around in my hair. Her fingers feel small. They feel nice near the back of my neck and I can hear the sandy sound they make as she moves them around on my scalp. I get a little shiver on my shoulders. "It's a bump," she decides.

"Yeah." I'm looking at the carpet. There's a little sticker or something stuck on it.

"Did you bump it?"

"I don't know."

"You'd remember if it really hurt."

"Yeah."

"Do you feel it?" She takes my hand and puts my fingers on it and starts them rubbing. It feels nice and smooth.

I nod.

"Have you felt it before?"

"Yeah."

"Why didn't you tell me?"

"I forgot."

In the doctor's office I'm walking around. I'm wearing my red dress with the little white ABCs all over it. I'm looking in the plants' pots. Mum's sitting in a chair watching me and looking around. When the doctor comes in he has a big envelope and I stand right near him while he takes the X rays out. I stand on the stool that he was going to sit on while he sticks them up on the wall. Then he flicks the switch on and it's like a bunch of skeleton heads. I stand still. I turn around and look at Mum. "It's a little scary looking isn't it," she says to me.

I jump down from the stool and go to Mum's lap. She has her arms out for me before I even get there. I turn around once more and look at the X rays and the doctor's pointing at them, talking but I don't hear what he's saying. I'm listening to Mum's heartbeat. Her sweater's itchy but I hear it. Her.

In the hospital my bed has a metal fence around it. When I change into a nightgown the nurse takes off my underwear too and I'm not used to sleeping without my underwear. There are other beds but no one else is in here. I can't sleep and I climb over the metal crib wall and walk out into the hall with my hospital bracelet tag on my wrist. A blond nurse picks me up and brings me with her. We sit at a desk with a panel in front of us and she pushes plugs into little holes and answers phones. In the morning Mum carries me down the hall. I tell her that when I couldn't sleep a nurse brought me out to her desk and let me sit on her lap. Mum doesn't believe me.

At the operation I lie on the table. The doctor's round face is big. His daughter's in the grade above me and her face is round and big too. He has a green hat and mask on like what Caleb wore at Halloween to be a doctor. He asks me, "Can you count backward from ten?" I can. Everyone else is dressed like he is. I can see he's smiling from his squinting eyes when he sticks the thing like a bowl over my mouth and I say ten and that's all.

WE'RE BACK in front of the mirror in Mum's room a while after the operation and she's changing the square Band-Aid at the back of my head. I want to touch the stitches and Mum lets me. My hair's growing back in too and it feels as prickly as the stitches. I can't see it all but to my fingers it doesn't feel like me. Each hair feels hard edged like metal. The stitches feel like bugs sticking there but at the same time it feels like a machine. Like Frankenstein.

Then Mum says "How's it feel to have a steel plate in your head?" like she read my mind.

I'm concerned. "What?"

She's laughing at my face. She kisses my cheek. "I'm just kidding, love."

I don't care. I'm just glad to be home and not in that metal bed with intercoms out in the hall. At night when I woke up in the hospital I'd get really scared. That's why I climbed out and found the blond nurse that time.

SOMETIMES WHEN Mum turns the light out at night at home I'm scared too. I think of things under the bed and all of those stupid things. When I was really little once I had a nightmare where I was falling off a cliff in my bed and then my room landed and everything seemed to be okay. But then right at my window this really mean-looking horse jabbed his head through the glass so it smashed and he started snarling around, then I woke up. It was pitch black and I wanted to go to Mum's room I was so scared. I got out of bed and thought I was on the wrong side for the doorway so I crawled over the bed to the other side. I found the wall and felt along it in the dark for the corner where the two walls meet. When I found the corner I started feeling around for the light switch. I kept feeling around on the wall with my hand and I couldn't find it. But I knew that just a few more feet away was the door to the hall and then I'd be able to get out into the hall and turn that light on. So I felt along a little farther but my hand couldn't find the door in the exact place where the door should be. It was all just wall, wall, wall. I was walled in. "Mum!" I screamed. I fell down on the floor, screaming for Mum. Then the light turned on and it was Mum in the doorway. She was way over on the other side of the room. It took me a second to realize I was just feeling around on the completely wrong wall but then I started crying. Mum said, "What are you doing way over there?" then came over to me. Sometimes even now when I get scared at night it's because

I'm thinking of that scary horse that smashed my window in my dream that time.

But sometimes when Mum turns the light out at night at home I'm not scared at all. I'm in my own bed. Sometimes when I can't sleep I sing a little in the dark. Mum might be out in the hall. She can hear me singing in my bed. She might say, "Pipe down in there, Janis," or "Can it, Aretha," to tell me to be quiet.

Sometimes I just lie there on my back looking up with my eyes wide open. It's so dark that my eyes are open wider than they'd ever be in the day. After a while I can barely see some of the sky over in the corner top of the window. It's black-blue. But the air in front of me is black. It looks like it would feel nice if I could touch it and feel it. I hum into it. I hum the same note and it sounds nice. I try to do it as long as I can in one breath.

When I stop it sounds even quieter. "It's dark," I whisper. I wait. The quiet sounds like it's buzzing it's so quiet. I whisper into it. "Mum," I whisper. I listen. There's nothing. "Mum," I whisper again. It sounds like the hum. It sounds like home. It's like a soft balloon with no edges that rises up and out. I say it out loud into the black air—"Mum"—and then it's just me and the sound in the dark before it sinks up into the night and falls in.

FOURTEEN

Short Recess

—᠗ I DON'T REMEMBER social studies that well but after it
we had recess again. It's a short one. It was even warmer than in the
morning recess so I didn't wear my mittens or even put my coat on
when we went outside. The warm air felt kind of weird. It wasn't
that warm at all, but compared to earlier. It felt nice to have my
hands out in the open air. The air was cold on them but I could feel
the sun on them too when it came out in flashes from behind the
mostly clouds. The snowbanks on the sides of the roundabout were
getting waxy looking and slushy. I could hear the icicles dripping.
The ice on the pond was melting. I wondered about the ice on the
other ponds around town.

I started hockey this winter but we're not really a team. It wasn't
really a team but I loved being there. I love how the sound of the
sticks hitting the ice claps up through the air in the rink. I love the
leather smell of my hockey gloves once they soften up. I like it too
when it's sort of warm and the mist rises up off of the ice.

Next year in hockey I'll be a Squirt instead of a Mite. I don't get how I'll be good enough to be a Squirt and get better since it's not like I'm practicing in between now and then.

"You'll see," Mr. Emerson tells me. Tessa says he was a hockey star once. "It's coordination. Your coordination improves."

"Just by—just it does?" I ask.

Mr. Emerson nods his head down in a single nod. He looks at me over his glasses. " 'Just it does' is correct."

MR. EMERSON BRINGS me and Cy skating on the pond at Bayside. Mr. Emerson's leather skates are so old that they look like deflated old-fashioned footballs that someone's been sitting on for a few years. The laces are like regular shoelace string. Once he puts them on they look more like skates. When he's skating he looks like he's going slowly because he looks so relaxed. But really he's going fast. He glides. He clasps his hands behind his back. He digs in with bent knees so his body's tipped forward just a little bit. His chin's tucked in. Each stride cuts long and deep. He skates around the edge of the pond like it's a rink while Cy and I pass the puck back and forth in the middle.

There's a lake too that we skate on. It's a huge lake. It's not that far from our house but I don't really know where it is. By the dump or something. We only go there a couple of times in the winter for the black ice. When Mum comes she can do little jumps and twirls. Her tracks are the best to look at.

WE PLAY street hockey at home, even in the summertime.

Cy comes over to me on the porch and stands me up straight. He has a pillow. There's another one behind him. They're from his bed. He has masking tape or that hockey tape that's like white cloth. "Here," Cy says. He puts a pillow on my leg. We've done this before. He hasn't even asked but I don't mind because I'm just glad I'm playing. I'm just glad I get to play.

The Tiny One

Cy puts the pillow on my leg and then tapes around it so it stays. The other pillow's blue. Cy goes and gets it and puts it on my other leg. His friend Mal comes back outside. Mal goes under the porch where the bikes are and brings out the net. They put it in front of the steps, right behind me, and tell me to stay there. Cy puts another pillow on my chest. He tapes it around.

Cy puts his helmet on me and then bends down to do the snap under my chin. When it snaps he looks at me. "Just stay there," he says. "Here. You can use this." He gives me a stick that he's holding under his armpit.

Mal and Cy take shots on me. One hits my helmet and I'm so surprised that it doesn't hurt that I laugh and start to walk away. "Hey," Cy reminds me to get back where I was. They're not pucks. They're like wads of tape. Cy shoots and it goes over my shoulder. Mal shoots and it hits my foot so I curl my toes. It stings. I think to put on my sneakers but when I look over at them I only see one and remember Sparky took the other one.

I forget Cy and Mal are shooting at me because I'm busy watching them. Mal can't move around without sticking his tongue into the side of his cheek. He flicks his bangs to the side like he's coming up from underwater or heading a soccer ball. Cy puts all of his lips over to one side like he's about to kiss something on a corner. I try both things with my mouth and Cy's way feels comfortable.

I look behind Mal and Cy playing because I see someone coming up the driveway in front of the Emersons' house. My throat gets hit by a humming puck and the slap feels wet. My throat feels like there's a dent in it. It's like getting my wind knocked out but up in my neck.

"Oops," says Cy. They don't realize yet that I can't make a sound and that's why I'm not crying. I hold my neck and drop the stick. "You're okay," says Cy.

Another shot flies past my head. My helmet's slid down so I can't see really but I see the legs of the person behind them walking toward us. They're man's legs. I point.

"You're okay," Cy says again. He's stickhandling around. He doesn't know what I'm talking about.

"There." I point again. The guy's practically here.

"Well all right, street hockey," the guy says. Mal turns around to see. Cy does too. People never just walk up here to the house. We're up on a hill, out of the way. We don't know what to say. Our visitor's smoking a cigarette. "And who's the goalie?" he says, pointing with his cigarette.

"My sister," says Cy.

"You all play ice hockey?" he asks.

"Yeah," says Cy.

"What position?"

"Wing. Or center."

"Never defense?"

Cy shakes his head.

The guy's mouth doesn't stop grinning while he talks. "Always good to be on the defensive, man," he says. He's wearing sunglasses so it's hard to say what he's looking at. He's sunburned. He's skinny. "Right?" He grins.

Cy nods. Cy's holding his hockey stick in front of him like it's a guitar.

"Right on," says the guy. He's almost giggling. He's nodding a lot. "You mind if I just . . . you know," and he sits down on the side of the driveway near the shed.

Cy looks at Mal and sort of shrugs and they start shooting at me again. The guy says "Nice" or "Ooh" like a commentator but he doesn't say "It's wide!" or "Shot—*score!*" like a real commentator or like someone who plays very much. Sometimes he's just giggling. Who is this guy?

Cy likes the audience. "You want to play?" Cy asks him. "There are sticks under the porch."

"No no no. Play on, man," he says. He's lighting a cigarette. He's sitting back and propping himself up with his elbows to watch. He rests his foot on his knee. Even from where I am I can see that his feet are big and dirty inside his sandals. They're long feet.

Cy comes up close to the net and then flicks the puck thing over my shoulder but it misses the net and goes up onto the porch.

I'm the one to go get it. It's hard to walk up the steps with the cushion padding on my legs but I make it. Down below they keep shooting anyway even though I'm not in net anymore. Cy has bare feet so he sort of tiptoes when he runs.

I walk around on the porch looking for the little wad of hockey tape puck. I can't find it so I stand still and look around trying to trace its path in my head.

"It went by the kitchen," Cy yells. He sees I'm standing still not knowing where to go.

I throw the puck at Mal and get back in net.

Mal hits a slap shot and it hits my neck but it doesn't hurt like the one Cy did earlier. "Sorry, V," Mal says softly.

Cy and Mal shoot at me for a while and then they slow down. They're getting bored of showing off.

The guy watching us play coughs and sits up. He lights another cigarette but it's not a cigarette this time it's a joint like Pete smokes. I can smell it. "I'm Larry, by the way," he says.

"I'm Cyrus. That's Mal. She's Via," says Cy. Then Cy goes and sits down on the grass near Larry.

I know the game's over so I put my sneaker on and then find the other one that Sparky took. He didn't take it far. It's under the bush where he digs a little bit of a hole and then nestles in to sleep on the clean dirt.

I touch my neck where the puck hit me. It feels like the kind of big mosquito bites that hurt. I walk to where Cy's sitting down. "Can you see?" I ask him, jutting my neck out.

"No," he says. "Well, wait," he says and waits for me to lower down to him. He looks at my neck. "It's right there," Cy says. He touches it. "It looks like a hickey," he tells me.

"What's a hickey?"

"When someone sucks your neck."

I look down at him. "You mean like a vampire? The blood?"

"No. It's like a kiss but with more suck to it. So it makes a red mark."

"Gross," I say. It sounds nice.

I look at Larry smoking his joint. He hands it to Cy and Cy takes a puff.

AT BAYSIDE Cy and his friends sometimes go out into the woods at recess and smoke. Only a couple times, he told me. When Pete's home he has a bong in his room and Mum calls it a bomb. I like looking at it because it's a clear yellow plastic tube and it makes me think of a squirt gun or the yellow plastic treadmill that I put the gerbils on. It's like the clear-yellow-handled screwdrivers that Mr. Emerson has in his woodshop that make me think of lemon-drop candies. Pete and his friends laugh and tell me to put my lips inside the round circle of the bong. I cough and they laugh some more. Marly says, "God, Pete, she's your sister. Not your dog," but she's giggly while she takes my hand and we go outside and sit on the lawn. Marly gets lazy and asks for a back rub so I give her one. She lies on her stomach on the grass and I sprinkle her back with my fingers for a tickle rub while we can hear the record player playing Van Morrison.

I'm downstairs at the piano and Mum walks up the stairs. When she's at the top I can hear her. "Peter. Give me that bomb of yours. I know you've hidden it somewhere."

I'm changing in my room and at the top of my window I can see Cy's feet dangling down from the roof up above. He's wearing his Jack Purcells with the flat blue soles on the bottom with the red stamp in the middle. I see his hand quickly dip down and flick the ash of a cigarette. I run downstairs to Mum and tell her Cy and his friend Charlie are smoking cigarettes up on the roof and she tells me it's bratty to be a tattletale. No one likes a tattletale.

The Tiny One

I GET INTO the hole where the tree's tipped over. It's not buggy or anything. It's torn-up dirt that's moist and powdery like really ground-up coffee. It's like a fort already without building anything. I can't wait to come out here with my cars. It's too late tonight. Is it? It's still nowhere near being dark. I crawl out to look around and see.

Mal's sitting on the ground near me. Cy's sitting on a stump. They're watching Larry. I look too. Larry's trying to shimmy up a tree but the trunk's too thick for him to really get around. It looks stupid. He lets go and goes over to another tree and steps up onto a branch.

"Come on," Larry says. No one answers. "Come on up," he says. He's reaching his spidery long leg up onto another branch.

"Nah," says Cy.

Then Larry's voice gets squealy—"Whoa, look at these leaves!" His voice is like a squeak. "It's too beautiful, man!" squeaks Larry.

Cy and Mal start laughing so I laugh too. Larry shakes the branch with his foot so it waves up and down. "What do I do about this tree?" says Larry.

"What?" says Cy.

"What?" Larry says back.

"What?" Cy says again.

Larry sighs. "Her body looks like a lot of fun," he says. We hear him through the leaves. "She melts my syndrome, man."

Cy sits up. "Who does? We're going inside," says Cy. "V's got to go to bed."

Larry jumps down from the tree and almost lands on his sunglasses.

Mal puts the street hockey net back under the porch and Larry lies down where he was before on the grass by the side of the driveway. Cy's sort of hanging there I think because he's not sure if it's okay to just leave Larry there alone or not. Marly comes out the door onto the porch to get me for bed.

"Who's this?" Larry asks.

Marly's at the top of the steps. "Who's *this*?" she says back.

"That's my sister," says Cy.

"Well hello, sister!" says Larry, like he thinks she's pretty.

Marly takes my hand and we walk through the kitchen. Mum's unloading the dishwasher.

Marly says, "There's like a drug addict out lying on the lawn, Mum."

Mum says "What?" but keeps unloading.

While Marly's tucking me in I can hear someone bouncing a basketball on the driveway. It's still light but it's darker. After Marly leaves me in bed I get up and go over to my window and look down to see if Larry's still down there. He is. Now Mum's out there on the grass beside him. They're eating Doritos. I can tell because of the red-and-orange bag.

I stand at the window and look down at them. The basketball bounces into my view and hits Mum on the head but not very hard. Cy comes and gets it and then moves back out onto the driveway where I can't see him. Then Larry gets up. He stands up and then he starts walking down the driveway in the direction that he came. I see him turn near the Emersons' and then I can see his head through the leaves going down the hill and then he's gone.

I look back at Mum on the grass. She's putting a Dorito in her mouth and smiling probably at Cy. I can hear the ball bouncing. It's slow bouncing like Cy's bouncing it and then holding it, bouncing it and then holding it, like that.

FIFTEEN

A Special Assembly

⟋ꙮ MISS HUNT TOLD us to line up for our special assembly.
I'd forgotten that we were having a special show-type thing for
Valentine's Day. We walked in a line down through the halls back
into the cafeteria but all of the tables had been moved to make
room for rows of chairs like at assembly but assembly's always in the
gym. It's some dance group had come from Montseratt or Peabody
or somewhere. Maybe Danvers.

THERE'S A NUTHOUSE in Danvers like a big creepy castle up
on the hill. It's near one of the rinks. Me and Dad drove up to it on
our way back to one of Pete's hockey games from the lumberyard.

Dad drives up the nuthouse's winding driveway just to see. The
pavement's so smooth and dark that I can hardly hear that we're
driving. "We'll just spin around," Dad says. He likes to scare me.
"We'll come out on the other side," Dad tells me.

I want to but I'm scared. I pull my feet up onto my seat. "Eeeee," I say. I pull my baseball hat down tighter. We curve along the quiet road. Up near the top of the hill there's a white-haired man on the side of the road with his feet in the leaves. He's dressed all in white. He should be wearing a coat. He looks at us blankly with his mouth wide open as we pass. He's walking away from the nuthouse at the top of the hill. "Better turn around, buddy," Dad says to him, even though he can't hear us.

When we come through the gates at the bottom of the hill Dad turns into the car wash. Once we're inside he doesn't pay attention to all the things coming at us because he's reading a magazine that he's folded over so it looks like one page. I look out all of the windows while we're in the car wash. There's something happening at each one. I love it. It's like going on a ride at a fair with whirling *Sesame Street* moppy guys rolling over the car and shining us up. It's like being under the sea with octopuses and seaweed heads mopping and grabbing at you.

THE MUSIC STARTED in the cafeteria and they turned the lights off before we all sat down so we'd hurry up. The third-graders were there too. I'd never been in the cafeteria in the dark before with the shades pulled down. Usually when they show us slide shows and stuff they do it in the gym. In the cafeteria there was a screen set up over near where we usually line up to get lunch. It wasn't a movie screen but like a screen that people might change their clothes behind, but bigger. Then, in the dark, the screen lit up. It lit up orange. Then we saw the shadow of a woman dancing. It was her silhouette. Everyone was laughing because we couldn't see her clothes so she looked naked. Then we forgot. She passed across the screen in twirls. It was excellent. The color changed. The song was Jimi Hendrix. It was "Little Wing" like what Pete calls me when I'm being an Indian— *Well she's walking through the clouds. . . .* When he sings *It's alright, she says it's alright, take anything you want from me* I feel like throwing my arms out and falling forward toward the music in a somersault.

The Tiny One

Then it was "Strawberry Fields." The screen was lit up pink and then green like a field and a guy was leaping around. Marly used to play this on the piano. I know the words from the music book. Last year I loved the Beatles. I'd sing Beatles songs and songs from *Oliver!* while I was up in my tree house and I'd pretend someone was filming me. This year it's Mick Jagger and Jimi Hendrix. I had a dream this year that Mick was licking the inside of my leg.

The guy dancing behind the screen was jumping around, dancing. He made his arms look like noodles when he moved but he was standing still and kind of looking like he was playing a drum. The light was just right, glowing pinkish red toward us in the dark and the music sounded so pretty. It was my whole head. I looked next to me at Caleb. His face was shiny in the light.

I touched Caleb's arm. I wanted to ask him something but I didn't know what. Caleb looked back at me quickly but then looked back at the screen and the dancers.

"Caleb," I whispered. I looked quickly up at the colorful screen and saw that lots of people were dancing. There were a bunch of dancers up there now.

"Caleb," I whispered again, and then I had to look back at the dancers because Caleb's face started quickly changing colors from the light and I didn't want to miss it. It was a heart up on the screen that looked like tie-dye that went from big to small, big to small, and it was changing colors. It was a Valentine's Day thing, I guess. Then there was a sound of something falling around us and then one hit me on the forehead and I saw it was one of those wimpy flattened lollipops wrapped in clear cellophane that you get at, like, the doctor. I like them, though. I like the orange ones.

All the teachers started clapping so we clapped too. When the lights turned on the dancers came out from around the screen to bow for us. They were all wearing red leotards and tights. None of them looked like I thought they'd look like. One girl that I thought was really pretty wasn't. One of the guys looked like this one friend of Sasha's but with a shaved head.

Caleb looked at me. "What?"

"What?" I said back.

Caleb was tearing the wrapper off of his green lollipop and it was crinkling. "What did you want?" he said.

"What?"

"You were tapping me," he said.

"Oh." I remembered. Now with the lights on I was scared to ask. Or, no, I wasn't scared, but I didn't know what to say. I didn't know what I was asking. I missed Amanda. "Nothing," I said. Caleb was looking at me. "Just," I said, "just that was cool, wasn't it."

"Yeah," said Caleb. He spoke through the lollipop in his mouth. "That was wicked cool."

WE DON'T GO to see dancers and shows and stuff very much at home. Or not at all, really. Like we never go out to dinner in a restaurant except for HoJo's on the road or stopping at Lorraine's for a sub or Nick's Roast Beef. Tessa brought me and Amanda to see the play *Peter Pan* in Boston once.

TESSA STOPS at the drugstore so we can get those booklet games with invisible ink for the ride into the city. Amanda's here for the weekend from New York and Tessa's bringing us into Boston to go see *Peter Pan*. I've never been to a play in Boston.

"The real theater with the big stage," Mum says. I'm sitting on my bed waiting for Mum to sew the button back onto my Mary Jane shoe so I can wear it to *Peter Pan*. It's hard for her to get the needle through because the leather's so thick.

Mum looks up at me and Amanda. She's holding some red thread between her teeth because she's about to tear it that way so she speaks without opening her mouth. She raises her eyebrows. "Maybe Peter Pan will even fly," she says to us.

I look at Amanda and then look back at Mum. "How?"

Mum's making a funny face because she's trying to push the

needle hard through the leather strap. "You'll have to see," she grunts.

"I wish I could fly!" shouts Amanda.

I laugh. "Me too!" I cry.

Mr. Emerson doesn't come with us. "Awful," he calls it. "Nothing worse in the world than musical shows." I think of *Oliver!* I sing "Where Is Love" up in my tree house and pretend I'm in a movie. I think of the musical at Sasha's school that almost made me cry that time.

Tessa's inside the closet looking for her pocketbook. Her muffled voice says, "What about *My Fair Lady*, darling?"

Mr. Emerson pats the counter. "Marvelous!" he says. He's quoting from it, I can tell. He speaks loudly so she can hear him. " 'Why can't a woman . . . be like . . . me?' "

We hear Tessa laugh. When she comes out of the closet, she's smiling. She looks pretty. She's wearing gold earrings that look like dragonflies. Her navy-blue coat is clean like a uniform. Her dark hair's glossy and loose but she has it back out of her face. "Don't you girls look beautiful!" she says to us. We have our parkas on but underneath we're wearing dresses. I usually hate getting dressed up but this time I don't mind. I'm wearing my gray flannel dress with woolly gray tights and my red Mary Jane shoes. Amanda's wearing my navy-blue velvet dress because her mom forgot to pack something nice. I usually hate wearing my hair down but this time it's okay. I've got a barrette on the side. Sasha painted it for me. It's light blue with a daisy daisy daisy painted along it. It's starting to chip. "All set?" Tessa asks.

Once we're in the city we go to a place called the Magic Pan for lunch. They make really thin pancakes and then put regular food on top, then fold it. Our waitress calls them "craps." Tessa explains it's a French word and says it the French way for us. Amanda and I smile when she says it in French. We try to say it too. Tessa says it again. It sounds pretty. It makes me think of a scallop shell or air. I get one with mushrooms and they taste good but they look like they have lotion all mixed up with them. It's snowing next to me out the window. People are walking by with their long coats flapping around their knees. The men are all dressed like Dad when he goes to work.

As Mum and I drive back from dropping off Aunt Nellie or Aunt Catherine at the airport we stop in traffic in the middle of the city. "See all the people, my love?" she says to me.

I nod. There are so many people that it's hard to see just one. They all seem to be crossing the street in the same direction just like the fish at the aquarium all go around the tank the same way.

We're at the aquarium and all of the fish in the tall round tank are swimming in the same direction like at free skate. Dad's holding my hand. "When do they switch directions?" I ask him. I mean the fish. I ask him again.

Dad looks down at me and smiles. "I don't know," he says.

I look at him. I'm surprised. I'm surprised he doesn't have an answer. His white collar's glowing in the dark from the black light. I look down to see if I have anything white on. Only my sneakers. They're glowing at the bottom of my black pants to make my feet look superpowerful. "Look," I say. I walk and look down at them sideways while I walk. "Look at my feet."

"See them all?" Mum says again. "All the people?" She didn't see me nod before. We're stopped in traffic in the city and people are everywhere you look. A handsome man in a suit holding a newspaper that he's rolled up into a tube looks at us through the windshield. He looks at Mum. I see him look back at her when he's made it to the other side of the street and gets up onto the sidewalk. We see two women bump into each other and then get mad about it.

"Yeah," I say. "I see them."

"And every single one of them has a mum just like you and a dad just like you."

"Mmm," I say. There's a man on the corner selling pinwheels and Red Sox pennants from a cart.

"Or at least at one point they did," Mum says. She flicks the radio on. It's snow like the TV set, then choked voices and squirts of music while she swishes the dial around. "Each one of them's born, each one of them dies." Mum's sighing. "The world's a big, big place," says Mum, "and you're my special, special girl."

After Mum says that I look down at my knees and they're small. I look at them and I feel proud like I'm chosen and we're all soldiers here living, chosen to live, and I get to be Mum's.

AMANDA'S CREPE HAS cheese inside of it. Tessa's is little pieces of chicken and rice mixed together. The mushrooms are salty and good in my mouth. When we're done Tessa orders us hot chocolate. She gets some too. We sit looking out at the whirling snow guessing where the people walking by our window are going. It's a man in a suit. "Work," says Tessa.

It's a woman with a purple coat. "Home," I say.

"Shopping," says Tessa.

"Skating," says Amanda.

Me and Tessa both laugh at her. "Skating?"

"Look!" Amanda points. We look. It's true. A pair of figure skates are dangling off of her shoulder as she's walking away.

Our waterlogged-looking waitress comes back. "Anything else?" she asks.

"No," says Tessa, "no thank you. We're just right."

In the theater at *Peter Pan* it's the biggest stage I've ever seen. I can hardly pay attention to what they're saying. I'm watching the colors, the movement, and I don't really care what's happening. Peter Pan's a lady with short hair and a squeaky voice. She looks kind of like Maria Von Trapp but I like Maria better. Wendy's a lady too. She's wearing an adult-size nightgown that's supposed to look like a girl's because it has a big bow in the front. The big bow on her head I guess is supposed to make her look smaller. I like Tiger Lily and Tinkerbell better than Wendy.

Amanda keeps looking at a lady to our left behind us in the audience who's making weird faces. When I turn around and look at the lady, the lady smiles and inchworms her finger around beckoning me. I don't understand. Amanda shrugs. The lady's over on the aisle one row back just a few seats down. When I look back again she does the same thing and winks.

When they sing on the stage the funny-faced lady behind us sings along with them and we can hear her. So can everyone else, I think. I turn around to watch her. She's patting the chair in front of her while she sings. The rows suddenly feel like pews at church. She starts talking while the actors on the stage are talking. She's acting like an old lady or one of those people who scream at nothing on the streets in the city. But she's all clean with dark lipstick. "Sure sure sure," the lady yells, while Tinkerbell's talking to Peter. "Yah yah yah," she yells up at Tiger Lily, slurring, "*I* have to be careful."

Then the lady gets up from her seat and walks down the aisle toward the stage, muttering. Someone has to stop her. They do. One of the ushers stands in front of her. We see him motion his arm toward the back of the theater like she better turn around. The lady doesn't care. She tries to edge by him but then he's holding her. We hear her start laughing hysterically. "She's kookoo," Tessa whispers.

"She doesn't look crazy," I say.

"Can't judge a book by its cover," says Tessa. Then me and Amanda laugh. We hunch down in our chairs and laugh because we're embarrassed for the kookoo lady and sort of scared for her too. Thinking of a book and its cover all flat and shiny keeps making me laugh. I don't know why. Sometimes you just laugh when you think of things. You just laugh out loud.

———

The Tiny One

LIKE IT'S FALL and we're sitting on the bottom limb of a tree waiting for recess to be over. Lulu just starts laughing. "What's so funny?" I ask.

Lulu keeps laughing.

"What?" I say.

And instead of saying "Nothing," she goes, "I was just picturing, like, a white bunny rabbit that has long bunny ears all over himself except for where his eyes are."

I picture it. I pause. I can see it. "It's like a porcupine!" I say. I think of all the soft white ears jammed all over it. I laugh. "But soft!"

Lulu's still laughing. "Yeah, but soft! Soft and poky all over and like cuddly!"

IT'S FUNNY THAT people laugh. It's weird. People open their mouths and make noise that they can't control and it means that they like something. Why? It seems so weird for a second. Something's feeling good in them. It's like a burst. It's like barking. Why? Thinking about how weird it is makes me feel like laughing.

Clapping's weird too. There's lots of clapping at Sasha's graduation. Sasha's graduation is outside and we're all sitting on white chairs in the middle of the audience. A big branch is armed out above us like a canopy bed. A gypsy moth falls from it right onto Mum's program and it makes a sticky thud when it hits the paper. The lady next to us says "Oh! How ghastly!" and winces away from it. She's wearing a neck brace the color of Silly Putty. Me and Mum laugh. "It just . . . fell," I say, summing it up.

"Shhh," says Mum, smiling.

The gypsy moth's curly and little. Gypsy moths are bad, though, even though they're cool looking in a glow-in-the-dark creepy way with their bright yellow and bluish spots. They eat the trees. I hold it on my hand and watch it lurch around. It's so small to eat trees. I should kill it to save the trees or should I not kill it because it's an alive thing. I get down by Mum's feet and push it back into the grass. It doesn't absorb into its world as quickly as I'd like. It lies limp on the top of the grass for long enough that I think it's dead. Then it goes. Where does it go? The little thing's got something to do.

ON THE WAY to Maine me and Dad drive through a town that has such humongous trees that they make the houses and churches look small. All their leaves fell off and then they looked like big giant skeleton hands reaching up through the ground. We're driving slowly through the town like we're going slowly just to look at how sick the trees are, but really it's traffic.

There are men up there in cherry pickers with chainsaws on two of the biggest trees. "Why are they cutting those guys down?" I ask.

Dad's driving and I'm leaning up front from the backseat so I'm talking to him right next to his head. "They're dead. So they don't fall down and hurt someone," says Dad.

"Dead?" I say it loud.

"They're diseased," says Dad.

"Diseased?"

"Diseased, yes. They're sick."

"That's sad, Dad," I say.

"Yes. Dutch elm disease."

I see the workmen carrying one of the huge limbs in a gigantic red sling. "It's so sad!" I say.

"You're right in my ear so don't shout," Dad tells me.

"It's too sad!" I say. "Why?"

"Why? Because it hurts my ear."

"No, why?"

"Dutch elm? Because it's a Dutch bug."

"No. No I mean. I mean like *why*, Dad?"

"Ah. Well. It, it came on a boat. Though, well, it might be that the name of this specific elm is Dutch elm. No, the bug is Dutch. We'll ask your mother. It came over on a boat. It's a bug that causes it. Like when you get sick."

"Yeah but Dad I don't die!"

"Right. Look, either move away a couple of feet from my ear or lower your volume. But right. You're absolutely right. You don't die when you get a bug," Dad tells me. "And we're lucky because the bug never made it to Sky Island so the elms there are fine."

"Can the bug fly?"

"Wind. Not really. But I don't see why it couldn't come over on the ferry with someone."

"On the ferry?" I'm shocked. We're on our way to the ferry right now.

"For all we know we might be bringing it with us right now," Dad says.

"Dad!"

"Via! Jesus! That's it. Sit back, would you?" He's swatting at his ear so swatting at me but I can dodge it. "You've got to settle down," he tells me.

"No one cares?" I ask. I want someone to make sure Sky Island won't get contaminated. I want that someone to be Dad.

"Settle down. It won't come on the ferry with us."

"But Dad, we've got to stop it, Dad!" I say.

"It's stopped. Now would you please relax. Sit back and look out the window."

At the ferry landing the threat is everywhere. Everyone's a possible carrier. Even Mrs. Kister who's always nice and friendly seems like she's being that way on purpose to pretend. Really inside her car she's got the Dutch bugs in a can that she'll let run crazy once we get across to Sky Island.

SASHA'S GRADUATION'S LONG. A girl talks up at the podium in her black cap and gown and she's holding a rose. I can't pay attention because I don't even get what she's saying but then

I pay attention because she starts crying. She's smiling but choking crying too. I look down our row to see if anyone else is crying and they're not. The girl bursts more into tears and then can't really talk at all and everyone claps.

I sit on Mum's lap and she redoes the bow at the back of my white dress. Her fingers feel nice and tickly on my back through the material. Then she gives me a little back rub. When she stops I have my head hanging forward and I'm drooling a little bit. I ask Mum for more but she keeps shushing me.

I'm so bored. I get down and lie down on the grass at Mum's feet. Her pumps are brown with black patent leather capped over the toes. I'm lying down and I'm resting my cheek on her foot like it's my pillow and I'm looking sideways through the forest of all the legs of chairs like tree trunks that stretch row after row. I wonder where the gypsy moth went.

The man up at the podium says a name, then there's clapping. Another name, then there's clapping.

I get up on my knees to look at Mum. She has a straw hat on and the little holes are letting sunlight through them so she has freckles of light peppered across her face. "Mum?" I ask. She's clapping.

"What is it, pumpkin," she answers. I'm surprised she answers so fast. I thought I'd be asking a lot. So much time is spent getting her attention.

"Um. Mum. Why do people clap?" I ask.

Mum answers me without looking at me. She's smiling. "Because they're graduating, love. This is a graduation." She's clapping. She's stretching her neck up to see over the people in front of us. "They're all done with this school."

Does she think I'm stupid? "Yeah but. I know. But why do people *clap*?"

She points in a direction and says something to Dad. Dad nods. She points in another direction and says, "That's the Harrington boy. Right there." Dad nods again.

I'm smoothing Mum's skirt over her knee. I tap her leg. "Mum?" I tap.

She's clapping and smiling, not looking at me. "Mum?" I tap her leg again.

She's telling Dad something. She's looking over heads. I rap on her leg a few times fast. "Hey!" I whisper. "Hey, Mum!"

"Hay is for horses!" Mum whispers. She's mad. "Don't jab at me," she says. She pokes at my side a few times and it digs into my ribs. It kind of hurts. "How would you like it if I poked at you all the time?" she says.

"Ow." I forgot what I'm asking. The applause sounds like someone falling down stairs. I remember. "Why?" I ask.

"Why what?"

"Why do people *clap*?"

"It shows we're proud of them. That's why."

"Yeah but. I *know* that. Why clap?"

They've stopped clapping and a deep voice is talking up at the stage. I'm impatient. I whisper loudly at her. "Mum!"

She's impatient too. "What *is* it?" she whispers.

"Why do people *clap*?" We're whispering, but fast.

"Honey, I don't know. You mean like instead of slapping their cheek? I don't know why. It makes a noise and it's nicer than hollering."

"Slapping their cheek?" I say.

Mum wrinkles her nose up and squints her eyes because she's imitating me. "Yeah. Or banging their heads together. I don't know why, Via. You figure it out. Now put a lid on it."

And I can't figure it out. In the car on the way home in the backseat Cy and I come up with alternatives to clapping. I try Mum's idea of a cheek slap. I do it just on my right cheek. Mum turns around and looks at me slapping myself over and over. "Dear me," she says.

I'm slapping my cheek over and over and I see Dad in the rearview mirror. I say it before he does because I know he's about to. I'm slapping myself. I say, "I'm a certified lunatic." I don't really know what it means but I sort of do.

Another one's with our voices. Me and Cy start humming

really low and then get higher and higher and louder and louder like a teapot that's coming to a boil. When we're as high and loud as we can go Mum raises her hand up in the air and yells, "I'm really against that one." Then she says, "What if people . . . what if people just . . . sang," says Mum. "What if people always sang the same song. Sometimes only a couple of words if it's just a quickie applause."

"Sing?" asks Cy. "Instead of clapping?" The idea's like it scares him. "Like sing *what?*"

Mum opens her window and takes her hat off so her hair blows around and we smell the fresh world outside. "I don't know," she says softly, but her head's moving from side to side slowly like she's drumming up a song. The wind's soft as it blows around in the car. She turns to look at Dad and we can see her face too, her hair blowing in whirls up above her head and in strands across her face. We're waiting for her to think of something. Mum dances her head around. *Heaven,* she sings, smiling, *I'm in heaven. And my heart beats so that I can hardly speak. And I seem to find the happiness I seek, when we're out together dancing cheek to cheek. Oh I love to climb a mountain and . . .* then she hums, then sings again *but it doesn't thrill me half as much as dancing cheek to cheek.*

"Pretty, Mum!" I say.

"Mmm," Dad says. "I like it. Breaking into song at a board meeting after a presentation. Or 'Ladies and gentlemen, the President of the United States,' and the Press Corps begins belting *Heaven, I'm in heaven. . . .*"

Dad's voice is deep. I can see his finger tapping the steering wheel while we're waiting at the red light. Mum leans over and smiles and kisses him on his ear. Then Dad turns his head and kisses Mum so they kiss on the lips one longish lippy smiled one followed by a short one then another short one to finish it and it makes me feel warm from the bottom up like something could crash right into me but I'd absorb it right in and it wouldn't even hurt.

"I've got one," says Cy. I forgot about him. I look at my brother. "I got one," he says. "This." Cy clicks his tongue against the roof of his mouth and keeps doing it. I start doing it too. It sounds like giant raindrops in a fairy tale. I like how it feels on the roof of my mouth. Mum joins us. Dad too. Dad stops doing it for a second to say, "I like this one. Slower," then begins again with the rest of us and we all slow down—drip drop lazy horse—"faster," and we speed up and my tongue begins to cramp up to the side and we sound like grasshoppers or some kind of popping seeds bursting open, bursting.

SIXTEEN

Sloyd

⌒ AFTER THE DANCE recital thing we walked down the hall to sloyd. It's a word no one knows where it comes from. Not even Mr. Emerson. It's Norwegian or something. But it's woodworking class. We're just old enough to go this year and it's everyone's favorite. We go down into a room underneath one of the sixth-grade homerooms. There are tables, vises, and machines. We wear goggles for the jigsaws. On the bigger saws Mr. Becker does everything. We saw things. We whack wood off ends. We chisel stuff along penciled lines or sometimes chisel out little ponds in the wood like if we're making a place where the people need to sit in the little boat. Most of the time all we do is sand things or tighten them into the vises to file down edges. The wood when it gets smooth and sanded feels like skin. It's soft and smooth like with a rounded bone underneath it.

In sloyd the thing that everyone wants to make are mini-baseball bats. We want to play with them since it'll be spring soon. Mr. Becker makes them on the lathe and we watch. He lets us take turns holding the chisel there for a while while the wood turns around and around so fast you can't see its edges but you can feel them chipping through the chisel.

So we went to sloyd and Mr. Becker told me to come into the other room where the table saw is. "I have a surprise," Mr. Becker whispered.

"For Valentine's Day?" I was excited. I pictured a cake or something that he needed me to help him with to bring it out to everyone else.

"Exactly." He smiled. I smiled too.

Once we were in the dark table-saw room Mr. Becker went into the closet and then came back out with a mini–baseball bat. It was varnished and everything. Its shellac made it look like the skin on a turkey on the dining room table before Dad carves into it. It looked so new and perfect that it looked like Mr. Becker bought it in a store. "Excellent!" I said. "How many do you have?"

Mr. Becker laughed. "Just this one," he said.

"For everyone?"

"No," he said, "for you."

"What?"

"It's for you," Mr. Becker said. He was edged back onto a stool with his arms a little out like maybe I'd sit on his lap. The room looked dark. "Don't tell," he said, and put his finger up to his lips like *shhh*. His straightened leg was blocking the door like a horse jump.

"Why?"

"Because you're my favorite," said Mr. Becker.

"Um. What?"

He was handing the bat to me. "Don't you want it?"

"I—" I wanted to run out the door but it was behind him and I'd hurdle his gate leg and I couldn't run away from a teacher.

"You can leave it in here so the others won't see it, then come get it later," he told me. "It'd be hard to sneak out with it at the end of the class."

"That's okay," I said.

"You can come get it later," he told me.

"No. That's okay," I said. I didn't like him anymore.

"You don't—don't be scared or anything," he said. "I just made it. I just made it for you."

"Um. Thanks," I said. I wanted him to move just a little so I'd have a straight line to the door and then out to everyone else. I could hear them out there—a hammer banging, then Brendan's voice low down under it. Russell's cough. Someone was imitating an airplane and then an explosion. Pretty much everyone was making tugboats except for Pierre and Darren were making little tanks.

"You can come back and get it later," Mr. Becker said.

"Um," I said, "no thanks."

"You don't want it?"

"It's weird," I said, and I felt my whole body kind of rise up on its toes even though I didn't go on my tiptoes in real life.

"What's weird?" asked Mr. Becker.

"I don't want the only one," I said. There was something else that I wanted to say but I didn't know what it was. I was feeling something more but it was, like, I don't know. I said, "I'll just, I'll make my own."

I walked to where Mr. Becker's leg was blocking the door and just pushed his leg out of my way. I walked around the corner quickly over to the table where everyone was and started filing down the side of the little boat I was making for Mr. Emerson.

AFTER SLOYD on my way back to homeroom I had to go to the bathroom, number 2. Mum calls number 2 kiki but I don't like that word but I don't know what else to call it. "Pooh" is a bear and "poop" is like when you're tuckered out. "Shit" is good but I'm too little to say it.

The Tiny One

"The cat shat all over the rug," Marly yells to everyone when she cleans it up.

I never have to go so bad that I can't hold it. Once, though, up in Maine I did.

I'M DOWN on the little beach near our house in Maine looking for blue sea glass but I've got to go to the bathroom. I'm wearing my yellow shorts with the buttons on the side.

I've got to go so bad and I'm too big to go in my pants. I run up the hill through the rock garden and down the little path and then I'm upstairs and I've done it.

It's in my pants. It's a mess. I take them off and my underwear's heavy. I go into Mum's bathroom. I don't know what to do. I don't want to tell her. I put my underwear in the sink and run the water. I don't know what to do with the globs. I don't know how to push it off of the cloth and push it down the drain. I take a toothbrush from the cup on the sink and use it as a scraper. I scrape it down into the water. I keep the water running. I clean myself off too. I ball up my shorts and underpants and throw them in the straw hamper. I've done it, all cleaned up.

Later on I'm on my bed looking at the pickup sticks that Uncle Terry brought. I'm humming. I'm looking at the box and all the different pictures on the back. I look over at the door and Mum's leaning in it like she might have been there for a while. She holds up a toothbrush. Mum can't help but smile a little because there's a little piece of poop on the bristles. Mum holds it up. "What gives?" she asks.

WHEN I CAME back from the bathroom on my way back from sloyd Lulu was sitting up on top of the cubbies where we wait for the buses and car pool to get called at the end of the day. It wasn't the end of the day though, yet. We still had math and stuff. Patrick was with her up there and they were looking down. "Here, Via," she called. "I saved you a seat."

I looked up at her. There was room to fit just me up there next to her. "I saved it," she said again. Lulu and Patrick were both smiling. I imagined myself up there with them and I thought of myself spitting at them right in their faces. I don't know why, I just did. "But you don't *have* to come up," Lulu said.

I was still looking at her. "I know I don't have to," I said. "And I'm not going to." It was mean but I didn't care. It felt nice to just flick her away.

"Well ex*cuse* me," Lulu said.

"Hey," I said up to Lulu, "the buses are here." I was talking about our adoption conversation out on the jungle gym at recess yesterday.

ME AND LULU ARE sitting on the jungle gym watching recess and then I hang upside down like a bat.

"I'm adopted," says Lulu, out of the blue.

"What?" I'm hanging upside down.

"We're adopted."

"Wait," I say. I come back up. I can feel the blood drift back down from my head like I'm a bottle of ketchup. "You and Brian?"

"Uh-huh."

"You're adopted?"

"Uh-huh," she says.

She's lying. She always wants attention. It's too much. "Since when?" I ask.

Lulu doesn't know how to answer, then she does. "Since when we were," she says. "Mom says."

Lulu knows how I used to think about adopted kids all the time. I don't know what to say. "Your mom?" I say.

"She told us last night. She said everything's the same but just she thought we should know."

"She did?" I ask.

"It's because Auntie Sherry told me that my dad was driving the bus and then we had to ask Mom."

"Your dad?" I ask. Lulu doesn't have a dad.

"Yeah."

"Driving what bus?"

"The Newbury bus." That was one of the buses to school.

"Your dad?" I say again.

"That's what Auntie Sherry said."

"I thought you didn't have a dad," I say.

"I don't know," says Lulu.

"Is it your real dad or just the one that adopted you?"

"Who?"

"The dad driving the bus."

She looks at me. "What?"

"Is the guy driving the bus your real dad or the dad that adopted you?" I want to catch her somehow.

Lulu looks at me. Then she looks over at the front of the school where the buses usually wait at the end of the day. "I don't know," she says.

"Auntie Sherry didn't tell you?" I'm sounding like a jerk.

"No," says Lulu. "Mom did."

"Maybe I'll go ask your dad bus driver about it at the end of the day when the buses are here," I tell her. That'll teach her.

Lulu's looking at her shoes. "Okay," she says.

"Is Brian really your brother?"

"I guess."

"Why's he driving the bus?" I laugh.

"What?"

"Has he always been driving it?'

"No."

"Why's he driving the bus?" I ask, like, what a stupid thing to be doing. She shouldn't lie. It's the attention she likes like when she gets jealous so easily or needs to go home with a stomachache. "Huh?" I ask. I want to kick her. "Why the bus?"

THE BUSES SOMETIMES COME like an hour or two early and wait outside like giant horses tied up. I saw them out there on my way back from the bathroom.

I told Lulu, "I'll just ask him if he has a daughter."

Lulu twitched her mouth to the side but she didn't say anything.

"Should I ask him if he has a son?" I asked her.

Lulu shrugged. She knew I was about to catch her in her lie.

"You want to come with me?" I asked. Lulu shook her head. She was sitting on top of the cubbyholes and she pulled her knees folding up to her face. She was pretending she was sick like when she's homesick. I felt a little bad. "You want me not to go?" I asked, but I'd go anyway, I knew it.

Lulu didn't answer. Then she shook her head against her knees and I wasn't sure if it meant *No, don't go,* or *No, I don't not want you to*. I was looking at her. "The Newbury bus, right?" I asked. Lulu kind of moved her head, but I was on my way out.

I walked up the tall steps of the bus. It was cold again. The man looked at me because there's no reason I should be getting on the bus. I stood in front of him. He was wearing a red windbreaker and he looked younger than Lulu's mom. He didn't look anything like Lulu or her mom or like he might have lived in that house. His hair was sandy and he had a sandy mustache. He looked sort of like a science teacher who was really tired. He wasn't old or fat or sick looking. He was a pretty regular guy.

"Yes?" he asked.

"Um," I said, "do you have a daughter named Louise Brown?"

He touched his mustache. "Yes I do."

I felt like someone had swatted the back of my head. I couldn't think of what to say. "Her name's Lulu," I told him.

"I know," he said. I couldn't believe it.

"She goes to school here."

"Yes," he said.

I didn't know what to say. "Okay," I said. I turned around. I jumped down the tall bus steps and ran back inside.

Lulu looked up at me with her eyes waiting. I was breathing deeply. "Yap," I said, "it's him." Lulu started crying. She still had her knees in her face so she cried into them. I know how that is how you can fit your eye sockets into your kneecaps.

"What's going on?" It was Honor. All day long she was being nosy.

"Nothing," I told her. I was standing by Lulu's feet.

Honor inched her head up to look at Lulu up on top of the cubbyholes. "Are you crying?" Honor asked.

"Leave her alone," I told Honor. "Go home and make cupcakes."

"Well sorreee," Honor said.

I climbed up next to Lulu and touched Lulu's head. I felt bad. I felt like a big black doom bird the size of a car might come down and grab me. I pulled my head into my shoulders a little bit. I hunched up and looked around. I couldn't help it. I felt like a squirrel that was ducking. I patted Lulu's head. "It'll be okay," I told her. "Don't cry."

Lulu looked up at me. She was wondering if I was going to be nice. Her eyes were brimmed with tears. They looked like marbles. "It'll be okay," I said again. She looked a little relieved before she put her head back down but I felt like it was worse than being mean because I was lying. I don't know if it'll be okay. How should I know? So I said really softly, "But it might not be."

Lulu caught me. She shot her head up. "What?" her head said. Her face was all smeared with tears.

I smiled. I was trying to be nice and not scared. "Just that I hope it'll be okay," I said.

Lulu put her head back down. I touched it again. "Don't worry," I told her. I sat beside her all bunched up. I had my arms folded around each other and my chin on my knees with crossed ankles. I was like a knot. I felt like a frayed knot.

THERE'S A JOKE Pete tells that goes: There are two strings hanging around out on the street. There's a bar across the way but there's a big sign that says NO STRINGS ALLOWED. They really want to go in, but they're not allowed. One of the strings just tries anyway. He goes across the street, goes in, and sits down at the bar. The bartender comes up to him. "Hey, you saw the sign, man, no strings allowed. Get out." There's nothing the poor string can do. He leaves. He goes back out to his buddy string and they mope around a little bit. They kick at pebbles on the street. They really want to go in.

Then the second string has an idea. "I've got an idea," he says. He twists himself around into a funny shape and pulls some of his string apart up at his head to make like hair. He crosses the street, walks in, and sits down up at the bar. He's all twisted up with his frizz of rope on top. The bartender comes over to him. "Look, man, how many times do I have to tell you guys? No strings allowed. And you, if I'm not mistaken, are a string."

"No," the string says.

"No?" asks the bartender. He's mad.

"No," says the string, "I'm a frayed knot."

LULU AND I SAT there being scared next to each other. Then Lulu looked up at me again. "Will you sleep over? Friday?"

"Yeah," I told her. But it made me think of one time at her house when I had sort of a nightmare.

I WAS SLEEPING over at Lulu's and I woke up in the middle of the night. "Via?" Someone is calling me. "Via!" And as I wake up in the dark the voice fades like a smell getting blown away. But it was loud. I'm crying. I'm at Lulu's and I fell out of the bed. I look up at Lulu sleeping and she looks like a dummy. I can't see her body going up and down with breathing anywhere. But she's alive, probably. I'm at Lulu's on the floor on the flattened pea-green rug that smells like a flea-and-tick collar.

A dog's out there howling in the kennel next door. It's slow and even. Just him in long howls. A pretty voice moaning, singing. It's the sound of a mouth blowing on a bottle, lip to lip. When I look out the window it's like I can see the sound across the dark blue sky and it's like a head bowed down.

Who's he crying to? The howling calls down a deep tunnel. The air out there. It's dark night. It's an empty prairie. It's me. I've joined him. Something's dropped hollow. Something fell. It's like I'm with the dog howling. We howl like a wolf with no mountain, no moon.

I'VE GOTTEN the scary feeling at home but not much. Once I saw Mum and Dad fight and I felt it. I was in the closet in the kitchen and they didn't know I was there.

I'M INSIDE the little cabinet sitting on top of the dry-dog-food bag. We've eaten dinner. Mum was in here before doing something with the oven but now the kitchen out there is empty with just the dishwasher going. After a while I hear someone come in. I can see a flash through the crack and I can tell it's Dad. I stay very quiet. The bag underneath me crinkles. I listen to Dad walking around out there. He's moving fast but I don't know what he's doing. He sounds like one of the horses in the stables at Charlotte's house when they want to get out.

Then I see him. I can see Dad through the crack. Through the crack he looks like a long, thin man. He's standing at the door that opens out onto the porch. The top of the door is a window with panes of glass like the French-door cabinets here in the kitchen. Dad's looking through the window out onto the porch. Then he lowers his head into his hand. He slowly shakes his head back and forth. He looks sad. Then all of a sudden he shouts something that shakes me so much that I don't even hear what it is and he punches one of the squares of glass in the window with his hand. It shatters out onto the porch. I hear the tinkling crash. He kicks the door.

I hear someone come into the kitchen. It's Mum but she must be barefoot because I can't hear her shoes. She starts to talk. Her voice is clear and almost loud. She says, "I only want to—"

Dad yells, "You! You get out of my sight."

"Shhh. I just wanted t—"

"Go!" Dad yells. I hear him thump the table like a slap with a low voice.

Mum leaves. It's just me and Dad. I'm alone with him and I can't get out. He groans. I don't want to look.

Mum comes back in and I hear her walk around the table to him. Mum speaks quickly and low. The air out there seems precise and different. It's like a dark wilderness but without the dark and without the wild. "You have *got* to get ahold of yourself!" Mum says to Dad.

I look through the crack. Mum's staring at Dad. I'm flinching but I can't get out. The shadow that's Mum hurries past me and then I'm alone with Dad out there again.

I edge my face away from the door. I sit back. I'm so scared. I hear Dad cough. I'm scared for him to know I'm in here. I don't want to have them know I saw. The light of the kitchen shines in gold cords through the cracks around my door. I sit back in the dark. I stay there, strung up between getting out and not getting out. I stay very still.

The light's like I've been underground when they come get me later. It's so bright. I'd fallen asleep in the dry-dog-food smelly dark. Mum's squatting down and picking me up. I look at her but I rub my eyes. The light hurts them. Dad's behind her. It's the kitchen. My hand smells like the dog biscuits. "Honey," Mum says. It's soft. She's whispering. She's pulling me toward her. "We didn't know where you were, pumpkin." She's lifting me up. I'm so sleepy my eyes feel like they're rolling back into my head. I try to keep them open to look at Dad. My cheek's mashed against Mum's shoulder while she carries me down the hall.

Dad touches my head. "Close your eyes," he tells me.

I wake up later and Mum's beside me in my bed. It's getting light out. I look out the window and the morning light is gray. It's the kind of morning when there's no sunrise but the light just comes silver then color like turning the hue up on the TV set. Mum rolls over so her face is facing me. She looks tired even though she's sleeping. Her mouth is pushed by the pillow so it's partly stretched open.

I look out the window again. There's no wind. It's like me and the window are at the trees' eye level and the trees are all standing still and somber out there like an audience looking in with the gray sky behind them feeling sorry for me. But they're rooted in the ground and can't even move, so I feel sorry for them too.

SEVENTEEN

Math

⟶ AFTER WE HUNG around out in the hall we had math. Lulu was sulking kind of and I felt bad. Friday I'd make it that we'd have fun at her house. We'd go make trouble or something. Or we'd go out in her playhouse and stick one of her gerbils up our shirts so it squirms. We do fun stuff there at Lulu's house sometimes. There are some good things. She lives on a kennel for horses and dogs and cats. She has a pool but it's shaped like a jellybean so when you run and jump in you have to be careful you don't hit an edge. There's the pit where we can go watch older kids on minibikes and look for those red shells for guns. We can look for *Playboys* under the wet leaves out in the woods. We can go run around in the paddock and jump over the horse jumps like we're horses. We can go up in the loft in the barn and sit on the stacked bales of hay and smell them and look at the charred part of the roof where the barn got struck by lightning.

––––––––––

DAD SAYS THAT lightning could easily get us because we're the tallest house on the hill.

Mum says, "Dad's just pulling your leg. We have a lightning rod."

"Up on the roof?" I ask.

"That's right." Mum's at the kitchen sink putting tiger lilies in a vase.

"Who put it there?" I ask.

"Who put what," says Mum.

"Who put the lightning rod up there?"

"Ask Dad," Mum tells me.

I ask Dad in the living room and he doesn't answer. He's reading something. "I don't know," he says. He says it slowly like he's not even sure what he's answering.

"Is it about submarines?" I ask.

He hears me this time. He turns his book around and looks at the submarine on the cover. "No." He lifts an eyebrow. "No, it isn't."

"What's it about?"

"A man and a woman."

"A boyfriend and girlfriend?"

"Two spies."

"Oh. Do they get in a submarine?"

"Not yet," he says. He's still looking at the cover. "So far they're only in the mountains."

"Oh. Dad?"

"Yes, Via?" This time he's with me.

"Who put the lightning rod on the roof?"

"I don't know," he says. "It was there when we bought the house."

"Maybe it's old and doesn't work, Dad."

"Maybe."

"What happens when it hits?"

"Lightning? It's a very loud noise. Then it smolders and burns."

On our way back from getting pumpkins in Ipswich we passed a tree that had been hit. It looked charred and crumbled apart like a little piece of war. It was hard for me to imagine something burning in the rain but I kind of managed to.

"Can it hit a person?" I know the answer but I want to hear it.

"It certainly can," says Dad.

"Can it kill you?"

"It sure can." Dad lifts his eyebrows up and grins. If Mum was here she'd tell him to stop scaring me. Dad's told me all about it before. Lightning can come in a window and follow you down a hall and get you.

Some people get struck and don't die. Their hair goes sticking straight up. Golfers are prime targets because they're out in the middle of nowhere with their golf clubs sticking straight up in the air which attracts the bolt. Mr. Emerson says that They get a golfer struck by lightning every couple of years just like he says every few years They throw a child down a well.

I PICTURE THEY and they're an army of men in olive green with their olive green helmets. Or They're black trousers and black polished work shoes from the knee down and I'm under the boardroom table looking at them, surrounded, their half legs of dark flannel like slats of a fence around me.

Dad says, "They've given us the day off," or "Why don't They just settle things and make the metric system universal?"

Mum's watching the news and says, "What in God's name are They thinking?"

Pete's talking about M&Ms, popping them in his mouth. He holds his palm up like he's an Indian chief saying "How." Pete says, "Melts in your mouth, not in your hands. They don't use the red dye anymore since it's toxic." Or "You know what They should do, They should do a movie about Pélé."

Marly's looking at the bulletin board by the phone. She says, "Why do They keep changing the train schedule? It's so stupid."

The Tiny One

We're in the car unwrapping our food from McDonald's. The smell of the fries wafts up and warms the damp car. Cy says, "I liked it when They have shamrock shakes. They should just have them all the time."

Marly's leaning against the sink drinking a glass of water and complaining about some friend of hers at school. Mum's at the kitchen table chipping wax off the candle holder with her thumbnail and a knife. Mum listens to Marly complain. Then Mum says to her, "Well, honey, you know what They say, 'Once a pickle, never a cucumber.' "

I TRY IT. I try soaking a pickle in water to see if it can go back to a cucumber. "Don't touch the experiment!" I'm whining.

Pete's picking the glass up and looking at it. "It's foul," he says.

Mold has grown around the edges like gray cotton candy. I've forgotten to change the water. I get a chair over to the counter and kneel on it and take the pickle out with a fork to look at it. It still looks like a pickle. It might be fading a little. It might not be such a bright green. Pete doesn't ask what my experiment is. He goes to the fridge and takes gulps of milk out of the NuForm carton.

SOMETIMES WE SEE people walking along the breakwater in Maine heading out to the lighthouse to check it out. It's long and thin like a road of rock that leads straight out to the lighthouse at the end that's there like a mailbox to the harbor. Dad told me a story about how once a little boy went walking out there with his dad. It wasn't raining but when they got out to the lighthouse it started to a little. Instead of waiting out at the lighthouse—they couldn't get in because it was all locked up—they walked back along the breakwater. Lightning came down and hit the little boy up on his dad's shoulders and they both died.

We're on the ferry looking at the breakwater as we rumble past it. Dad's next to me. I look up at him. I ask, "How old was that little boy, Dad?" Dad looks down at me. He doesn't know who I mean. "The one at the lighthouse." I kind of want him to scare me. "The one on the dad's shoulders, Dad."

Dad looks out at the water like he's trying to remember if he forgot something. He's squinting because the air is misty fog so it's blowing in our eyes. Then he looks down at me, squinting. "Just your age," Dad says. But he says it sort of sad. He picks me up.

WE WERE GETTING out our math books. My class is on the green Spectrum books. Me and Billy are already working on the orange ones since we're way ahead. We just finished our yellow ones. When you walk down the hall you see the other levels of Spectrum books sometimes underneath people's jacket hooks or sticking out of book bags. The purple ones are the highest level and when I pass them in the Upper School they look serious, but I can't wait until I get to them. Miss Hunt told us to get our work sheets out. I like numbers. They're not words, but they're related. I write them on my book 123456 . . . and keep going. I like words better though. I really liked it when we were learning cursive writing but that's way over. We all know how to do that now. But I loved it. We were learning a lot of spelling then too and I like that. I practiced a lot.

I PRACTICE WRITING cursive in the air. I practice spelling too. It's not really practice, though, because I'm not doing it to get better at spelling or cursive; I just do it because I can't help it. It's like a habit. I use my pointer finger and write the word in the air in front of my face. "We want this place looking spick-and-span," Mum says.

I say it slowly as I spell it out with my right finger about a foot in front of my face. I watch my finger as it writes—"SPICK-AND-SPAN."

Mum claps her hands. "Shipshape," she says.

I whisper and spell. "Ship. Shape."

Mum laughs. "Busy conducting your own little orchestra?" she says.

I stop. "What?"

Mum wiggles her finger around out in front of her face to imitate me.

"What?"

"We might have to have you committed if you keep that up," says Mum.

"Keep what up?"

Mum makes her eyes cross-eyed and tilts her head to the side. She twiddles her finger around in little circular squiggles in front of her face so she looks crazy.

"I look like that?" I ask. I might.

She hands me the Windex. "Here. You can squirt your words all over the windows with this."

"Win-dows," I whisper, and write it. I can't help it.

"Your brother used to do the same thing," Mum says.

"Peter," I write. "Brendan. Patrick."

St. Patrick chased all of the snakes out of Ireland. Ireland's green from the pictures and so's the name Patrick. Chased them where? They slithered into the sea? "I'd imagine they did, yes," says Mum.

"Did they drown?" I ask.

"That'd get rid of them," says Mum.

"But how did one guy get *all* of the snakes," I say.

"Reality's suspended a touch, love, when you're in the world of saints. That's why saints are saints." I get it. I know about them. Teresa ate leper flakes. Other ones swallowed plague phlegm. The best are the ones that floated. When I learned that the devil was a fallen angel I felt sorry for him.

"Is Jesus a saint?" I ask Mum.

"He's the Son of God."

"Is he a saint too?"

"Um. Find out at Sunday school," Mum tells me. "That's your assignment."

CY SPRAY-PAINTED his name on the side of one of the fences around where we keep the garbage. I go outside with the flashlight to look at the raccoons paw around in the trash. I see them. They're not scared of me at all. I have to make sharp, fast movements to scare them away otherwise they just look up at me, then go back to tearing apart the garbage bags, then look up at me again while they eat. When I shine the flashlight in their face their eyes reflect the same way the reflectors do on the back of my bike.

I have one of those big orange flags on the back of my bike now. It goes up a few feet and then at the top is a little orange pennant so cars can see you better. I saw it on TV and asked for it and Dad was really happy I wanted it and brought one home the next day. He was really happy when I said I wanted a ski helmet too. Toby Frost and his older brother both wore helmets when I went skiing with them since they both race. The whole time I was with them I wished I had one too. I felt like a soft head under my hat.

I follow the raccoons that scramble all over the trash with the flashlight to see where they go. There are two of them and they skim across the driveway and then slip under the hedges to go over into the woods.

I turn around and look at the house in the dark. I can hear the crickets *ree-ree*-ing. I'm in the driveway and I shine the flashlight against the side of the house by the kitchen. There's a postcard on Mum's desk of someone drawing with a torch. He isn't writing a word but he's doing a drawing of, like, a bull or something. I try it. I make huge circles with the flashlight. I make huge circles against the house with the light. I do it really fast and the circle seems to stay.

I hear the screen door crack open. I hear Mum but I can't see her. "Almost time for bed, love," she says.

The Tiny One

I write it against the house—L-O-V-E. I write it with the flash-light against the house. It's so big. I try to write it fast enough so it stays and I can see the whole word at once. It's there. It's lit up. It's like the name of my house in the dark.

I'M IN THE KITCHEN spelling words with Windex on the windows helping Mum clean them. I have the Windex and I write "CLEAN" across the glass before I wipe it. While I'm getting the paper towels my Windexed word "CLEAN" drips down the glass so it looks like Halloween or something. I wipe it. Mum and Dad have people coming over for dinner, that's why Mum wants the place so spick-and-span. Cy and I are going with the Emersons to see the movie *Moonraker*. There's a guy in it named Jaws with blades for teeth. "He's huge," Cy tells me. "He's like my size if I were him and you were a normal person." Cy means the difference in size between us. "He goes like this to everyone"—Cy lifts me up by grabbing my turtleneck at the shoulders and then rams me against the wall so my feet aren't touching the ground. He pins me there.

The first movie I ever went to see Mum brought me to see *The Reincarnation of Peter Proud*. People smiled at me in the theater because I was so small. I slept on Mum's lap. She thinks I don't remember but I do. It was dark and the naked people beat each other with oars while they were out in the middle of the lake in a rowboat. They drifted through the dark green water down to the bottom of the lake. Their hair swished around like sea grass. Their heads bled into the water and the blood looked like ink because it was so dark. Their skin underwater looked pasty and green and I have dreams like that sometimes underwater, not of dead people, but I also have dreams sometimes like I'm floating above a great huge forest looking down on all of the trees and the leaves look soft like feathers and I float up, higher and higher.

WHILE I WAS getting my orange Spectrum math book out of my desk there was a pretty postcard in my desk on top of my books. It was of a snowy mountain scene with a blue sky and at the bottom it said NEW HAMPSHIRE in red script. I flipped it over. It was Brendan's writing. It said "Happy Valentine's Day. Love, Brendan." Brendan's doing his state project on New Hampshire.

AFTER CHRISTMAS before we go back to school we go up skiing in New Hampshire for New Year's. I have a plaid shirt from Christmas that I want to wear every day. It's gray, blue, and white.

We stay in a rental house that has dark rugs and fake wood on the walls. There's a huge moose head above the fireplace. When we come in Mum looks at it and says "Charming" because she hates dead animals. Dad hunts for little birds sometimes when they go on a trip. I don't know where they go. Once, after he came back, me and Cy looked at the little dead birds in the freezer. They looked like the kind you see out on the driveway only their feathers were all gone. We looked for the bullets and in some of them we could see them. They were under there, like splinters. They looked like BBs from a BB gun but purpled sort of through the pink flesh like the mimeographs at school.

We're eating dinner in the rental house and I'm wearing not the gray plaid shirt but a red one that's pretty good too. Mr. Emerson says it's a Royal Stewart. Mr. Emerson says that different plaids have different names.

WE'RE IN MR. EMERSON'S GARAGE and Mr. Emerson is putting gasoline in his lawn mower.

"There are names for plaids?" I say.

"There are indeed," says Mr. Emerson. He's down on his knees with the funnel like the Tin Man's head and he's sticking it into the lawn mower's little red hole on top.

"There are names for *plaids*?" I say it again. I'm amazed. It's not like they're colors.

"I'm as astounded as you are, my child, at the breadth of classifications with which mankind surrounds itself," he says. "They're used by the Highlanders of Scotland. Each represents a clan."

"A clan?"

"Yes. A family." He's pouring the gasoline. It always smells really good at first and then it makes me feel carsick.

"Like a uniform for a team?" I ask. "The plaids?"

"Very much like a uniform for a team," says Mr. Emerson. "Then that pattern. For the clan."

"A clan?" I say again.

"Yes. A family. A tribe, so to speak," says Mr. Emerson.

"Like an Indian tribe?" I ask. I wish my family had a plaid. I'd pick the navy-blue one with dark green. I tell Mr. Emerson which one I'd pick, the navy blue with dark green.

"Black Watch," Mr. Emerson tells me. "A splendid, sober choice."

"That one has a name too?" I ask. I can't believe this discovery. I say so. "I can't believe this," I say.

"As your life progresses, my child," Mr. Emerson tells me, "you'll find there are a number of patterned fabrics with names all their own. Gingham, for instance. Houndstooth."

WE'RE EATING DINNER in the rental house with the huge moose head. I'm wearing my Royal Stewart plaid shirt with my new navy-blue wool baseball hat on backward, which is how I like it these days.

Mum hits the table with her hand so it shudders and we all look up at her from our stew. She's at the head of the table and she suddenly looks weird like something scared her but nothing happened.

Dad says "Mum?" and she doesn't answer. Mum puts her hands out in front of her like she's putting them on either side of a tree trunk and then makes fists.

Dad gets up from his place. I see his napkin all balled up fall to the floor. Dad says "You choking, Mum?" and starts slapping her on the back. He hits her in thumps on her back.

Pete says "Grab her from behind," but then Mum starts coughing deep coughs and then she sort of throws up in her hand. They're chunks of the meat in the stew we're all eating. They're all covered in muck that looks like gravy that's the color of the walls of this house. Mum holds it while she coughs some more. Her eyes are red and watery. She smiles. Her voice is raspy. "Excuse me," she says.

WE'RE IN NEW HAMPSHIRE and it's snowing and it's night-time and Mum won't let me go night sledding with everyone else because I have a cold. A couple of Pete's friends are up here and a couple of Marly's friends too. Cy and Mal come to the door of our room that I'm sharing with them with the bunk beds. I'm lying down on the top bunk. "Come on," Cy says to me. He's standing in the doorway. His scarf is wrapped around his head a couple of times.

"I can't," I tell him.

"Don't be a wuss," Cy tells me.

"Mum says I can't," I tell him.

"Just come anyway," he tells me. "It'll be great," he says.

"Yeah," says Mal next to him.

It's a good idea, but Mum says I can't. So I don't.

BUT IN NEW HAMPSHIRE Mum does wake me up to go for a walk with everyone under the full moon on Sugar Hill. It's so bright I can see my hands. I can see everything. The white snow everywhere is light blue. You can look down the hill from the road we're on and you can see the steeple of the church next to where Pete's old girlfriend got into a car crash and poked her lung. You can see the hill below us all bluey white and then the trees dark and velvety around its edges like we're up in the clouds. I can see our shadows in the moonlight on the blue snow. I can see Mum smiling. I lie down in the blue snow and make a snow angel. Sometimes on Mum and Dad's bed we do flying angels. One of them lies on their back and then puts their feet on my chest, holds my hands, and lifts me up, flying.

We walk down the blue-white road on Sugar Hill in the bright dark. Pete's friend Jay starts singing "Moonlight Mile." We keep on walking in the bright night and there's a VW bug parked on the side of the road, shiny in the moonlight. It's shaking. Mum and Pete start laughing at it. I don't get what's funny but then Pete's friend Jay says, "Someone's going at it," and we walk by and then I know what he means.

PETE'S FRIEND JAY is around a lot. Pete comes home from boarding school on weekends sometimes with friends. So does Marly. I like it when they're all around. In the spring Pete and his friends play shoe golf out on the lawn. Most of them look like Jesus Christ. "You Can Get It If You Really Want" plays out of a speaker out the window of the living room. When I hear the song and listen I always see a blue bottle way up high on a shelf surrounded by clear glass bottles. I can't reach it, but if I really want, I can get it. I see the same thing for "You Can't Always Get What You Want." It's the same blue bottle but this time it really is way too high up so I can't get it even though I want to.

I'M SITTING ON the edge of the terrace with my legs dangling over. I can almost touch the grass. I sit and watch Pete and his friends play shoe golf while I drink a glass of milk and eat a piece of salami and some carrot sticks for my lunch. Cy's playing with them and he looks like just a normal kid next to all these big and hairy men. When I look at Pete's legs and tell him he looks like a werewolf he says he is.

I'm on the terrace. The terrace is puzzle pieces of slate with green grass and moss tufting up around the edges of the pieces. On the slate I can see tiny tiny red spiders dribbling around.

Pete's friend Jay has his pair of shoes in his hand to get ready to play shoe golf with them. He starts clopping the heels together so it sounds like a horse walking along a street.

Pete's new friend Mike comes and sits down next to me. He's a new friend of Pete's. I don't like looking at his face. It's too friendly. I like looking at his chest and arms like now when he doesn't have his shirt on. They're not as friendly. They're strong. He has a part of a shell that hangs around his neck on a piece of black leather. I like looking at that. I look at his collarbone and I'd like to hold on to each side of it like handles on my bike and hang from them.

CY BROKE HIS collarbone when he was a baby. So did Marly.

"They *both* did?" I say to Mum. We're in the kitchen and I'm eating a bowl of Sugar Smacks.

"They *both* did," Mum says and flicks the dish towel at my face as she passes me.

"*Both?*" I say again. I like her answering me the same way I say it.

"*Both,*" she echoes, teasing me.

"How?"

"They fell out of a chair."

It's the dumbest thing I've ever heard. "Out of a chair? Together?"

"No. Each on their own."

"A *chair!*" I'm laughing. I'm sitting in one. It seems so hilariously funny. "Out of a chair!"

"They were babies, honey. They could hardly sit up."

I can't stop laughing.

"Well I'm glad you think it's such a gas," says Mum.

The Tiny One

DURING PETE'S SOCCER GAME I roam around in the cattails with a girl whose name I don't know. We can hear music coming from the window of a dorm. I come back and sit on Mum's lap. Mum yells into the playing field. "Come on! Hustle!" she yells. I see Pete out there. They're in blue. Pete kicks and scores. After he makes the goal all the other guys run up to Pete to pat his back. I see Pete's friend David. I watch him. He's dark and strong and I try to see his face but it doesn't stay still for long enough. He's like a panther my favorite animal but he's also like a wolf my other favorite. I'd like to jump on his back and hang on up around his head.

When David's sort of close to us and heads the ball I look at Mum and smile. She's looking at the game. When David's right in front of us and kicks the ball up and away all the way to the other end of the field my stomach lifts up and I look at Mum and smile again. This time Mum looks back at me and raises her eyebrows. She smiles at me smiling.

The players run flashing in and out of the dark shadows into the syrupy long light. The sun's begun to flatten itself out so the field's in spiky shadows and the colors are all a shade darker. I lie down on my back with my knees up. The orange and yellow leaves on the trees look glassy with the light shining through them. I hear the whistles from the game, muffled cheers, the hollow sound like a cork being pulled when the ball gets kicked long and hard. I hear a plane buzzing. I look straight up at the sky. It's huge like a blue yolk above me that I wish I could poke with a needle to let the color of it spill out. It's fall. I stare up at the sky. I get that feeling that I don't understand that's happy and sad at the same time.

I'M SITTING ON the edge of the terrace with my legs dangling over and my lunch on a white plate on my lap. The salami has a piece of peppercorn in it that looks like a scab. Pete's new friend Mike is sitting next to me. Out the window from the living room we can hear the nice whiny sound of that song about Mother Nature and 1970.

Mike's not used to being around kids, I can tell, since it's like I'm a new thing for him.

"Where did you get your sneakers?" Mike asks me.

I'm resting my plate on my lap but I kick a foot up to look at my sneaker. It's a red one. I shrug. "I don't know," I say. "Mum."

"I like them," says Mike.

"These are my sneakers," I tell him. "These are my sneakers I wear when I go to repair the water tower."

"When you what?" asks Mike.

"Nothing," I tell him. I'm ripping the salami and putting a piece in my mouth.

"Do you like salami?" Mike asks me.

"Sometimes," I tell him. I think to point out the peppercorn like a scab on the salami but I don't feel like being so friendly. My milk is in between us and I'm scared Mike might spill it.

"Do you play shoe golf too?" Mike asks.

Who is this guy? "I'm too little to kick it very far," I tell him. These guys wind up and it goes flying, over the lilac bushes and around to the back of the house.

I look at Mike. He's eating a piece of my salami. I say "Hey, Mikey, he likes it" like the commercial and I think I'm being really clever.

While Mike's trying to talk to me I look over behind the swing set and I can see Cy's out there in the woods with Mal on the space trolley. I can't really see, but I can hear it rattling and whirring along its cord.

MARLY'S FRIENDS SMOKE cigarettes and sit in bikinis out on the terrace in the long lawn chairs. They bring the phone out there and talk. They talk a lot. Behind them out of the speaker Bob Dylan's yelling about a red rose. Phillipa braids my hair into little braids all over the place. Some of them give me piggybacks or bring me with them into town when they go to buy cigarettes and magazines.

One night Marly and her friend June go skinny-dipping in the rain in the Emersons' pool and they bring me with them. Marly takes my hand and speeds way up so I get pulled. The pavement's gravelly on my feet and wet with the rain. June's in front of us in the dark and she starts to run. We're almost there. Marly undoes the hitches at the fence and reaches underneath a thing and suddenly the pool lights up like some sort of show. It's so blue in the dark. It's so blue. The rain rains. Each drop's lit up on the water because of the light inside the pool so they're lit up all over the place and they look like sparks. They look like live things. June jumps in and her splash sparks around. June comes up from underwater. Her curly hair's smoothed down.

"Look how it's all lit up," Marly tells us. "Like mercury. It looks like little mirrors getting splashed around." A big burst of wind blows around. I'm not sure I want to go in anymore. "Ready, V?" Marly squeezes my hand. She squeezes my hand tight and then gently jumps while she's still holding my hand so I go with her.

We're under and shapes warp around. When I come up the rain's on my face. The wind's blowing the trees around above us but I can't see them I just hear them. I swim to Marly and hold on to her neck. "See?" she says. The wind's on my face. I can see the drops in my eyelashes. "See?" Marly says again and hugs me closer. Her face is lit up too.

Marly sways us over toward the edge of the pool. "Look," says Marly, "they look like little ants."

"Where?" I ask, my mouth open. I don't see them. Then I do. On the bricks on the side of the pool little raindrops dart around. They're beaded and shooting around across the wet brick. "Oh yeah," I say, and then I hold on tighter around her wet neck to hug her.

———

PETE AND HIS FRIENDS PLAY Wiffle ball too. I play Wiffle ball but I can't throw my shoe very far in shoe golf. It whacks straight onto the ground. But spring smells good. The lilacs speak up. I go into them or under the rhododendron bushes at the bottom of the driveway. There's a plastic bag matted under the leaves and an empty pack of cigarettes that's mashed flat and has dew underneath the Saran Wrap part. Marly tells me how she used to come down here to meet the tooth fairy. She'd close her eyes and put her hands cupped together in front of her and they'd be filled up with gumdrops. I don't like gumdrops but I like them once I scrape all of the sugar off of them.

I try it. I get in there inside the lilac bush—there's almost a real room inside with roots for chairs to sit on and everything—and hold my hands out with my eyes closed and wait for a little bit until I get too bored.

PETE SAYS he caught the tooth fairy in a jar once. "You did not," I say.

"Mmm-hmm," he says.

"In a jar?" I ask.

"Right."

"Tooth fairies aren't that small," I tell him. That's not what I meant to say. I'm not meant to believe him at all. I'm not meant to even believe in the tooth fairy.

"This one was," he says.

"There are different little kinds?" I ask.

"Different little kinds of fairies? Sure."

EIGHTEEN

The News

⸺ᴼ ꜰɪʀsᴛ ᴏɴ ᴛʜᴇ ɪɴᴛᴇʀᴄᴏᴍ they called my name smack in the middle of math class. Miss Hunt was up at the board writing times tables in blue chalk and the answers in pink chalk. I was thinking about what it would be like to have a buffet table of candy and a little paper plate that you'd put your candy on like it's dinner and then when you finish you'd go back up to the table and get some more. Each candy would be like food. The red chewy things would be like the meat. The whitish taffyish stuff could be like the mashed potatoes. Sour apple stuff like string beans. We could eat it all with white plastic forks and knives.

Pᴇᴛᴇ sᴀʏs ᴛʜᴀᴛ one day people probably won't even eat food. It'll be all in a pill that'll come on a plate like when the blue girl in *Willy Wonka and the Chocolate Factory* eats one of the pills she's not supposed to. She tastes all different courses of a meal all in a tiny capsule—or no not a pill, it's gum—roast beef, gravy, dessert, and the whole thing. Pete says that one day people probably won't ever have to learn or study; they'll just have chips planted in their head and they'll know all languages and everything just by having it put into their brain.

Right as the intercom was saying my name during math class—it was like winning a prize or something; I've never been called on the intercom to come down to the office before—right as the intercom was calling me, Mrs. Browning from the Upper School appeared in the door of our classroom like she was sneaking in. Her head was ducked down and her shoulders were tucked up and she was smiling her mouth open but it wasn't a smile; it was a face that says silently *eek* like *Sorry to barge in* or like she'd just made a really loud noise or dropped something and it broke. It made the muscles in her neck string up and look like thin cords draped down tight from her chin. We were all looking at her. She was there in the crack of the door, half in our room, half out. Her rectangle glasses were down on her nose. She was looking at me. I watched her. She wiggled her finger at me and mouthed something. She wiggled her finger at me again and whispered, "Come with me, dear."

I got up from my seat. I passed Caleb and I could see the static on the top of his head. His blades of hair were fuzzed up from the top of his head and looked like the tentacles of a sea animal. When Mrs. Browning closed the door behind us it smothered the sound of Miss Hunt's chalk tapping the times tables against the blackboard like Morse code. Then we were in the quiet hall, me and Mrs. Browning.

Mrs. Browning had gotten me out of class before. Usually she calls me out and then out in the hallway we stand among the jackets hanging on their hooks and she asks me how Bethany's doing. She tells me to be nice to Bethany so that the rest of the class will welcome her and be nice to her as well. She explains how it's hard to be a new student with kids who've been in the same class since they were small. I'm lucky to always be in the same school and have the same friends every year. I thought she was going to talk about Bethany, especially since Bethany was out sick.

But this time Mrs. Browning kept walking down the hall. She didn't start talking about Bethany. She kept walking down the hall. She turned around to look at me without stopping walking because I was still standing at our corner by the coats where we usually stay and Mrs. Browning talks. While Mrs. Browning was walking away she beckoned me by patting her hip on the side of her thigh, *Come on,* like she was calling a dog and I was the dog. I walked with her. I listened to her heels in the hall. I skipped a little to keep up with her stride and I could feel my loose shoelace whip my other leg. I could feel my tights slipping into my sneaker and bunching up back behind my heel.

While we walked I looked out the window at the empty driveway circle that the cars round around in a traffic jam to pick us up at the end of the day every day. We passed the buses where Lulu's dad was and a couple of car pool cars were out there, really early, but to beat the rush. The flagpole in the middle of the roundabout usually has a little circle of bushy flowers in a ring around it at the bottom but they aren't there now since it's winter. On the other side of the driveway the playground was all empty. It looked like a deserted village—the jungle gym an overgrown igloo, the monkey bars like some kind of hardware store, the swing set like a car wash or something. The snow was on the ground. Looking at the playground like it might be a ghost town made me want to laugh. Usually it's so full of sniffly kids with pom-poms on their heads, like earlier in the morning before school started when it was overrun when it should have been empty. Usually it's so full of running around and pushes, yelps floating up into the air like baby echoes or falling birdcalls.

Mrs. Browning slowed down to fix something around her shoe. Then she stood up and we kept walking. We turned the corner at the water fountain and then we turned the corner again at the eighth-grade homeroom. We came toward the office where the hall's linoleum changes to big shapes of slate like hopscotch squares. Mrs. Browning took my hand and she did it the wrong upside-down way so I couldn't hold her thumb mound like a handle the way I hold Mum's. It felt backward and inside out but interesting like when I have a dream that I can't explain but it's something like where my foot's resting in the arch of my other foot and how it's resting there is very important to something someone's trying to tell me and a place I'm trying to get to but can't. I held Mrs. Browning's hand and avoided the cracks on the floor.

When I looked up from the floor and holding Mrs. Browning's hand I saw Dad. He was in his suit and he was standing in front of the office with someone else and I thought it was Uncle Jimmy who's not really an uncle but we call him Uncle anyway. Uncle Jimmy was holding their overcoats.

Dad had his sleeves rolled up and his tie was still on. He smiled when he saw me. As we got closer Dad clapped his hands together slowly so they didn't make a sound. "Have everything?" he asked.

I looked up at Mrs. Browning. She raised her eyebrows at me instead of asking out loud if I did.

Have everything like have everything what? Dad's never at school.

"Go run and get your things," Dad said. "We're going home."

My things. Dad. Home. As I ran back down the hall my stomach felt giggly and I kept flexing my limbs and my stomach, my butt and between my legs, just because I felt excited. My parka. My books.

When I came back into math class breathing heavy everyone looked up at me. They all looked sleepy and the sound of Miss Hunt's voice was so boring. Kids in school. It was like the air was thick and warm and slow around them and I was coming in from the hall outside where everything was quick and cool and fast. In here in the classroom the air was sluggy and smelled like Mrs. Crockel's bad breath. I was about to have a new afternoon. I smiled at Lulu. She mouthed *Where are you going?* and I shrugged. I put my coat on but I still felt shivery and keyed up. I was tingling all the way down to my toes and between my legs and I felt like pushing the big glass window smash open with my arms and laughing. I sprinted down the hall past the water fountain. I jumped squares in the floor, leaping streams and crevices, and back to Dad.

You push the heavy yellow door open with its bar across it in the same motion you do when you're pushing oars before you pull them back toward you in a rowboat. I pushed it open and then Uncle Jimmy put his hand up above my head and held it open. Dad took my hand the right way, it fit in, and we walked down the stone steps to the car. It was parked right in front of the school office where I'd never seen it parked before.

I got into the back seat. Cy was back there. He was in the car already back there. It wasn't the normal car. It was the one that Sasha usually borrows. Cy was looking out the window. I couldn't see his face but he was looking out the window and his breath was steaming up the window where his mouth was. Dad got into the front seat. Uncle Jimmy was in the driver's seat. I wanted to ask where we were going and why Dad wasn't driving but I didn't. I wanted to ask what we were doing. I thought maybe they were taking me and Cy skiing because I thought Mum and Dad were going to go next weekend. I thought I remembered that they were going to go with Uncle Jimmy and maybe this was a surprise trip.

Dad turned around in his seat up front to look at me. He looked at me. He sucked his lips into his mouth so they disappeared, then released them. His dark eyes looked dark and clear. His eyes circled my face and then landed on my eyes. "Mum's been in an accident," he said. I looked at him. I looked at Uncle Jimmy. I looked at Cy. Both of them were looking away. I looked at Cy. I wanted to hit him in the leg so he'd look at me. I looked back at Dad. I knew he wasn't joking but still it wasn't funny. Accident sounded like smashing glass. I thought of Mum in a hospital bed with a clear dome mask over her mouth. I saw her in a wheelchair somewhere like in a library. I put my hands in my pockets. They're worn thin and I could feel the tiny balls on the material. Mum calls it pilling. I could feel my mouth start biting my lip. I looked back at Dad. He was looking at me. It was just his head because he was looking around the seat to look at me. Then Dad's head said, "She died instantly so there was no pain."

I've never felt like I was dreaming before when I've been awake. I've never felt like I'm in a nightmare. Dad's eyes were watered over like they were layered with shellac. Dad was suddenly Dad without Mum. I looked at Cy. It scared me. I was scared but what I felt like was like I felt extra clear, like life isn't real. I felt like I could jet straight up through the roof of the car.

"Come up here," Dad said to me. It was like I was a prisoner captive in that car that wasn't moving. I wanted to rock it so it would fall tipping onto its side. Then we'd have all had to get out and talk about that. Dad was looking at me. He patted his lap the way Mrs. Browning patted her hip to call me in the hall. I looked at Dad's face. His face looked crooked and so did everything in the car. Everything was like pointy and scared. Dad looked scared. My hand looked flat and scared. The flagpole in the middle of the circle was standing frozen and so skinny like it was terrified to move. So were the trees.

"Come up," Dad said to me again. I was scared to move because I had the feeling the air was so brittle I'd break something. But I still felt excited. I still felt like I couldn't really move enough or breathe enough. My throat was closed over making a noise like a whistle for a second and I felt a flash of desert expanse like a split second of iced emptiness flared up under our car, raising up. I couldn't breathe. My eyes were full of it. I think I tried to say her name while I was trying to breathe. Watery Dad said, "Come," and I stepped over the gearshift to get up front. The gearshift poked the side of my thigh and I got on Dad's lap. He was Dad without Mum. I couldn't get it. Dad hugged me and I wanted him to squeeze me so my guts would come out my ears and mouth. I could feel Dad's chest shaking. He was smoothing my hair. I looked back. Cy was crying. Cy was crying so hard that he couldn't stop to look up for a second. He was Cy without Mum.

The Tiny One

I felt something I've never felt before, quickly, something slipping. Like as if the ground is really just pokeable cardboard and can just be poked through with a ski pole or a foot taking a step, falling through, falling through ice and there's no water underneath, just air and nothing, but fast.

Uncle Jimmy started the car and my heart felt like it was floating like air in my chest since I couldn't feel any of my body it was like I was all just my clear eyes. The outlines of things were sharper. The air in my nose went in and out. I didn't get what was happening or why I felt so wide awake. On Dad's lap I tried to tense up my whole body to hold on to it.

Out the window, while we moved along, the side of the road looked fuzzy but clear too the way a 3-D sticker looks when it's flat but it doesn't look flat and the background cuts farther deeper than it is. I looked out the window at the trees on the side of the road, the flat marsh, the ocean when we got to where I could see it. They all looked like they were speaking to me, to us. They all looked like they were frightened frozen but they were holding us to the road as we drove along. They all looked different. The world didn't have her. The world doesn't have her anymore.

As we drove up the driveway I pretended it looked the same but I couldn't even remember what the same was.

I had been chewing on my cheek and then I noticed because I tasted blood. I touched it with my finger and then looked and saw the red. I looked up at our big house and there were lots of cars in our driveway like it was church. It didn't look like home anymore. It looked open and exposed like a big giant foot could easily come whenever it wanted and squish it splintered apart.

When we came in the door a couple of women like Mum squatted down and kissed me near my eyebrow and on my cheek and I wiped it off and I saw Cy going through the people in the front hall and go running up the stairs, skipping steps in his stride.

I went running to follow Cy upstairs. When I got up there Cy's door was shut and I couldn't open it and it made the hallway look different because his door's never shut. I hit it. I hit on it. Cy wouldn't answer so I kicked it. I couldn't really hear him through the humming of the people downstairs but I kind of heard a muffled "No!" I heard the stairs squeaking with someone coming up them so I went running into my room and flopped onto my bed.

When I looked up Lenny and Dan's mom was there in my room with her plaid headband. Lenny and Dan's mom has wrinkles from a frown between her eyes which make her look mad all of the time but once you know she's hardly ever mad then she looks pretty and the frown wrinkles aren't scary at all. She went to my bureau and opened different drawers like she was looking for something and then she found it and pulled out a green sweater that I don't like very much. Then she came closer to my bed.

"Where do you keep your pants?" she asked. Her perfume smelled bad in my room.

I pointed to the bottom drawer. I got up and got them myself. I took off my skirt and put my brown corduroys on and then bounced back onto the bed.

"What we're going to do," Len's mom said, "is we're going to go to school and pick up Lenny and Dan. Then we'll go to our house for the rest of the afternoon. How's that sound."

I didn't know what to say. I wanted to stay with Cy. I thought of him on the other side of the wall on his bed. I thought that he must have known what to think.

I closed my eyes on my bed and started to kind of cry. I wanted Len's mom to go away. I closed my eyes into my baby pillow. I wanted to kick my feet. I felt like I was running. I was coming running. I'm coming running. Home. I'm running up the hill. I'm running up the hill and then when I turn toward the house I smell Mum up in my face, in my mouth. I smell. The wind has it too. I'm running toward it. This house and the water below. Home. Nothing will ever stop me. I'm coming in fast. I only wanted to play. Nothing can stop me. Mum! Nothing can stop me and I run so fast.

PART IV

Night

NINETEEN

After

⟿ I WENT with Lenny and Dan's mom but I don't remember it that well. Before we left I wanted to find Dad and stay with him but I didn't want to make a big deal.

I don't remember Lenny and Dan's that well. We didn't go pick them up at school. Somehow when Len's mom and me got to their house, Lenny and Dan were there already with some dark-haired lady in a pink sweater and a lime-green headband. I don't really remember. Dan had to go to a piano lesson. I remember me and Len sat on his bed up in his room stretching out his Stretchy Hulk as far as we could. I was sitting on Lenny's pillows at the head of his bed and I pulled the Hulk's legs while Lenny pulled the Hulk's arms. Me and Len sort of talked about how weird it was that we'll never see Mum again, but we didn't know what to say. We talked about Carl Yastremski and the Red Sox. We talked about the Abominable Snowman.

I remember a few things, though. While we sat on Len's bed

with the Hulk I remember thinking of Mum looking for four-leafed clovers up in Maine behind our house where the laundry room is.

IT'S HOT SUMMER and I'm walking down the steps to our house in Maine and Mum and Pete's friend Seamus are lying on the grass outside the laundry room. They're looking for four-leafed clovers. They're fiddling their hands in the grass so they look like they've lost something in there. Mum's lying on her side with her elbow cocked to rest her head in her hand. With her other hand she's brushing over the grass slowly like she's testing water in a bathtub, sliding her hand over the tips of grass back and forth like her hand's one of those metal detectors at the beach that people walk around with to find stuff, like a divining rod. I can hear "You Are the Sunshine of My Life" twinkling out the door from inside the kitchen.

Mum sees me coming down the steps. "You want to come help us, pumpkin?" she says. I know what they're doing. I never find any. Mum finds them and then presses them in between pages of a book on the shelf in the living room.

"No," I tell her. I'm coming down the steps. I never find any and plus I want to go play Kick the Can down on the wharf with Ethan and Amanda and some kids we met off of a cruising sailboat that's passing through.

"It's good practice," says Mum.

"Practice?" I say. I go stand by them and look down. I want to lie down on the grass in the center and have Mum rub her hands on me instead of the grass looking for four-leafed clovers. "Practice for what?" I say.

Mum's dreamy down there on the ground on her grass. "I don't know," she says. "Anything."

AND WHILE LENNY talked about Yaz and baseball I remember thinking of blowing out my candles at my birthday party a while ago. My friends are all around the dining room table. Brendan and Caleb are next to me. Charlotte's too scared to come in because she doesn't know anyone so she stands in the dining room doorway. Presents are stacked up unwrapped to my right. The glow of the candles on the pink cake is up in my face. All the kid voices are finishing the song—". . . *to you*"—real loud. I'm about to blow. Mum's face is there smiling. Mum's face is there saying, "Make a wish," smiling over the candles everywhere down on my cake.

I WAS GOING to tell Lenny what I was thinking of but it wasn't a story, just pictures. He wouldn't care. But he was at my birthday party.

"Remember my birthday party?" I said to Len. Lenny was digging goop out of a cut on the Stretchy Hulk's arm with a purple crayon.

"Yeah," said Len, "that was good."

I remember looking up at the poster Lenny has by his window. It's of a deer walking through really green woods and I thought of Maine again. I see deer up there in Maine all the time. Usually it's the girls or the young ones without all the antlers. They go bouncing over the side of the road and you can see their cute pom–pom cottontails. Or I hear them cracking sticks under their steps in the woods. Usually there's more than just one. In the woods sometimes when I hear them I pretend that they're Indians over there through the branches. I missed Maine.

DAD STARTS the engine of the Aquasport and it roars like it's our animal being woken up, ready to go. Me and Ethan dangle our legs over the side so our bare feet hang down toward the water. We hold on to the metal railing at the front of the boat like it's a handlebar. We chew on the canvas ties of our life jackets because they taste good like salt.

Dad unties us. When we pull away from the dock, we go in reverse. Me and Ethan watch the dark green water beneath our dangling feet. The bubbles of air boil up to make white foam doilies that fan out over the water's surface in overlapping flat marbled balloons.

Then Dad shifts the boat into forward. We weave slowly through the moored boats in the harbor like they're trees and Dad's following a path to get through them. Once we get past all the boats and we pass the red nun, Dad speeds up so the bow tilts up.

It's like flying. We soar over the water. The water below our feet looks flat like a floor that we're zooming across. I put my head over the railing and stretch my neck out a little so I can't see the railing at all, so I can't see any of the boat that I'm sitting on. Then it's really like Superman, like I'm flying a few feet above the water, fast. All I hear is the wind in my ears like its sealing them shut and the engine curlicuing up into the air. The wind makes my eyes tear. We speed through rooms of warm air, then cold air, then normal air. We move through gusts of wind that ruffle the water so it looks like schools of fish are swimming underneath.

We chop over the little waves, then drive smooth again. A big fishing boat leaves its ropes of wake and Dad slows down so we don't hack against it. We dip into it, holding on, and me and Ethan's feet get wet and then we go fast again. Dad follows the road of white foam that the fishing boat left in its trail.

I look at Ethan. My hair's blowing sideways. His is too. Where the wind makes a part in your hair it feels like a bald spot. Me and Ethan make our hands into shapes like a swan's neck or like we're holding puppets and point them cutting into the thick wind. Our hands are like rudders and if you move them just a little bit, up and down, they swoop like roller coasters or jumping porpoises. We squint into the wind. Me and Ethan yell singing *Bum Bum Bumble Bee Bumble Bee Tuna I love Bumble Bee Bumble Bee Tuna!* while our boat veers past Goose Rock Light like a giant spark plug plugged into the ocean and then out into the bay with the wide ocean.

Then we get to Brimstone and all the cool black stones. The Brimstone stones are like smooth-skinned people with sunny skin that you want to rub up against. They're everywhere. You can't even find a regular rock even if you look. There are none of those big Maine craggy rocks that look like roast potatoes. The brimstones are in all different sizes, like potato size, jellybean size, football size, pea size, almond size, pear size, coin size, oblong, round, everything, but all smooth and when you rub them against the skin on your face they get shiny from your oil. When you hold them in your hand and rub them with your thumb they feel like they belong to you. Me and Ethan look for the good ones and keep them in a little pile near the picnic basket for Mum to take them home. They're heart shaped, paw shaped, Madonna shaped, egg shaped, anything shaped if you can find it. They clink together in a really good sound. They feel good when I'm lying on my stomach and Ethan puts a bunch of them on my back.

Me and Ethan walk around a little bit on the hill. We walk through the scruffy grass. The seagulls get antsy and cry at you like barking dogs protecting their little areas. There are tons of them. Me and Ethan don't stay up there for long. The beach is the best and you just want to be with the black stones, looking at the ocean.

Then we're in the boat heading back home to Sky Island from Brimstone. My skin's all salty and the sun's going down. I'm sitting on the seat with Mum with a towel around me. I'm eating a peach. There are some clouds over near the sunset. They're pink and orange swipy swirls that go up to the middle of the sky. They look like glowing tails of a horse that are flared. I love this day. I love peaches. I love the way the ocean's so dark blue and the sky's so pink and orange. I love the way I feel the vibration of the boat's engine and that we're in a boat moving across water, going home.

Mum's next to me. I feel like I wish I could say something but I don't know what it is. Ethan's sitting down on the floor in front of us rolling a Nerf football under his bare foot. He's whistling to himself but I can't hear the whistle because of the humming engine and the wind. I can see it from his lips and the way he's moving his head. I'm leaning into Mum and her arm's around me. My peach is so good. The sunset's so big. The water's blue and, like, long. I shake my head around in the wind. I want to do something like gulp it all in or get it and catch it somehow.

"Look, Mum," I say, "look," meaning the sunset. I point at it with my foot. I know she sees it because we're heading straight for it, but I can't help it, I want to point it out to her. I want to show her more but I don't know what. I want to get everything and have her see it. "Take a bite of this," I tell Mum. I want her to taste the peach too. It's a perfect one. I want to take everything and put it all together somehow but I don't know how.

Mum smiles at me. She's smiling at me because she sees how I feel. She lowers her head toward my ear so I can hear her over the engine. "You must always remember, my pumpkin, that there will always be days like this." She's smiling. "Always," she says again.

I WAS LOOKING at Lenny's poster of the deer. I asked Len, "Have you ever seen a deer before?"

"Um," Len said. "Yeah. Lots." Lenny was trying to glue the cut on the Stretchy Hulk. I wanted to tell him to just use Scotch tape or a couple Band-Aids instead of glue. It would hold better. "I've seen tons," said Len.

"Me too," I told him. "One time I saw one swimming way out in the middle of nowhere."

Len looked up at me. He had the bottle of glue in his hand. "On a lake or something?" he asked.

"No. In the ocean."

WE WENT DOWNSTAIRS into Lenny and Dan's kitchen be-cause his mom made peanut butter and jelly sandwiches. I hate peanut butter and jelly sandwiches. Sometimes I can eat them, though, but in Len's kitchen it was like I wouldn't have touched them even if someone gave me money to do it.

THEN PETE came to pick me up. Pete hugged me in the car and started to cry but told me everything would be okay. I told him I just felt like Mum was away on a trip, maybe. I also told him that I didn't think she wanted to die. When Pete started to cry, I cried too. We rode home without the radio. I pretended we were in a boat, that the car was a little covered boat that Pete was steering, and that the road was a river.

When we got home there were people still waiting around. The TV room was full of people and there were people out in the hall still. I went into the TV room and looked at all the faces and then saw the ones I was looking for. Cy and Marly were on the couch. Marly's eyes were red. Cy looked tired. Otherwise they looked the same. I went and sat between them and they moved to give me a little room so I could fit.

There were lots of people around. It was the news on TV. Father Kelly was talking to Dad in the doorway. Dad was drinking a drink and so was Father Kelly. The fire was going. I watched the flames. I don't really remember.

Then Marly brought me upstairs to go to bed. While I was in my room with Marly, Pete brought in a little brown glass bottle that looked like cough syrup. Pete said, "Dr. Hooper dropped this off a little while ago," he told Marly. "He said it would help her sleep."

"You mean me?" I asked. I was under the covers but sitting up.

Pete looked at me and smiled. He had a spoon from the kitchen in his other hand. "Yes, you," he said.

Marly was unfolding a blanket for me. "Maybe we should all take some of that," said Marly.

Pete was still smiling. "Sure," he said. He was sitting down on the bed trying to open the cap to the medicine or whatever it was.

Then Dad was in the doorway with Sasha. "How we doing?" he asked. But he looked terrible.

"Don't worry, Dad," said Marly.

Some guy came and told Sasha that she had a phone call, so she left.

Dad came down to kiss me and he smelled like wine. "My big girl," he said to me. He kissed my forehead. He said, "You'll have to help me from now on." It was a weird thing to say, I guess, but it was all weird. Then Dad went back out because he was sort of starting to cry a little. It scared me.

We kept hearing the phone ringing and it sounded like a cocktail party I could hear down the stairs in the front hall with all the people coming in and out. I could hear ice clinking in glasses.

Then Cy was in my doorway. He came in and sat down on my bed next to Pete. He lay down sort of on my legs so he could look around Pete and see my face. I saw him look up above my head at the postcard of the pope I have on the wall, then over at the picture of Jimi Hendrix, then the big round pin of the Fonz that says SIT ON IT that's pinned to my wall hanging.

Pete got the cap off the bottle and poured some of the medicine into the tablespoon. It was dark purple. "Mm," said Pete, "smells good."

"What is that?" I asked. I just realized that I was the one who had to eat it. I wasn't sick but I didn't protest since I felt different than I'd ever felt before anyway.

"It'll make you sleep and have good dreams," said Marly, "a spoonful of sugar," she said.

Then Marly sat down on my bed too so I had all three of their faces looking at me like a good dream. All three of them were there, looking at me.

"We can watch and see how it'll make you drowsy," said Cy.

"Yeah. I want to see that," said Pete. "Open the hatch," he told me.

I took the spoon in my mouth and the syrup was grapy and thick. It was pretty good. "It's good," I reported.

Marly clicked the light off. "Don't go," I said.

"I'm not going anywhere," she said, and sat back down on my bed.

Sometimes when Marly comes up to say good night to me she lies down next to me and falls sound asleep. I love it when that happens.

"Stay till I fall asleep," I told them. Their heads were dark spots but I could sort of see their faces.

"We'll stay," said Marly.

"We're staying right here," said Pete.

"Yeah," said Cy.

"Now close your eyes and think of something nice," said Marly. Always when I'm falling asleep and trying to think of something nice I think of the same field in Maine right on the water at Caulkins Cove where me and Mum go clamming and the wind's all over on the grass and makes the wildflowers bob around. It's where Mum found that red heart piece of jewelry that time in the mud. But this time I hardly had time to think about it I fell asleep so fast.

And Dr. Hooper's medicine made me have not good dreams but kind of scary ones.

In my dream I was in the car with Amanda in the back seat. I was sitting behind her mom who was driving. Her dad was in the passenger seat. They were bringing me home. We drove along down by the water before we turned into our driveway. The ocean was windy and blue. I could see the islands—Resolution, Revelry, and Swann's Light. It felt like we were on an island like in Maine instead of just the point that Slate Avenue is on. The ocean looked pretty. I said, looking at the water, "The inner bay must be really nice today," thinking there was another body of water farther in where the land really is.

We turned up our driveway and then turned toward the house. As we came toward it I could see a black animal sitting on the steps of the porch. It was sitting on the side of one of the steps like the cats do. It was black like one of the cats or like Sparky but I could tell it wasn't one of them. It was in between, like the size of a big fox. It looked like a black fox.

We pulled in and parked to the side of the steps in front of the rhododendrons. The animal came over to us. Amanda's dad started to get out of the car. I told Amanda's dad not to get out because it wasn't one of our animals, that it was a wild animal. I looked at it out the window and it looked like a snake even though it stayed like a fox. It slithered even though it was walking. It was smooth and snaking around. It was scary, but it also was like a cool animal. It didn't pay any attention to Amanda's dad getting out of the car. It was over on me and Amanda's mom's side.

Then Amanda's mom got out and the black animal swished its tail around and then bit at her hand. It was clamped onto her hand. She couldn't shake it off. While she was trying Sasha was coming down the steps to greet us. When the animal saw Sasha it let go of Amanda's mom's hand and came over to check out Sasha. Sasha ran and jumped into the back seat through Amanda's door and tried to close the door quickly but the animal thing sort of managed to start to get its head partway in the car door so we were trying to slam the car door on its head so it would get out and go away.

While Amanda and Sasha were trying to fight the animal off and close their door, I got out of the door on my side and ran up the steps onto the porch and then into the kitchen to go get something, I don't know what, Cy's BB gun maybe, or a broom to scare it away with. No one was in the kitchen. I walked down into the hallway and Mr. Emerson was sweeping the floor in front of the TV room. Mr. Emerson was in our house, sweeping. He had a big, floppy straw hat on his head.

I was so glad to see him, even in the weird hat. I was so glad to see him and he's been away in France for so long. I said, "Mr. Emerson! There's this thing out there!" I was scared. "This *animal*!"

Mr. Emerson stopped sweeping and looked up at me. "Certainly, my dear," he said, not surprised at all. "It's an acumen."

———

WHEN I WOKE UP I went downstairs to go look up the word in the blue dictionary by the TV set. Pete's friend Jay was asleep on the big couch so I tried to be quiet. Everyone was sleeping. I looked up "acumen." I expected to see a little scratchy black drawing of a fox. Something about it sounded like a stamp, though, the kind of official stamp they use like the ones Dad has in his passport.

I looked up "acumen." It said "*n.* superior mental acuteness." I looked up "acuteness." I didn't understand the meaning. I didn't really get it and I didn't really get how I could dream a word that I don't know but that's out there in the world. There wasn't anyone to ask. There wasn't anyone to tell. Everyone was sleeping. Everyone was sleeping and Mum was gone now.

TWENTY

Home

⎯☙ V I A ' S   G O T her fancy wool coat on over her Easter dress. She's sitting up front in the car on the way to her mother's funeral. She's between Sasha, who's driving, and her father, who's in the passenger seat. Her brothers and sister are in the back seat behind her. It's a quiet car.

We all have mothers. We all have fathers. We all have what's us not being here before we're born and after we die. We all have this. We all have what's there before we're alive that we can't see, and what remains after we die which we'll never know. You can lose more than you'd ever thought you'd find. But you can also find more than you'll ever lose.

Via the girl has found something. The sky is white like frozen milk. The trees and clapboard houses stand lining the road like an audience watching their solemn procession pass. And as the quiet car glides through the town of Masconomo, past the crescent of beach at the base of Slate Avenue, past the slope of hill with the low stone wall, past the scruffy red farmhouse at the edge of the woods, past the gas station, the grocery store, past the library's clock, Via feels something going. Something is gone and it's much more than her mother. It's that girl.

It's that girl in the pigtails walking to school, that girl in the T-shirt swinging down from a swing, that girl in the sneakers kicking at rocks, that girl in the towel running back from the pool, that girl in the raincoat headed over next door, that girl in the life jacket up front in the bow, that girl in the high-tops whittling the stick, that girl with her hair brushed who waited, who watched, who jumped in the water when no one else went, who came into the kitchen and no one was there, that girl in the rowboat rowing back in, that girl at the window, that girl at the door, that girl in the wind, who hummed, who laughed, that girl who yelled "Wait!" or "One more for me!"; who wiggled her tooth, who dangled her legs, that girl at the beach drawing lines in the sand, that girl up at bat, that girl who dug holes, that girl who was spun, that girl on the snowbank looking up at the birds, that girl in her bed singing slowly to sleep, who blew out the candles, who fell from the tree, who whispered so softly "Shhhh, come with me," who stomped in the mud and tracked it indoors, that peony girl, that yawning girl, that girl with the fever and drink by her bed, who's building a fort out of branches and leaves, who's up in her room and won't come down, who's rounding the house, who's coming inside, who's tearing in circles through the crowded loud room, who's weaving through waists of belt loops and skirts, who's searching through grown-ups all talking so much, who's looking through faces like tulips up high, who's looking for one face among all the others, who's seeing her mother, who's seeing her mother, then running back on outside. Who first finds her mother, then does all the rest.

The sight of her mother was rooted under that girl's days that grew up from it, its hourliness of living, its sounds of her words, its backward bends and kicks forward in the air. And once that girl found her mother, everything else would settle and slow down, all points would focus, beautiful and clear, stable and set. All would return to its best—everything done up, right side right, the stars above and the trees outside, the sky so big and the world of air, the ocean out flat with its horizon line—it would all fall back to its careful close distance, patient, and there with that nameless sensation of whole relief, whole gratitude, and whole joy.

THE REVERES ARE nestled close together in the front-row pew of the church. Via is watching. She's partly on Pete's lap and she's turning around watching all of the people. The church is so full of them that they spill out the front door onto the street. She looks up at the balcony in the back and there are men up there in a row like books on a shelf, each of them holding a gold trumpet.

Father Kelly's robe is clean and white. The dark coffin is covered in yellow daffodils. There are daffodils on the altar. After Father Kelly talks some, the trumpets begin playing. Via leans back into Pete and kicks her leg up onto her father's lap. She looks up at the high ceiling and over at the painting of angels above the altar, listening to the trumpets blow.

She holds a big bouquet of daisies in her fist. Later on when the service is over, she'll hand them out one by one to people on the steps outside as they're leaving. But for now, she holds them. Sitting stunned in her seat on Pete's lap, her hair brushed down but with some winter static fuzzing up, sleepy-looking Via is surrounded in a gentle radiance that only a death can bring. It is a glow of life. It is a glow of who's living in it.

The music stops. She turns around to see why. The church is silent. She can hear people rustling paper a little. A baby cries out in the back. Father Kelly moves a chair that squeaks when he sits down in it. Someone blows their nose while someone else coughs. But the air's without music and it's stopped. It's empty air, suspended and dry.

Then the trumpets begin again. The trumpets begin again and there are the high ceilings, the flowers, the people, and the angels painted on the wall above the altar underneath all of the glinting stained glass that are like charms of color. It's all there again. The trumpets begin again and here, relieved, as the music starts again, Via becomes engulfed in that feeling that yes, certainly, of course, there is something remarkable here. There is certainly something remarkable here. Like the Sistine Chapel or the Taj Mahal, like music that pulls you and you can't tell how, like a cathedral with all of its time and deaths and ages put into it, like an empty room with another presence, a good presence, like someone dead come back, an empty chair but someone sitting in it, something present, something strange, yes, there is certainly something here, something remarkable, like the ocean and seeing it stretching on, moving, rolling cold, rolling strong, blue and gray and blue and green, with all of its whitecaps and foam fringes, its movement and depth, its calm, on and on, the stars, on and on, like a roaring waterfall that never stops, power, like a jungle, something ancient, something mysterious. Like rain. Like long warm ropes of rain and the human sound of rain breathing. Like faces in windows calling you home, like flying, like flight. It is a blustering heart. This is hands and eyes and the wrists of dawn. We rise up forward in unison. We tip forward. We remember. We are there. We fold in and reach out. We return. This is the heart of life beating and the body in bed. This is you. This is us. This is love. This is home. This is love in a place where it always has been, and where we know it will always be.

TWENTY ONE

Via

◦ EVERY DAY from now on forever I won't see Mum. I don't get what'll happen now. I feel sad and I feel so weird. I don't get it. It's like something special that scares me but I like it too. I don't like it at all but I can't explain. Something has stopped. I feel sad but it's like there's something shining in it. I can't explain it. I feel so sad but I also, also I feel, like, lit. I can't explain. I close my eyes and it's shining. I open them and it's shining too. I don't get what's going to happen now. I'll just keep doing what I did before. I'll keep looking for her just like I did before. I can find her even if she's gone. I'll see as much as I can. I'll look for her. It feels like I'm falling out of sleep. I'm falling up. I'll keep up. I miss her. Because too much gets said that just gets forgot about. Because so much gets seen that just goes down a drain. I'll look for Mum. And I'll find her. I'll look hard. I wish I didn't have to. But I do.

That's what I feel like now. Like someone sprinkled special glittery dust all over me that went right through my skin and is all over in me now. Not like crammed in, but powdered all over the place like that fertilizer that Dad sprinkles in the garden or like powdered snow that's dusted down and will never melt. It's the tiny one thing in me that's at the bottom of all the rest, that I know will never go. It's the tiny one thing in me that will, like, hold me forever to looking for Mum. It makes my eyes like watcher eyes. That's what's in there. It's like the dust of magnets or something that will pull me to her. I'll always try to see. I'll get better and better at it every day. I'll watch and remember. I'll look. Because it keeps life from getting lost and wondering where she went. Because it keeps life.

Acknowledgments

UNENDING GRATEFUL ACKNOWLEDGMENTS go to my brothers and sisters: Carrie, Susan, Dinah, George, Sam, and Chris; my stepmother Wendy; Mary Caulkins and the Caulkins family; Jean and Gordon Douglas; Melanie Jackson; Leonard Lueras and Taman Merta Sari; Jordan Pavlin; Justin Smith; Gwen Strauss; and Maxine Swann.

Permissions AcknOwledgments

A NOTE ABOUT THE AUTHOR

Eliza Minot graduated from Barnard in 1991 and lives in New York. *The Tiny One* is her first novel.

A NOTE ON THE TYPE

The text of this book was set in Bembo, a facsimile of a type-face cut by Francesco Griffo for Aldus Manutius, the celebrated Venetian printer, in 1495. The face was named for Pietro Cardinal Bembo, the author of the small treatise entitled *De Aetna* in which it first appeared. Through the research of Stanley Morison, it is now generally acknowledged that all old-style type designs up to the time of William Caslon can be traced to the Bembo cut.

The present-day version of Bembo was introduced by the Monotype Corporation of London in 1929. Sturdy, well-balanced, and finely proportioned, Bembo is a face of rare beauty and great legibility in all of its sizes.

Composed by Creative Graphics,
Allentown, Pennsylvania

Printed and bound by The Haddon Craftsmen,
Bloomsburg, Pennsylvania

Designed by Cassandra J. Pappas

NOV 17 1999

DATE DUE 11-24-99

OFFICIALLY
DISCARDED
ELMONT PUBLIC LIBRARY

STEWART MANOR BRANCH
Elmont Public Library
Elmont, New York

The borrower is responsible for all
books and other materials drawn on his
car   e

28 DAYS

Do not remove date card from pocket

STEWART MANOR BRANCH